DIRECT SUNLIGHT

STORIES

CHRISTINE SNEED

TriQuarterly Books / Northwestern University Press
Evanston, Illinois

TriQuarterly Books
Northwestern University Press
www.nupress.northwestern.edu

This is a work of fiction. Names, characters, places, and incidents either are the
product of the author's imagination or are used fictitiously, and any resemblance
to actual persons, living or dead, business establishments, events, or locales is
entirely coincidental.

Printed in the United States of America

10   9   8   7   6   5   4   3   2   1

Library of Congress Cataloging-in-Publication Data

Names: Sneed, Christine, 1971– author.
Title: Direct sunlight : stories / Christine Sneed.
Description: Evanston : TriQuarterly Books/Northwestern University Press, 2023.
Identifiers: LCCN 2023000562 | ISBN 9780810146167 (paperback) |
    ISBN 9780810146174 (ebook)
Subjects: LCGFT: Short stories.
Classification: LCC PS3619.N523 D57 2023 | DDC 813.6—dc23/eng/20230105
LC record available at https://lccn.loc.gov/2023000562

In memory of my grandmothers

Dolores Walker, June Webb, and Katherine Sneed

CONTENTS

The Swami Buchu Trungpa

Her mother had been sober for seven months when Nora moved to Paris with her employer, a man from Queens who had changed his name from Jim Schwartz to Swami Buchu Trungpa twenty years earlier. Around the same time, he'd quit his job as a mechanic at a Saab dealership on Long Island and reinvented himself as a spiritual adviser and yoga instructor. His father owned the dealership, and although the swami had never admitted it to Nora, she had a feeling his father wasn't unhappy to see him go.

Whatever his previous disappointments might have been, he'd done well as a spiritual adviser, having steadily acquired supporters and acolytes over the last two decades. With Nora's assistance, he was now preparing to open a juice bar and yoga studio in Paris's eleventh arrondissement on the boulevard Voltaire with money he'd inherited from one of his longtime followers—an undertaking he'd told Nora had first occurred to him during a weeklong retreat in the Berkshires that she remembered chiefly for its bad weather and the raccoons nightly ransacking the trash.

She had lived for a year in Paris during college and for two more in her late twenties. Buchu was relying on her to obtain the necessary commercial permissions in France and to handle the legal protocols, which were intentionally onerous. Before they'd left New York, her job with Buchu International was part-time assistant and full-time girlfriend. Now she was both full-time assistant and girlfriend, and she knew others wondered how long she would last in either role after they settled in Paris. She didn't really care what other people were saying, however—she was returning to France, something she'd wanted to do for the past several years but hadn't known how to orchestrate without a partner or an employer, and now she had both.

Regina, Nora's mother, did not like the swami, who reminded her of Nora's father, in both looks and temperament. Nora didn't see the resemblance, but Regina accused her of not wanting to see it. Her mother was also upset that Nora was now a long plane ride away. Regina was busy in Portsmouth with her friends and hobbies and AA meetings, living off money inherited from two dead husbands, but it didn't matter—she wanted Nora closer.

"You can come visit me anytime," said Nora. "And stay as long as you'd like to."

"But not with you and the swami botulism," said Regina. "He'd have a fit if I showed up on your doorstep with my big wheelie bag."

"Don't call him that, Mom," said Nora. "He wouldn't mind you staying with us for part of your visit."

Her mother snorted. "A day or two is about all I can imagine him allowing."

"You could stay with us for a week. That'd be fine." But she knew her mother was right—Buchu wanted privacy and his living quarters were his most sacrosanct space. Three days would probably be his limit, and Regina was, at best, trying company with her strident opinions and her aversion to crowds and unfamiliar food. She was also more snappish than usual as she clung to her recent sobriety.

"There are a lot of former drunks in Paris, I was happy to discover," said Regina. "I can find English-language meetings in the city every day of the week."

"Give us a couple of months to get situated," said Nora. "It's only been four weeks since we got here, and the amount of paperwork I have to do to open the studio is mind-boggling."

"I thought you were opening a fast-food place."

"It's a juice bar. It'll be downstairs from the yoga studio. I told you that."

"I'm not sure who you think is going to buy your overpriced potions," said Regina. "I wouldn't."

"You don't have to. It'd be a very long trip for you for a spirulina smoothie." Nora was standing in one of the two east-facing rooms of her and Buchu's apartment, phone to her ear, the sun striking the windows of the building across the street. Three stories below, on the rue de la Folie, a woman in a short red dress and matching heels was walking a terrier toward the park a block and a half away. Buchu was in his meditation room down the hall with the door closed and had been in there for the last two hours. Nora had a feeling he'd fallen asleep.

"I have to go, Mom. I need to make a couple of other calls before it gets any later."

"I haven't had a drink in seven months and twenty-six days."

"I'm very happy to hear that," said Nora. "Keep it up."

"I want to," she said.

There were two kinds of replies her mother was expecting, and Nora chose the kinder one. "You will," she said. "You can do it."

"We'll see," said Regina.

When Nora first met Buchu four years earlier, her mother was a year into her third marriage and had been alternating between sobriety and active alcoholism for more than twenty-five years. Her first husband, Nora's father, was alive and prospering in Anaheim, where he owned a chain of cafés that served bad coffee, Bill's Beans & Things (her mother hated the name and made fun of it relentlessly: "Things? Couldn't he have chosen something a little more specific?"). Her second husband, Howie, had died of cancer eight years earlier. Of him she had a much more sentimental view—along with his ashes, she still kept his pool cue in the hall coat closet.

Her third husband, Vance, was a recovering alcoholic who fell off the wagon during the second year of their marriage and dragged Regina back down with him. Several months after they were both drinking again to the point of nightly oblivion, he was killed in a car wreck but managed not to kill anyone else. Regina was at home when it happened, passed out on the sofa, and didn't wake up until the next morning when a sheriff's deputy arrived and pounded on her front door, all attempts to phone her having failed.

About her mother, Buchu had said, "She is like a great gaping cave into which sunlight disappears forever."

Nora did not share this assessment with Regina, which, although cruel, was not wholly inaccurate. In Paris with Buchu, she hoped to find a way to detach herself more fully from her fear of her mother's self-destructive proclivities, and it was this same desire that had first led her to Buchu's temple in the East Village where he held meditation sessions for neophytes on Tuesday and Friday evenings. Following the sessions were Trungpa Talks, some of which lasted ten minutes, others two or three hours.

"Three hours? Can I leave early if I have to?" Nora asked the ex-boyfriend who recommended she try one of Buchu's sessions, their relationship one of the losses Nora suffered after having been raised under her mother's slash-and-burn rule. Trusting anyone was all but impossible.

"I wouldn't advise it," he said. "But don't worry. You'll like the swami's talks." ("They'll be good for you," she could imagine him thinking, but he knew enough not to say these words aloud.) He likewise assured her there would be no pressure to join anything, no sales pitches, no chanting or group confessionals—nothing but an intelligent man sharing some of the observations he'd made about the human experiment during his fifty-one years on earth.

Now Buchu was fifty-five and she was thirty-four, and their lives were elaborately entwined. She loved him but doubted it would last forever, which was one reason why her mother disliked him. Didn't Nora want more from him, or at least some kind of declaration, if she was moving her life across the ocean for this pseudo-swami with his large head and bony bare feet? (Buchu did, in fact, wear shoes, but not in the apartment.)

No, Nora didn't mind the terms of their relationship, and Buchu appreciated her attitude. He'd sensed when first setting eyes on her that she was a special case, a woman who recognized the ephemeral nature of all human commitments. She'd understood implicitly what he meant: at some point he would want to have sex with other women. But who was to say she wouldn't be tired of him by then too? No one believed her when she said this though, not even Buchu.

He emerged from his room half an hour after Nora got off the phone with her mother, the scent of lemongrass incense trailing him down the hall. She heard him go into the kitchen where she knew he'd be looking for a snack, but other than apples and an overripe banana, he wouldn't find much. She needed to go to the Carrefour Express a few blocks away and had intended to do it before noon, but between the phone call with her mother and the cyberspace black hole she'd been sucked into before the call, she hadn't done it. Outside it was a humid, midsummer day, and she knew if she left the apartment and picked her way through the narrow Parisian streets with their meandering tourists and harried natives, she'd feel better almost instantly, but she hadn't yet peeled herself away from her desk, and now it was nearly two thirty.

While Buchu banged around in the kitchen, she stayed in the study, peering at share capital forms from the Banque Nationale de Paris, intermittently looking online for fruit and vegetable growers within a 150-kilometer radius of Paris from whom they could buy the produce for the juices and smoothies. There were farms with greenhouses that operated throughout the winter, along with the farms of southern France, but orders from the latter would include higher transportation costs. Nora knew before they moved to Paris that there would be dozens of details to attend to, and they seemed to be multiplying now as they drew closer to the day, still looming ambiguously ahead—five months, seven, seventeen?—when they would be ready to open for business.

"Why don't you take a break," said Buchu, his voice startling her from the doorway.

She turned toward him as he took a large bite of apple, a bright green Granny Smith, and crunched it noisily. He was wearing gray yoga pants and his favorite black T-shirt. His thick hair, brown with silver threaded through it, was tied back in a ponytail. He was tall and filled much of the doorway. Wherever they went, people cast admiring or curious glances his way, but his body, so firm and straight and strong, was beginning to hunch forward, and his knees bothered him, sometimes badly. Nora was sure one or both would need to be replaced in another few years, if not sooner, but he wouldn't discuss it.

Her stomach growled. She hadn't yet eaten lunch.

He heard it too and said, "Your body obviously agrees with me."

"I think my mother wants to come for a visit," she said.

Buchu blinked, his heavy-lidded eyes briefly fluttering with what she knew was annoyance. "So soon?"

Nora nodded. "I asked her to give us more time to settle in. I want to be closer to finishing the incorporation for the studio before she comes, and that's probably at least a couple of months away, if we're lucky. I'm still working on the share capital with Rémy and the bank, and next week we're planning to order the announcement for the publicity requirement."

He looked at her as he took another bite of apple, nodding vaguely. She could see he wasn't really listening. He had only a hazy notion of how much work—how many sheerly bureaucratic, hand-wringing steps she and Rémy, the business formation expert she'd hired on the advice of a former boss, were trudging through, all in a highly specific, stultifying order, with extreme tact and patience, not to mention an open wallet.

The money was the swami's—or rather, Buchu International's—but the time and perseverance were all hers.

"Perhaps you could tell Regina to hold off until the new year," he said.

"I'll have to go home for Christmas if she doesn't come here before then."

His sigh was a long, slow gust of aggrievement. "Please insist that she wait until October, if not later. You and I haven't had much of a chance to settle in yet. Hardly more than a month."

"I told her that," said Nora.

"She won't insist on staying here, will she?"

"Buchu," she said. "You know we have to let her, at least for a few days."

"We can pay for her hotel."

"It's not the money. You know that."

He was shaking his head in a loose, boneless way that meant he was exceptionally annoyed. "You know she'll drain you," he said, his grizzled eyebrows arching as he spoke. "After the first day, you'll say to me you wish she hadn't come."

"That might be true, but she is my mother. I do want to see her."

"Do you?"

"Of course I do."

He took a final huge bite of the Granny Smith. He always ate the entire apple, only spitting out the seeds. She listened to him crunching and held back a sigh. She needed lunch. She needed to leave the apartment.

"She doesn't like me," he finally said.

"She doesn't like many people," said Nora.

"But me especially," he said.

"She doesn't dislike you," she lied.

He smiled and shook his head again. "You and I both know she does. You don't have to pretend."

7

She stood up from the desk and nudged past him into the hall. She could smell the incense on his clothes and hair. "I have to go out," she said. "Do you need anything from Carrefour?"

"Almonds," he said. "And some dark chocolate. But not too dark."

"I know the kind you like," she said.

"Yes, I'm sure you do." He leaned over and kissed her. There were apple seeds in his palm. She heard them ping against the hardwood floor as he put his arms around her. She could tell he was feeling amorous, but she wasn't, not remotely. She pulled away and he looked at her intently, one hand on her arm.

"You look very pretty, Nora," he said.

"Thank you," she said. "I'll be back in about an hour. Will you be here?"

"I'm not sure. I'll leave a note if I go out."

"All right, I'll see you later." She squeezed his hand. He took her other hand and held on to it. She shook her head. "Tonight, all right?"

"All right," he said, disappointed, the look on his face briefly revealing the vulnerability he went to great lengths to suppress. She wished she would see it more often, as she had when they were first together. She had never said no to him then. She hadn't ever wanted to.

The streets were filled with sunbaked, glinting cars and men in summer suits and women in sleeveless dresses walking fast. French people, other than teenagers, seemed perpetually to be in a hurry, everything at the pitch and pace of near-emergency— such a different atmosphere from the one in her and Buchu's hushed apartment where fans, in the absence of air-conditioning, drowned out much of the street noise. The day after they moved in, they'd gone out to buy five of them, along with potted plants for every room, colorful throw rugs, and a big bed that was the most comfortable bed of Nora's life. They'd also bought a sofa and an armoire, bookcases, two armchairs, a kitchen table and chairs. In addition to these purchases, there were boxes of books, trinkets, and clothes still on their way from Manhattan.

Buchu had never been interested in asceticism. He liked luxury; he admired prosperity and posh homes but was mostly tight-lipped about these preferences. But he was not a hypocrite—as far as Nora knew, he had never pretended to lead a monkish life.

In Paris, he seemed content with the change in their environment, although there was no reason for him not to feel at ease—his spacious apartment in Williamsburg awaited him anytime he wished to return. One of the two assistants who'd remained in New York dropped by twice a week to check on it and water the plants. Much of his spiritual practice continued as before, with most of it now conducted online: he held weekly online meditation sessions and still gave Trungpa Talks. He'd also promised his followers that he would return to Manhattan after the yoga studio and juice bar's launch, but it was likely he would henceforth divide his time between New York and Paris.

Nora intended to stay in France full-time, but she hadn't yet told him. As she walked to Carrefour, she glanced up at the blond stone apartment buildings and the newer storefronts with their promotional signs fading in the July sun, the sidewalk cafés flanked by cheap pizza parlors and wig shops, some of them blaring music from speakers suspended above their doors. She didn't know she was smiling until men started smiling back at her, nodding as they passed. Someone was watering potted geraniums on one of the high window ledges, droplets flecking the bare skin of her pale arms and a few bigger droplets landing on her head. Another woman, a half step in front of Nora, cried out, "Zut!" and hastily patted down her hair. She and Nora looked at each other and laughed.

At Carrefour as she hovered over the lettuces, her cell phone rang. "I bought a ticket," her mother announced. "It wasn't expensive! I'll be there next Wednesday."

Nora felt her breath catch and hoped her mother hadn't heard. "Are you serious?" she said, already certain of the answer.

"You don't want me to come," Regina crowed. "I knew it!"

"That's not true. But airfares are always so expensive in the summer."

"I'll just stay in a hotel and you don't have to see me," said Regina.

"Don't be silly. Of course I'll see you. You can stay with us. How long will you be here?"

"I don't know yet. I got a one-way ticket."

Nora stared blindly at the lettuces. She'd have a good time trying to explain this to Buchu. "Why did you decide to do that?"

"Why do you think? I wasn't sure how long I'd want to stay. Five days, maybe five weeks. I didn't want to limit myself."

Five weeks! Nora felt her stomach leap. Under the store's bright lights, the pale green heads of butter lettuce, both her and Buchu's favorite, looked bleached.

"Hello?" said Regina.

"I'm still here," said Nora. "Send me your flight information. Are you flying into Orly or Roissy?"

"I don't remember. Does it matter?"

"Roissy's a little easier for us because it's on the north side of Paris, closer to where we live, but I can take a train to either of them."

"I'll have my schedule already figured out for the first week. There really are a lot of meetings to choose from."

"Good, Mom. I'm glad."

"Maybe I'll meet someone. Wouldn't that be exciting? A handsome, sixty-something Frenchman who speaks fluent English would be perfect."

"You have to wait a year, don't you?"

"Oh, you know. Not everyone sticks to that rule. Probably less than half of us old drunks do."

"Please try not to get too carried away, Mom," she said. "I have to go now. I'm at the store. I'll check in with you later this week."

"Okay, dear," said Regina. "I'm very excited. I love you."

"I love you too."

As she put away her phone, she looked down at the butter lettuces again but left them untouched on their shelf beneath the escarole and arugula. The store was busy, full of older men and women pushing handcarts and nannies with strollers. Someone took her place at the cooler the second she went off to look for Buchu's chocolate.

"A one-way ticket?" he said, his voice rising in alarm. He stared at her in disbelief. "What on earth is she thinking?"

"I don't know. I doubt she'll be here for more than two weeks. I'm hoping less, obviously."

"She can't stay with us. It's just not possible. We can find her an Airbnb in the quarter. Let's do that right now."

"Buchu, she has to stay here for a few days. We already talked about this."

He looked sharply away. Nora felt a surge of anger at him and her mother—why was Regina insisting on a visit now? Why couldn't she and Buchu be a little less selfish? "I have to go out for some air," he said ominously.

Nora said nothing. He looked at her, waiting, but when she didn't reply, he got up and left the kitchen where they were still eating dinner. She heard him slip quietly down the hall before he opened the heavy oak door that led to the landing and the narrow stairwell with its timed lights that sometimes prematurely clicked off. He'd left his plate on the table, his curried rice and vegetables half-eaten. Nora looked down at her own plate and pushed it aside, the evening, like their dinner, a waste.

He didn't return until after midnight, smelling of cigarettes and wine. He came into the bedroom and stripped off his reeking clothes and climbed in next to her and put his hands on her breasts and she turned to him, surprised by her own desire, despite her residual anger at his earlier petulance. It was over in ten minutes and afterward she fell asleep hard, a stone dropped into a pond. Her dreams were populated by small, furiously barking dogs and buckets of water pouring down on her head.

In the morning she felt groggy but got up at 7:15 anyway, Buchu still sound asleep, naked and gently snoring. Four years ago, his arrival in her life had felt messianic. At the time, her mother's drinking and calamitous third marriage were summoning waves of near-paralyzing anxiety whenever Nora thought of Regina. Buchu's interested gaze upon her, his voice and ease within his body, his large pale hands resting on his knees as he spoke, had alternately soothed and excited her. He taught her how to meditate, and how to suffer less over what she could not control. She hadn't been able to stop thinking about him—for almost three years it was like this—before she grew habituated to his beauty, his confidence, his long, somnolent silences. He was not so different now from who he was then, but it wasn't until they were preparing to move to Paris that Nora admitted to herself he was as needy as her mother, and with time, it was probable he would ask for even more from her.

Regina had in fact booked a flight to Roissy, and Nora took the RER north from the city and stood in the echoing, aging airport with the dozens of other restless daughters and husbands and wives waiting for their families and lovers to be released from customs and the baggage claim, the opaque doors opening and closing every few seconds to disgorge lone weary travelers or small clusters of people dragging suitcases and bleary-eyed children behind them. Her mother, when she finally appeared, was pink-cheeked and fresh looking, her face lit up with the pleasure of new and glamorous experience. She had only been to Paris once before, more than a decade earlier, when Nora was still in college. Regina was drinking then, and the visit had been an arduous, uphill climb of recriminations and tears and apologies, neither Nora nor her mother ever reaching the summit and finding relief.

Regina threw her arms around Nora and held her close for several seconds. Nora felt a sudden premonitory fear that her mother was off the wagon again, and cautiously sniffed her for traces of inflight wine. All she detected, however, were the scents of Regina's herbal shampoo and the slightly sour tang of her sweat.

"I'm so happy to be here, sweetie," said Regina, girlish and grinning. "I watched two movies on the plane. One about two gay boys, and the other about bank robbers who love horses. They were both pretty good. I stayed awake!"

"It's good to see you. I'm glad you're here, Mom."

"Me too. Now let's get this show on the road. I have to be at a meeting in two hours," she said, looking around as if expecting a cab to materialize before them. They were still inside the airport, passing a sandwich kiosk and another selling pastries and coffee where a small line of people waited listlessly.

They stepped through another set of sliding doors, out into the humid morning air where Nora flagged a cab and helped the bearded cabbie hoist her mother's suitcase into the trunk. Within seconds they were settled in the back seat, the cabbie signaling and pulling away from the curb.

Her mother leaned her head against Nora's shoulder. "I won't be a bother to you and the swami botulism," she murmured. "I promise."

"Mom, stop calling him that," said Nora, but she laughed. Her mother did too.

The cabbie pressed on the accelerator as he nosed the car onto the autoroute, other taxis and snub-nosed utility trucks driven by tradesmen speeding ahead of them as they merged. Nora felt herself relaxing in tiny increments as they hurtled toward the city and the quiet apartment where Nora knew Buchu awaited their arrival with annoyance and dread.

But he wasn't there when they arrived, and he hadn't left a note on the table in the foyer where they kept a key bowl and a small vase with fresh flowers Nora replenished every Saturday morning.

This week there were daisies and pink rosebuds in the vase's slightly murky water. Her mother stopped to touch the petals. "So pretty," she said, looking at them fondly.

Had she started drinking again? Nora recognized the good humor, the pliability, the sweetness that often heralded Regina's return to vodka and tonics, to white wine and red and bourbon on the rocks. Maybe she was wrong this time, but she'd only been wrong once before.

Buchu had offered up four days. Her mother would stay in a nearby Airbnb for the next four. After that, she would decide if she wanted to extend her stay or fly home. The willingness with which her mother had agreed to this arrangement had startled Nora, but she knew enough not to question her motives aloud.

"Where is he?" Regina asked after they'd stashed her luggage in Nora's study, which was serving double duty as the guest room. Buchu's meditation room was off-limits to everyone but Nora and himself, she sometimes meditating with him for an hour in the morning. It hadn't even been discussed that he might offer it to Regina in order for Nora to continue her work on the yoga studio more easily.

"I'm not sure," Nora admitted.

Her mother rolled her eyes. "Well," she said. "That's just fine with me."

"Do you want to take a shower or rest for a few minutes before I take you to your meeting? Where is it?"

"Near the St. Eustache church."

"That's over by Les Halles. It's not very close. Wasn't there anything in this neighborhood?"

"Bev recommended this group to me. She said there are lots of Americans in it." Bev was her mother's sponsor, a retired high school history teacher who lived with six finches named after her favorite presidents: Lincoln, Jefferson, Carter, Obama, and the two Roosevelts.

"All right, whatever Bev says, but we'll need to take another cab. The metro might be pushing it if we have to wait more than a few minutes."

"Bev said I'd love this group."

"How is Bev?" said Nora.

"She's gained some weight, but otherwise, she's fine."

"It looks like you've lost some," said Nora.

"I have!" said her mother, beaming. "I've cut down on sugar."

"Good. No diabetes for you."

"Oh, Nora," she said, shaking her head.

"I'm serious, Mom."

"Don't be a smarty pants."

"I'm not being a smarty pants. Your doctor said you were pre-diabetic, so this is good news."

"I forgot I told you that."

"Well, you did."

Nora dropped her mother off at the meeting, handing her the apartment's address on a scrap of paper for the cab ride home before she went down into Les Halles métro station and rode the train back to the eleventh arrondissement. She hoped Buchu would have resurfaced by the time she came through the door, but there was still no sign of him. She tried his cell but he didn't answer. He was going to pout the entire time Regina was in Paris. He'd promised Nora he wouldn't, but she knew it would be impossible for him to honor this promise. He was supposed to be skilled at transcending pettiness, but when it actually mattered, his record was at best one in two, especially since he'd inherited the money that had made their move to France possible.

The most powerful lesson Nora had learned from him was that no one, other than the dead, could ever reliably detach from the ego. When his acolytes flocked to him after a session in his practice space in the East Village, looking up at him with adoring eyes, Nora sometimes was seized with impatience. *I know him*, she wanted to say. *He's as flawed as you are.* But of course she never did. They all loved him, and she did too, most of the time.

She went into the kitchen, snatched a box of chocolate cookies out of the cupboard, and stood eating them at the window that overlooked the street behind their building. Halfway down the block, she saw a tall man standing in the middle of the sidewalk, a newspaper open in front of him. After a baffled few seconds, she realized it was Buchu. She called his cell a second time and watched him take it out of his pocket and glance at the flashing screen before tucking it away again. He reopened his newspaper with no indication the call had caused him even a half second of self-doubt.

Birds were chirping shrilly beyond the window through which she stood gawking at Buchu and wrestling with her anger before it pinned her down. She left the apartment and charged around the corner to confront him. He would hate seeing her so furious— why was she giving in to her anger? he would immediately wonder. *Because I want to! Because it's how I feel!*

When he heard her coming, he looked up calmly from his newspaper, as if expecting her. "I need a standing desk," he said. "We should go look for one. I'm really enjoying myself out here."

She stopped a few feet in front of him. "What? What are you talking about?"

"I think I should buy a standing desk," he said reasonably.

She stared at him. "Why didn't you answer my calls?"

He gazed at her for a moment before folding his newspaper in half and placing it under his arm. "Let's go inside," he said, reaching for her hand.

She refused to give it to him. "You could at least have said hello to my mother before you came out here to read the paper in the street like some kind of imbecile."

"Nora," he said, pained. "Please."

"I think she's started drinking again."

He said nothing.

"Did you hear me?" she said, her voice booming in her ears.

"Yes, I heard you," he said, almost cold.

She glared at him. "And?"

He peered down at her and shook his head. Cars were passing and she could sense the people inside looking at her and the swami. "Your mother is a grown woman. You can't police her like she's your prisoner or your child," he said.

"It's like you're both my children," she cried. "How did I let this happen?"

He regarded her solemnly. "Nora, come on now. We haven't 'happened' to you. That's a horribly facile way of thinking."

She was so very tired of his smugness. He met her gaze placidly, his two-day-old beard making him look even more handsome than usual. Neither of them spoke. She didn't know what she wanted to say. After a moment, she turned on her heel and left him where he stood.

He didn't follow her. She could hear the paper rustling in his hands, and when she was back upstairs and spying on him again from the kitchen window, he'd returned to reading as if she had never been there at all.

Later that afternoon, after he came up from the street and apologized to Nora and her mother for missing Regina's arrival, he took Regina's hand and bowed over it. Her mother blushed as Nora looked on, startled by her mother's susceptibility to Buchu's histrionic charm. Regina even had a small gift for him, a sleek black notebook in which she suggested he record his thoughts. He smiled and thanked her, and Nora was grudgingly impressed that her mother remembered the type of notebook she'd once told her he liked best.

"For his memoirs," said Regina after he'd retreated to his room, her characteristic tartness having returned. "He's probably already on volume two hundred and six."

"Mom," said Nora, laughing a little. "Very thoughtful of you."

"I thought so too," she said primly.

There were no more tantrums, no more scenes on the sidewalk—she and Buchu both deciding to act as if their public standoff had never happened—and relatively little bickering between Nora and her mother over the next three days, nor did Nora find any proof that Regina was drinking again. Her mother seemed unequivocally sober, but happier and more even-tempered than Nora remembered seeing her in many years. It was Paris, Nora realized, that had drawn her mother out of herself, sloughing away her customary gripes and grievances.

On the fourth day of her visit, Regina repacked her suitcase without complaint, and Nora helped her wheel it over to the small Airbnb apartment they'd found for her on the rue Merlin. Buchu was in his room giving an online Trungpa Talk, his sonorous voice droning through the closed door. Before he'd gotten online, he hadn't said goodbye to Regina, despite Nora's request earlier in the day that he do so. Her mother would likely be back at the apartment before she flew home, but whether she would see him again was anyone's guess, and Nora was too tired to insist a second time that he offer some gesture of farewell, knowing Regina didn't much care if it happened or not.

"I could live here," her mother proclaimed, scanning her new lodgings. "Maybe I should." The walls were painted sunset orange, and cotton batik covered the sofa and two armchairs in the sitting room; the apartment also had restored hardwood floors, southern-exposure sunlight, and bookshelves filled with English and American novels. The owners had clearly taken care.

"It is a great place," said Nora.

Regina eyed her. "Your swami would hate it if I lived here."

Nora made a sound of dissent.

"He would. He wants you all to himself," said Regina.

Nora looked at her before she turned toward the window. "Don't you think most men are like that?" she asked.

Her mother hesitated. "I suppose they are."

Nora turned and met her mother's gaze. "When you got here, I was worried you'd started drinking again."

"No, no. Over eight months now without a drink." She gave Nora an appraising look. "I don't think you're very happy with Buchu anymore."

"I'm fine," said Nora lightly. "I've been so busy working on the permits for the studio that I haven't had much time to think about anything else."

"But when you're done with that, what then?"

"I don't know. I'll have to see."

"I really think you can do much better than the swami botulism," said Regina.

"I don't want to talk about it, Mom. Not today."

"You never want to talk about it," she said. "But at some point you're going to have to."

Nora didn't reply.

Her mother sat down on the sofa, sinking into its plush cushions. She kept her eyes on Nora. "I know it's not really any of my business, but I don't think you're happy."

"Please stop worrying about me. Everything's fine."

They looked at each other steadily before Regina said, "I think I need a little nap."

The afternoon light in the room was still bright, dust motes suspended in the air behind the sofa. It looked to Nora like an enchanted picture from a child's book of fairy tales—so beautiful that she felt a peculiar devastation—duty bearing down on her, the obligation on some future but foreseeable day to disappoint someone she cared about. "I'll be back for you at seven," she said. "We'll go somewhere nice for dinner."

"You're a good person, Nora," her mother said drowsily. "I've always thought so."

"Thank you, Mom," she said softly, glancing down at the floor.

When she looked up again, her mother's eyes were closed. "I'll see you later, sweetie," said Regina. "Please make sure the door locks on your way out."

Nora touched her mother's hand, the skin still supple from years of nightly creams. "I'll see you at seven."

Her mother nodded but said nothing more.

At dinner that evening, the glow and goodwill from earlier in the day had ebbed. Her mother's salad was overdressed. The server was visibly annoyed when they didn't order wine. Nora found herself saying, "Elle ne boit pas. Vous comprenez?" and staring him down.

Her mother became agitated after he stalked off. "Did you just tell him I'm an alcoholic?"

"I just said you don't drink. That's all."

"But he must have understood what you meant."

"I doubt it," said Nora. "What would you have liked me to say?"

"You didn't have to say anything. I'm certain we aren't the first people in the history of this restaurant not to order wine with dinner."

"He was being rude," said Nora. Along with making a face over her refusal to order alcohol, he'd insisted on speaking English even though she spoke French to him—fluently, for God's sake. She wasn't some pidgin-speaking American tourist who could barely pronounce "bonjour"!

Her mother glared at her. "And you think he's going to be nicer now?"

"No, but I want him to know we're not bumpkins."

"Ah ha," said Regina. "So you're trying to save face. But it's at my expense, Nora."

"That's not true. He was condescending. He thinks he knows everything about us, but he doesn't. I hate men like that."

"You do?" Her mother took a sip from her water glass, looking at her over the rim. "Could have fooled me."

"Stop," said Nora, suddenly furious. "You're being just as much of a jerk as he is."

"I want you to understand something," said Regina coolly. "Every single time I go into a restaurant, I want to drink. I want to drink until I'm so drunk I can't stand up. My mouth has been watering since the second we came in the door. No, that's not true—since before we came in the door. The fact we're even sitting here while other people are drinking is killing me. But here I am anyway, making an effort. Do you have any idea how hard this is? I don't think you do, Nora. You can say you do and maybe you have an inkling, but I can tell you that it's much easier to be you right now than it is for me to be who I am, someone who used to wake up drunk and half-frozen in the backyard more times than you would care to know. Or how about this? Someone who used to drive her car into the ditch in the dead of night—but somehow I managed to get it out and creep my way home before the cops spotted me and threw me in jail."

Her mother took another sip of water and looked at her dispassionately. "Please stop crying, Nora. As you can see, I've survived all that foolishness, and I'm not planning to do any of those things again. But I don't ever want you to tell another waiter I'm an alcoholic. Have you got that?"

Nora nodded, her eyes burning from the effort of holding back another flood of tears. Her mother looked fierce and confident, but above all, relieved, as if she'd been waiting a long time to unburden herself. Nora hadn't known about the blackouts in the backyard, but she had imagined innumerable catastrophes befalling her mother— how many hours of sleep had she lost over the years? How many phone calls had her mother made or answered while drunk, either she or Nora hanging up—two minutes, ten minutes, an hour later—when one began accusing the other of neglect or selfishness or cruelty?

But here Regina was in spite of the long, clanking chain of one bad choice after another. It was finally over, she was saying, and Nora was trying to believe her.

"I'm sorry, Mom. I won't do it again."

Regina was nonchalant. "Thank you. It's not too much to ask, is it?"

"No. I'm sorry," Nora repeated, her eyes still watering. She was going to cry again and stared down at her lap, her hands gripping her napkin, twisting it into a rope.

"No more crying," said Regina. "I'm okay now, and I'm not going to do any of those things again. I mean it."

When the check came, Nora discovered the server had over-charged them, and when she asked him in French to remove the charge for an entrée they hadn't ordered, he took the check away without a word and made them wait twenty minutes for the correction. Her mother remained tranquil during the delay, looking out the windows that faced the street, watching the steady stream of passersby, while Nora fumed and muttered about the server's rudeness.

After they'd at last paid the bill and were sprung loose into the night, her mother put her arms around her and pulled her close. "I hope that supercilious shitbag falls into the Seine on his way home tonight," she said into Nora's ear.

"That's exactly what he is," said Nora, laughing, her eyes threatening to leak tears again.

"You can thank Vance for that one. The son of a bitch at least managed to leave me with a few good insults before he drove himself headfirst into a tree," she said.

She flew back to New Hampshire the following week, promising Nora she would return at Christmas. At the airport there had been an apology, Regina having trouble meeting Nora's eyes as she spoke. "I shouldn't have yelled at you the other night at that restaurant."

"You didn't yell."

"I'm still sorry," she said, hugging Nora hard, her cheek pressed against her shoulder. "I'll miss you, sweetheart. I can't wait to see you in December."

"I'll miss you too, Mom."

"You'd better," said Regina, her smile tremulous. "You can come visit me too you know. Anytime you want."

"I know. Thank you. I'll see how it goes."

Regina stepped back and looked at Nora intently. "I want you to know that I'm doing fine. I really am. You don't have to worry about me anymore."

Nora took her mother's hand in both of hers and held it. "I believe you, Mom, and I'm so glad you're doing so well."

"Good. No more crying, okay?"

Nora shook her head. "No more. I promise."

Buchu grew quieter after Regina went home, sensing Nora's retreat from him. They moved around the apartment politely, almost as strangers, occasionally coming together for meals and sex. "Where have you gone?" he asked over dinner a week and a half after the visit, blinking at her wearily.

"Nowhere," she said. "But I'm a little tired, I guess. There's still a lot of work to do for the studio."

"At least your mother isn't drinking again," he said.

"No," said Nora. "She doesn't seem to be."

He said nothing.

"Why?"

He shook his head. "I'm surprised. That's all. We'll see if it lasts."

"I think it might this time," she said.

"I know you're angry with me," he said. "But I can't help it if I don't like her, can I?"

"No, I suppose you can't."

He sighed and touched her hand across the table. "You still suffer too much on her account."

A siren blared below them in the street. Nora felt herself holding her breath, waiting for it to recede. "What I would like is for you to try a little harder to hide your dislike from her, if not from me," she finally said. She squeezed his hand once before letting go.

He nodded. "Fair enough."

"You wanted to move here," she said. "So we did."

"You wanted to move here too. Don't pretend this is all for me."

"I'm not choosing between you and her," said Nora.

"Haven't you already?" he said.

"By coming here, you mean?"

"Yes."

"No, that's ridiculous," she said.

Of course he didn't see her point of view. His parents were dead. His mother had died when he was in his thirties, his father ten years later. Buchu had no children of his own, but was briefly married in his twenties. From what Nora could tell, he'd floated along on a tide of healthy self-regard for the past twenty or so years, answering only to his whims.

"I'm not saying you can't talk to her or see her," he said, "but there's a significant part of you linked to her that refuses to open up to me. That's what I find troubling."

"If you liked her, even a little bit, I don't think you'd feel that way."

"Maybe not," he said.

She sat at the table for another minute, neither of them speaking. She stood up and went into the hall, taking her keys from the bowl before she went downstairs and outside to the street. She wanted him to come after her but knew he wouldn't. To his mind, it was the role of great men to keep from bending, to make decisions and stand firmly by them.

A very poor plan, in her view, one formulated for wartime, not for Tuesday nights with no character other than their resemblance to Monday or Wednesday nights.

She walked toward the Marais with its clubs and restaurants that stayed open very late, much later than she was usually awake. She could traverse the city north to south, spend the whole night walking from the Porte de Clignacourt to the Porte d'Orléans and back. What would Buchu think if she didn't come home? He would worry, but he wouldn't ask where she'd gone, or why, when she finally returned.

All around her people were walking with their faces lit up in anticipation of happiness. A few moved blank-faced toward the future, open to nothing, or possibly, anything. Cars sped down the boulevard, lining up abruptly at stoplights. Girls in short skirts called to boys who leered at them from across the street. Her mother was doing fine. It was a Tuesday night near the end of the summer. There was a river to the south and hills to the north—everything she looked at was, startlingly, as it had always been.

Where Do You Last Remember Holding It?

During the summer before her senior year in college, Erica noticed her mother, Julia, had begun to misplace her keys nearly every day and forget appointments and the names of people she'd known all her life. As these lapses became more frequent, Erica started to see them for what they probably were—harbingers of something serious and irrevocable—but her older sister, Marianne, refused to acknowledge their mother's fracturing memory, and throughout Erica's senior year, Marianne maintained an aggressive, confrontational optimism. She insisted their mother's forgetfulness was the sign of an overfull schedule, of not enough sleep or iron or Vitamin D. Maybe she was depressed but didn't want to admit it. Maybe it was a mental hangover from the holidays or too little fresh air. Ultimately, it was Erica who demanded they take Julia to the doctor, and after a series of tests and referrals, she was diagnosed with dementia. She was a few months shy of sixty-five.

Erica had graduated from college two weeks before the diagnosis, and in some ways she was more shaken by the news than her mother and sister appeared to be. Marianne was somewhat insulated from the whole ordeal, and with her job as a junior attorney for a firm in Chicago, was wholly independent of their mother's financial support for the first time in her life. She shared an apartment with two other women in the city, but during law school she had lived at home in Evanston, waitressing part-time and scraping together some of her tuition from tips. Now it was Erica's turn, Marianne insisted, to live with their mother again, but of course Julia wasn't the same person she'd been as little as six months ago.

There was no other feasible option, however. Their father had died six years earlier from a heart attack, and they didn't have the money to put Julia in a home, where they didn't want to put her anyway, not until they had to. She wasn't even eligible for Medicare yet.

"I'm going to need help," Erica told her sister. "You have to stay with us a few nights a week. I can't be a twenty-four-hour babysitter. I was supposed to be in Italy right now."

She and two friends had planned a backpacking trip in western Europe as a graduation gift to themselves, the trip conceived months before Julia began getting lost on the way home from work and previously routine errands. Sometimes she would call Erica in tears, asking to be picked up, having also forgotten Erica was almost a thousand miles away.

"I *have* to stay with you? Mom doesn't need a round-the-clock caretaker. You'll be fine."

"I think she does," said Erica. "Or she will very soon. I can't do it all by myself."

"I'm sorry your trip to Europe didn't work out, but it'll still be there when everything with Mom is more settled," said Marianne.

They were in the kitchen, Erica putting away the plates and silverware from the dish rack, her sister a few steps away, not helping, staring at her phone, as she often did when they were together. It was a Friday in mid-June, a cloudless blue sky framed by the windows, crows calling hoarsely to each other from the treetops. Erica had spent the day cleaning out the closets, preparing a large donation for the Salvation Army.

Her mother had initially fretted over the old clothes and shoes and ancient, crumbling paperbacks Erica was stuffing into paper grocery bags, but after a while Julia had retreated to the backyard and sat down in the shade of an oak tree to watch chickadees and wrens flit around the feeder. She'd seen a hawk in recent weeks, hunting for smaller birds in the yard, and was keeping an eye out for its return. Erica thought this a futile project but kept her opinion to herself. Her mother needed something to occupy herself with besides television, or search-a-words and crossword puzzles, or the knitting she did to keep her hands busy, none of her scarves or hats as yet trailing off into an unsalvageable tangle.

"Easy for you to say," said Erica.

Marianne glared down at her phone. "It's true. Maybe you can go next summer instead."

"And maybe you could move back here for a little while. It wouldn't be that hard to find a subletter." Erica could feel the burn of tears in her eyes.

"My roommates wouldn't want—"

"I don't care, Marianne. You need to help us."

"Girls," Julia called from the next room. "Don't bicker. I can hear everything you're saying."

Much of the time, their mother was more or less herself. She dressed on her own and fried an egg for breakfast and showered and brushed her teeth, but some mornings she didn't want to get out of bed. Some mornings she stared up at Erica from the pillow before closing her eyes again until noon, or she confused her with someone else—her own mother, who had been dead for ten years, or her sister Alice, who lived in Florida with her third husband, from whom Julia had been estranged since their mother's death. They'd fought over the terms of the will—among other things, it was Julia who inherited the heirloom Wedgwood, which Alice had openly coveted for years. She accused Julia of conspiring with their mother before she died, which Julia had not done.

Previously Erica had thought the fight petty and infantile, but now she wished they had never quarreled. They could have used Alice's help. A different kind of aunt might have offered to come to their aid with grocery deliveries or a few days' visit every couple of months to help them look after Julia. They had cousins, Alice's son and daughter, and on their father's side there were more cousins, but they had never been close to them. Their two aunts and the uncle on their father's side were all well into their seventies and not in good health themselves. Erica knew that she and Marianne would somehow have to manage their mother's worsening condition on their own.

Marianne gave her a dirty look, Erica mouthing back, "What?" before her sister stalked into the living room, Erica following with reluctance. She had the guilty, fleeting thought that she could go out to the garage, take the car, and drive away for the night without a word, abandoning Marianne and Julia. But she wouldn't do it. She was not that kind of person, even if impulses like this one were now assailing her every day. She wondered if her mother had experienced similar bouts of rage and resentment when she and Marianne were very young. With their father at work all day and Julia at home alone with them—all those innumerable repetitive tasks, all the hours she spent with no adult to talk to—how had she survived? She had, however, Erica reminded herself. Her mother had made it through those years and delivered her and Marianne safely into their own adulthoods.

But perhaps even worse than her and her mother's disorienting role reversal was being forced to witness the incremental effacement of Julia's personality, her charm and kindness and efficiency. Her mother's green thumb, her love of new books from the library and postcards sent by friends from far-flung cities, the Saturday morning farmers' market with its familiar, friendly vendors, her early morning walks—they were all falling away.

Presently, her mother sat with her knitting on the sofa, her brown eyes lucid as she looked up at Erica and her sister. She was a real estate agent, a good one, before she'd had to give it up. When she turned sixty-five, she'd start drawing on the 401(k) she had from the realty company where she'd worked as office manager before transitioning to Realtor. She also had some disability insurance. These were the things Erica thought about now. Before graduation and her move home, she had been a film studies major with plans to relocate to Los Angeles where she would find a job as a production assistant and write screenplays in the interstices. She would meet people and work hard and somehow become important.

At the moment, this trajectory was receding from view in tandem with Julia's mental retreat and erasure. The unfairness and cruelty of it all simultaneously made Erica want to scream with rage and collapse into sobs. Nick, the classmate she was seeing during the weeks before graduation, had stopped returning her texts after she told him about her mother and why she wasn't moving to L.A. He was in San Francisco, having landed a programmer's job with a video game company. Before they'd both left campus after graduation she'd hoped, despite the odds, they might keep seeing each other, but along with the trip to Europe and her mother's deteriorating condition, she understood that he was another loss.

Julia was still looking up at her and Marianne, knitting needles clicking. She had finished a scarf yesterday and was now working on a cardigan, though Erica doubted her mother would be able to finish this more complicated project. "You girls don't have to be here with me every minute of the day," she said. "I can still look after myself."

"Did you take a shower today, Mom?" asked Marianne.

"Yes," said Julia.

"Are you sure? Because last time—"

"Yes, honey, I'm sure."

"Then why are you still wearing your pajamas?"

Julia was in her summer nightgown, but her face was made up and her hair combed. "Because they're comfortable, sweetie."

Erica sat down and put her arm around her mother's shoulders. Despite its neatness, Julia's hair smelled unwashed, but Erica let the matter rest. Julia's neurologist, Dr. Baer, had said the pace of her mental decline would likely continue to be gradual, but of course this was only an educated guess. He had sympathy for them, Erica could see, but his sympathy had the perverse effect of upsetting her. What they needed was help at home, and in this regard he could offer them nothing.

The whole situation felt like a malicious trap, although in less emotional moments, Erica recognized it was only bad luck. To make matters worse, Marianne refused to acknowledge how unfair it all was—to all of them—and her mulish insistence on taking the moral high road made Erica feel even angrier and more lost. Couldn't she agree, at least once, that it was a total fucking shit show? They were losing their mother, slowly, and Erica had to watch from the front row. Marianne at least had her job and her apartment to block her view, and Erica deeply resented her for it.

As if sensing these thoughts, Marianne shot Erica a look of guilty defiance. "I have to go," she said.

Erica stared at her. "You can't. You were going to sleep here tonight." They were supposed to eat dinner together too. Marianne had taken the train up from the city after work, but now, twenty minutes after her arrival, she was already announcing her departure.

"I can't. Sorry. It turns out I—" She looked down and shook her head. "I can't stay."

"Unbelievable," said Erica.

"Let her go," said Julia. "You and I can watch a movie and have some ice cream."

"After you eat dinner, Mom," said Marianne. She glanced again at Erica. "I have a date."

Erica looked from Julia to her sister, Marianne's eyes dodging hers. "How nice," said Erica, her voice rising. "Don't let us get in the way of your busy social life."

Marianne said nothing.

"Who is he, sweetheart?" said Julia. "Someone from work?"

"No, I met him online."

"God," said Erica.

"Make sure you meet him in a public place," said Julia.

"Of course, Mom," said Marianne, still evading Erica's gaze.

"Make sure you don't accidentally sleep with him," said Erica.

"Erica," said Julia sharply. "Your sister wouldn't do that."

Marianne shot Erica an angry look. "You're such a jerk. You could be just a little bit happy for me. I haven't gone on a date in almost a year."

Erica stood up from the sofa and stomped upstairs to her bedroom, not wanting to witness Marianne's escape. The house was hot and smelled of dust and old clothes. The air-conditioning needed to be looked at. If her mother or Marianne couldn't remember who to call, she'd have to figure it out on her own. She also wasn't sure if they had the money for a repair, but it would have to be done—summer hadn't even officially started yet.

A few weeks passed. The weather grew hotter and more humid. Erica asked her mother if she knew which company to call about the air-conditioning, but as she expected, Julia didn't know. The last time it was serviced, Erica's father was still alive and he had taken care of it. Marianne was no help either. "Just do an online search and pick someone," she advised petulantly.

Erica ended up going next door to ask the neighbors for a recommendation, and three days later a taciturn repairman arrived, a guy named Toby in a sun-faded White Sox hat whom Erica thought she recognized from high school. He smelled of cigarettes and aftershave and didn't meet her eyes when she spoke to him. He was good-looking and his behavior—he seemed annoyed with her, though she couldn't figure out why he would be—perversely attracted her to him, but she didn't try to make him talk. She recognized that she didn't want anything from him but sex, although this would probably be all he would want from her too, if he wanted something other than to be paid for his work.

He changed the air filter and checked the compressor and left her with a bill for $120. The whole visit had taken less than fifteen minutes.

The next day, her diploma arrived in the mail. She pulled it out of the envelope and peered gloomily at the thick cotton paper, the embossed gilt lettering—what did it really mean, for now and for the foreseeable future? Her mother was persisting, on the whole, still recognizably herself most of the time, but one afternoon the week after the Fourth of July, when Erica let her drive to the drugstore, Julia didn't brake for a stop sign, and at another intersection a minute later, she nearly hit a woman in the crosswalk, deeply unnerving all three of them. Regardless, Julia had no interest in forfeiting her driving privileges, despite having been told by her neurologist before these near misses that she would probably have to give them up sooner than she'd want to. And now that moment was already here. Henceforth, Erica would have to keep the car keys hidden, rendering her mother truly homebound. It was a terrible day.

Clouding up the picture further, suddenly Marianne had a boyfriend. The man she'd met online in mid-June, Jordan something or other, a commodities trader, had announced to her on a romantic evening walk along Lake Michigan, fans' roars reaching them from the Cubs game a mile away at Wrigley Field, that he wanted her to be his girlfriend. He had already deactivated his online profile and hoped she'd be willing to do the same.

"We're now officially a couple," Marianne said wonderingly to Erica and Julia a few days later.

She was so happy she started crying. Julia hugged her, tears springing to her eyes too. Erica stood next to them, riven by jealousy and a quicksand feeling of futility. When Marianne turned to her, Erica hugged her back, numb and wordless. Her sister smelled of coconut sunscreen; her cheeks were flushed, her face glowing. It was possible she had never looked better. Erica hadn't received a text from Nick in San Francisco in weeks. They were unofficially no longer a couple, if they'd ever been one.

Her sister brought Jordan home to meet them the following Sunday. He was so good-looking and so breezily charming Erica could hardly look at him and her sister without feeling a surge of jealousy so powerful she wanted to flee to her room. Not that she believed in karma, but sometimes she had to wonder—because how was it that Marianne now had so much when she herself had almost nothing—no paying job, no boyfriend, no place of her own, only the impenetrable fog of her future and their poor, unraveling mother who was hanging on for the moment, but no one knew when that would stop being the case.

When Marianne introduced her to Jordan, Erica tried to shake his hand, but he pulled her into a hug. His body was all hard muscle, broad shoulders, warm skin, his gray linen shirt open at the neck. He had a full mouth and blue eyes. He was as striking as any of the movie stars she'd had silly but ardent crushes on during her adolescence.

How long until he cheats on her? Erica wondered, the thought there before she could turn it away. Men like that . . . She and her friends in college, the ones she was planning to go to Europe with, had sometimes made a game of repeating those words like an incantation, adding on to them in a fit of drunken, escalating one-upmanship:

Men like that don't have to beg for it, ever. Men like that have their cake and eat yours too. Men like that will screw you and forget to shut the door on their way out. Men like that . . . well, what did you think *would happen?*

Erica had never gone out with a man like that, nor, as far as she knew, had her sister—until now. They'd both always ended up with guys who were cute, brainy potheads or debate team nerds or reformed frat boys who worried about liver failure and whether picking up the check constituted a microaggression.

But Jordan—this beautiful, friendly commodities trader—he seemed almost to be another species. Julia stared at him all evening, girlishly abashed whenever he found her curious, admiring eyes on him. "And who are you?" she kept asking. He or Marianne would patiently answer her as if each time was the first time they'd heard the question.

Late that night, after Jordan and Marianne had driven off in his black Tesla, Erica texted Nick in San Francisco. *Come see me,* she begged. *You can stay here at the house. My mom won't care.* He didn't reply.

She texted him again the following morning: *Can we at least be friends? I miss talking to you.* To this, a few hours later, he replied *K.*

Fuck you too, she typed but erased the words a few seconds later.

She called the air-conditioning company and asked to speak with Toby. He returned her call while she and Julia were eating dinner—grilled, marinated eggplant and a caprese salad. Perhaps the only good thing to have happened during the weeks she'd been isolated at home: she was learning how to cook.

"Is something wrong with your AC again?" Toby asked. There was no hello, only this question asked with muted resignation. Erica supposed he was in the habit of fending off complaints, justified or not.

"No," she said. "But I was wondering—" She laughed weakly, ashamed of her loneliness, her witless lunge for the first man who came to mind. Nonetheless, she was going to go through with it. Hanging up seemed a far worse alternative. "Do you want to go out sometime?" she said, her voice halting. She was standing near the sink, having gotten up from the kitchen table to talk in semi-private. She sensed her mother's eyes on her back.

There was a long, unnerving pause. When he finally spoke, he sounded puzzled. "You mean, like on a date?"

"Yes. Unless you have a girlfriend or something?"

"Or something." He paused. "No, not anymore. I was engaged for a little while but that didn't work out." More silence followed.

"I'm sorry," said Erica.

His laugh was small and embittered. "Nah, it was a good thing." He exhaled audibly. "What the hell. Let's go out."

"Are you sure?" she said.

He laughed again, less angrily. "Yes. Why, don't you want to now?"

"No, I—I do."

"How's tomorrow? Seven? You want to get a burger? We could go to Nevin's, I guess. If you like that place."

"I like it. Sure."

"You're on Judson, right?"

"Yes."

"I remember. I'll come get you. The blue house with the big tree in front?"

"That's us."

Marianne did not want to come up to Evanston to stay with their mother while Erica went out with Toby, but Erica wheedled and cajoled and finally cried over the phone until her sister agreed to do it. She and Jordan were supposed to see a movie, but fine, they would go on another night if it was so damn important to Erica that she come up to the house so she could go out with some loser from high school.

"He's not a loser," said Erica.

Marianne snorted. "Well, you'll find out soon enough."

"You can bring Mr. America with you if you can't stand to be away from him for the night."

"Maybe I will," said her sister. "I'm sure you won't mind if we do it in your bed."

"Don't you dare."

"I'm kidding. Jesus," Marianne snapped. "I wouldn't do that. Jordan wouldn't either."

Toby was a few minutes early picking her up. She was still upstairs getting dressed when the doorbell rang, and she yelled down to her mother to answer it, which was risky—Julia had recently taken to walking around the house in her underwear. Marianne was supposed to have arrived by 6:45, but she had texted to say she was running fifteen minutes late.

The doorbell rang a second time. Erica called again to her mother, but there were no sounds of movement on the first floor.

"Coming," Erica shouted, smoothing her skirt as she ran down the stairs. At the bottom, she heard a toilet flush, her mother emerging into the hall that led from the kitchen to the foyer. She was fully clothed, pants zipped, shirt buttoned.

"Who on earth is that?" she asked, looking worriedly at Erica.

"It's a friend. I'm going out with him tonight. I told you a few minutes ago."

"No, you didn't," said Julia.

Erica turned to the door and opened it. Toby had shaved, his cheeks smooth, the skin soft-looking and lightly tanned. There was no Sox hat this time, his short hair neatly combed. He was in jeans and a baby-blue polo shirt and looked like a preppy version of his tradesman self, but behind him, parked at the curb, was the Weathermakers van he had arrived in on the day he'd come to repair the air-conditioning.

"You look nice," said Erica, smiling up at him. She touched his forearm, her hand leaping toward him without her having consciously willed it.

"So do you," he said.

"Who's this?" asked Julia. She stood at Erica's side, clasping and unclasping her hands.

"Mom, this is Toby. He was here the other day to fix the air conditioner. We went to high school together."

Julia's face fell. "Why is he here now? Did it break again?"

"No, no, it's working fine. We're going out for burgers. Marianne's coming to stay with you."

Toby stood nonchalantly before them, filling the doorway, the evening light watery and golden behind him, his expression unreadable. She hadn't told him about her mother's condition, but she imagined he would say very little about it. His calmness soothed her.

"I don't need your sister to babysit me," said Julia.

"I know, Mom. She just wants to see you."

Julia frowned. "I need some time alone once in a while, for Christ's sake. You and Marianne should know that."

Half an hour later, when Erica sat across from Toby in a booth with cracked red upholstery, after Marianne had arrived from the city with takeout Chinese in a greasy white bag, Toby asked Erica why she'd lied to her mother. "Why couldn't you tell her your sister was coming to keep an eye on her?" he asked.

She laughed a little. "Why do you think?"

"Can't you tell her the truth?"

"No. It would upset her."

He shook his head. "Jesus. I don't envy you."

"I'm sure you don't."

"I mean, who would?"

She laughed. "No need to mince words." She raised her beer glass, toasting him, before draining half of it. Her throat and sinuses burned from the coldness.

"Sorry," he said. "It's just—what the hell do you say?"

"Nothing, I suppose. Let's talk about something else, something lighter." She took another drink of her beer. "What do you think happens after we die?"

He grinned, the first sign that he had a sense of humor. "I have no fucking idea."

She had a second beer before their burgers arrived. She ordered a third beer, keeping pace with him, but he didn't finish his third, whereas she did. When she stood up to go to the bathroom, she felt dizzy, her hand flying out to grab the edge of the table. She whooped involuntarily at her clumsiness. Toby looked at her with a mixture of concern and wariness, though he was also sort of smiling. "You're drunk," he said.

"Maybe," she said, nodding, her head loose on the stalk of her neck.

"No more for you," he said. "Okay?"

"Aren't you responsible."

He nodded, his expression grave. She still had no real idea how to flirt with him. "My mother's an alcoholic," he said.

She stared at him, the words hitting her hard. "And mine's losing her mind," she said quietly. She was trying not to cry and turned abruptly away, toward the bathrooms at the back of the dining room. Each step felt ponderous and deliberate. It had been two months since she'd had this much to drink—her last night on campus, the night before graduation.

The beers at Nevin's came in pint glasses. All around her, people her age or further into their twenties stood in pairs and small groups, drinking and playing darts and eating the kind of food she didn't cook for herself and her mother, not anymore. The noisy, clammy bar felt alien and dispiriting, the opposite of suspenseful or exciting. She realized she was very tired, that she should apologize to Toby and ask him to take her home before she embarrassed herself further.

He'd paid the check when she returned from the bathroom, but she didn't ask him to take her home. She didn't want to go yet; she wasn't sure when she would. She hadn't had a night to herself since graduation, that day of wind whipping off her and her friends' mortarboards, scrambling their gowns about their legs, everyone all smiles and long, emotional embraces. Her mother had hung on, only once publicly losing her bearings.

Toby gripped her elbow as they left the bar and walked to his van. After she was seated inside, she discovered her wallet was missing. She had brought her handbag into the bathroom where three other women were gathered, laughing at something on one of their phones. She might have left her bag gaping open by the sink while she peed, but she could not remember.

"It must be in the restaurant," he said. "I'll go look. You stay here, okay?" The wan light from the streetlight made his face look sallow and earnest.

"I doubt it's in there," she said, her voice cracking. "I think someone might have stolen it." She reached toward him, unable to meet his eyes. She worried he was angry with her. All she'd done the whole night was make one plea after another for his pity, but he put his arms around her, drawing her close to his chest. He was so warm and almost familiar and his whiskers were already growing in. She could feel their rasp on her cheek, and she couldn't help it then—she started sobbing, her body shaking from the force of her grief.

He held on to her, one hand tentatively touching her hair. "Erica, hey. Don't cry," he said. "We'll find it. Where do you last remember holding it?"

Her nose was running, leaking onto his shirt, but she didn't pull away. She cried and he kept his arms around her while outside on the sidewalk, groups of college kids ambled by, summer school students at the university less than a mile away, their conversation and laughter pausing as they glanced into Toby's van. Erica could feel their detached, curious eyes on her before they moved away. So recently, she had been one of them.

"I don't want to go home yet," she said, and Toby nodded as if he understood. He tightened his arms around her. There was more laughter on the sidewalk, more strangers passing in cheerful, impervious groups.

He sighed. "No, of course you don't," he said so quietly she had to strain to hear his words. She wanted him to kiss her, but he didn't. He was patient and considerate, much more so than she was.

She could picture her mother at home, nodding off in her favorite chair in front of the TV, her sister lying on the sofa, staring down at her phone. She knew Marianne would rush off as soon as she walked in the door, the takeout containers and dirty dishes still on the kitchen table, although maybe this time her sister had put down her phone long enough to clean up. Unlike Erica, however, Marianne would be able to summon a cab and return to the city where Jordan was doubtless waiting for her. Erica would be left behind to help their mother up to bed and to sit with her until she fell asleep. And it was she who would answer when Julia called out in the night, asking for a glass of water, asking after she finished it where Erica had gone, begging her not to leave again.

The Monkey's Uncle Louis

Louis's younger sister Anne had adopted a monkey, news she shared with him over the phone, her call waking him early on a Tuesday morning, on the first day of the fall semester. She wanted to know if he'd like to come to Florida to meet the monkey. It was a white-bellied capuchin, a female. She was very sweet-natured, smart, and funny. Anne sounded smitten, a little dazed—the happiest she'd sounded in a while.

"I suppose I could," he said. "The first few weeks of the term aren't too busy." He could hear noises in the background, a series of beeps followed by laughter. "What's her name?" he asked.

"Bill and I haven't decided yet," said Anne. "I'll send you an email with the names we're considering."

"All right. If you want to."

"You're not happy for us," she said flatly.

"That's not true. I am happy for you," he said. "You sound good."

"I'm glad you think so."

Before they hung up he asked, "Is it legal to have a monkey in Florida? Don't you need a permit or something?"

His sister hesitated, a sound escaping her throat that he'd been familiar with since childhood. She was trying not to cry. "Yes, of course. We have one, Louis. We're not criminals."

The email with the proposed monkey names arrived that evening while he was eating dinner alone at an Olive Garden near his house. He only cooked on weekends, when his wife was home. Nearly every Friday, she flew back to Chicago from Hartford where she worked as a hospital administrator, or he flew to her. They'd been making these trips for six of the nine years they'd been married. Louis was a tenured professor in American history at a college three miles from their house, and when Sandra was hired by the hospital in Hartford, they'd both agreed his job was too good to give up, with its summers off and benefits package and periodic sabbaticals. They had a cat, Jules, but no children; Jules was Sandra's cat and pre-dated Louis, although the cat lived in Chicago instead of Hartford. In the last year, Jules had developed diabetes, and in Sandra's absence, it was Louis who administered the insulin shots, the cat submitting to them with disappointment on his owlish face, his tail flicking back and forth while Louis inserted the needle under the skin behind his neck. His disappointment was even plainer when he peered each morning into his food bowl: the vet had put him on a special diet, one with more protein but less flavor.

Dear Louis,

Here are the names we're thinking about for our monkey. Can you rank them from 1 to 5, with 1 being your first choice, and send them back to me?

Lucinda
Molly
Jeannie
Becky
Claire

*Bill and I would love it if you'd come down the next weekend
you're free—what about Labor Day? If Sandra isn't planning
to be in Hartford that weekend, maybe she can come too.*

Love, Anne

P.S. We are already so in love with our little monkey!

He had misgivings about his sister's plan to make a home for a wild
creature that was likely soon to bring its new keepers to their knees.
What would happen if in the middle of the night the monkey escaped
the house and, homesick for its native jungle, started screeching from
the treetops and rattling neighbors' doors and windows?

Online he found a video of a gang of capuchins chasing after
four fawn-colored Chihuahuas, someone off-screen laughing
maniacally. The Chihuahuas looked terrified, their eyes bulging
even more than Louis thought was normal. The monkeys screamed
and pogoed up and down when they overtook the horrified dogs.

Another video showed a tufted capuchin feverishly pulling
socks and underwear out of a chest of drawers and flinging them
over its shoulders.

Dear Anne,

Just curious, do monkeys like bananas as much as they say?

*Of the names you sent, I think I like Lucinda the best,
Claire probably the least. (It's a nice enough name, but maybe
not quite right for a monkey?) I don't really have strong
feelings about the other three names, but I suppose Molly
would be my second choice.*

*I'll see what Sandra is able to do regarding a visit. Labor
Day might work.*

Hello to Bill from both of us.

Your brother, Louis

P.S. I guess this makes me the monkey's uncle.

At first Sandra didn't believe him when he called to share his sister's news. "I'm too tired tonight for jokes," she said.

"It's not a joke. Anne and Bill really have adopted a monkey."

There was a long pause before she said, "Can they return it?"

"I don't know. I didn't ask."

"What's wrong with a dog?"

"Nothing," he said. "But apparently they wanted a monkey."

"I don't think I can change my plane ticket for next weekend without a big penalty," she said. "What if you go the weekend after Labor Day when I'll be here? Or we could meet down there the following weekend."

"I'll check with my sister. I do think we should both go."

"What if that monkey gets into our room in the middle of the night? I don't know if I'll be able to sleep."

"I'll protect you."

"We'll see," she said dryly.

"Which name do you like best?" he asked. "Claire, Lucinda, Molly, Jeannie, or Becky? Anne wants to know."

His wife was silent for a moment. "Your sister has lost her mind."

The monkey, whom Anne and Bill had named Molly, stared worriedly at Louis from her perch on Bill's shoulder when he and Sandra arrived at the front door of her new home. She was dressed in a diaper and a pink T-shirt with *Daddy's Girl* in cursive on the front, a chunk of mango oozing in one of her small hands. She was tinier than Louis expected, at most five pounds. Jules weighed ten. The monkey's head and chest were blond-furred; the rest of her was covered in brown fur. She made a hissing noise and bared her teeth, revealing two sharp-looking fangs. Sandra hung back, hesitating. Louis put his hand on her arm.

"Oh, don't worry, she's harmless," said Anne with an anxious laugh. "Such a little love." She caressed the monkey's miniature head. Ducking away from Anne's hand, Molly continued to stare distrustfully at Louis and his wife.

Bill and Anne stepped away from the door and led them into the front room, the monkey craning its neck to keep its eyes on them. "I've put you in your usual room," said Anne. "It's right next to Molly's."

"Molly has her own room?" asked Sandra. She looked at Louis in alarm.

"Don't say anything," he mouthed.

They passed the living room, where a large playpen had been installed in the space between the sofa and the television cabinet. Wooden alphabet blocks, a large plastic pineapple, a one-eyed Mr. Potato Head, and a constellation of small stuffed animals—frogs, kittens, and two monkeys that resembled Molly—were scattered in and around the playpen. Louis wondered how long it would take the monkey to start hurling the blocks at the windows or at her new parents. Next to the television crouched a stuffed monkey much larger than the two on the floor.

"Of course she has her own room!" said Anne. "We didn't want her to get into the habit of sleeping in ours, but she does come in sometimes in the middle of the night, wanting to cuddle."

Bill looked at his wife. "I think we're going to have to start locking our bedroom door when we turn in."

Anne shook her head, her dark curls bobbing. "No, no, we can't do that. Molly wouldn't like that."

Sandra glanced at Louis again, but he pretended not to notice. "She's very cute," he said. "Very precocious too, it sounds like."

"Yes, she's extremely bright," said Anne. "The breeder we got her from up near Orlando told us she's one of the smartest monkeys he's ever known."

"Maybe she'll ace the SATs and get into Harvard by the time she's twelve," said Sandra.

Anne didn't laugh, but out of loyalty to his wife, Louis did. "That's funny," he said.

"I thought so," said Sandra.

"I hope she gets a scholarship," said Bill. "I don't think we could afford any of the Ivies."

Molly finished the mango and let out a deafening shriek. Bill winced and put a hand over his right ear. "Ah, Molly, no. I told you not to do that." He tried to catch the monkey's eye but she leapt off his shoulder onto Anne's head and covered Anne's eye sockets with her small but deft hands, both of them sticky with mango juice. With an embarrassed laugh, Anne tried to pry the monkey loose, but Molly refused to be dislodged.

"Take it easy on your mom," said Bill, putting a cautioning hand on Molly's back. "You know she doesn't like it when you do that."

Molly blinked up at him and opened her mouth but this time no sounds emerged. Louis eyed her fangs; he doubted his sister was considering having them filed down.

"I need a nap," said Sandra. "Would anyone object?"

"No, go right ahead," said Anne, still blind. "We can all take Molly to the beach this afternoon. I need to make her lunch now, and I have sandwich fixings for you whenever you're ready."

Louis looked from Anne to the monkey, sensing they were both suffering in very personal ways; his brother-in-law also seemed tired and dispirited. Louis was certain that living with his sister required more stoicism than he himself would have been capable of. Anne was almost pathologically thin-skinned and anxious, but Bill, for reasons he and Sandra had speculated over many times, remained committed. His own marriage, Louis supposed, was doubtless a source of speculation for Anne and Bill too.

"Lock the door," said Sandra after they were alone in their room, one of its dusky pink walls streaked above the baseboard with what looked like dried mud. "That monkey must know how to use a doorknob if she sneaks into their room at night."

"She's cute," he said. "Don't you think?"

His wife gave him a wry look. "Yes, she is, but what's she doing here? She's a wild animal."

"Don't talk so loud," he said. "They can probably hear us."

"Good, because they should listen to what I'm saying."

He shook his head. "Don't be cranky. You didn't have to come."

Sandra snorted. "You told me I had to."

"I didn't say you had to. I just thought it would be a good idea if you did."

"That's basically the same thing," she said, flopping down onto the bed. She sat up again a second later, her expression pinched, and groped under the pillow. "What is this?" she said, pulling out two very brown and squashed bananas. "The monkey's secret stash?"

He laughed. "I guess they weren't kidding about how smart she is."

Sandra looked disgusted. "I knew this would be a bad idea." She thrust a hand under the other pillow and extracted a third banana, this one blacker than the other two. "How long do you think this has been here?" She waved the black banana at him.

"Probably no more than three weeks. I think that's how long they've had her." He went over to the streaks on the wall and bent down to sniff them. "Smells like banana," he said.

"Wonderful," said Sandra. She got up and dropped the squashed fruit into a trash can by the dresser. "I think we're going to have to ask Anne to change the sheets. I'm not sleeping in a bed that smells like rotting bananas. We're lucky there aren't any fruit flies."

Somewhere in the house they heard the monkey screeching. "I hope your sister has gotten that creature off her head by now," said Sandra.

"I think we'd better tell them about the sheets later," he said.

Anne had a rainbow-colored leash for the monkey and a matching harness, which she assured Louis they'd be using at the beach. Molly sat quietly on Anne's lap as Bill drove them toward the ocean, Louis next to Sandra in the backseat, the air conditioner not cooling down the car fast enough; he'd already sweated through his T-shirt and could feel his boxers bunching against his groin. A half-open diaper bag sat on the hump between him and Sandra;

inside, he could see two Ziploc bags bulging with Cheerios and Goldfish crackers, two juice boxes, and several diapers. There was also a tiny pair of pink socks and what looked like a onesie. He wondered who among his sister's and Bill's friends had been introduced to the monkey, and if any of Anne's friends had thrown her a shower. He hoped so, but didn't ask. Sandra would think he was a lunatic and chastise him later.

"Uncle Louis," said Sandra, noticing where he was looking. "Don't steal your niece's Goldfish. I see you eyeballing them."

"Don't you dare eat those," said Anne. She'd put on some makeup, red lipstick and black mascara, and had tied up her hair in a yellow bandanna, over which she'd placed a pair of sunglasses, large black ones that covered half her face.

"I'm not going to eat them," he said. "Sandra's trying to get me in trouble."

His wife pursed her lips. "If you thought you could get away with it, you'd eat them."

"You need to bring him some snacks of his own," said Bill, meeting Sandra's eyes in the rearview mirror. "Anne brought me a Power Bar."

"I brought us all Power Bars," said Anne, a hint of smugness in her tone.

"That was nice of you," said Sandra, who Louis knew didn't like energy bars of any kind. Neither of them had mentioned the rotten bananas or the sheets yet. Sandra was waiting for him to do it, but he was stalling, certain it would spoil their beach trip.

The afternoon was punishingly hot, the air torpid with humidity, the fronds of the palm trees bordering the streets limp in the sun. He'd forgotten that September was sometimes as unbearable as August. Most years he and Sandra visited at Thanksgiving or Christmas, the weather in both Hartford and Chicago by that point reliably bad. He and his sister were all that remained of their close family; their mother had died two years earlier, their father ten years before her. Bill had grown up in Fort Lauderdale, and his parents and one of his two brothers still lived nearby. He doubted that any of them had met the monkey—Anne didn't like her in-laws, who she thought blamed her for their lack of grandchildren. Bill's brothers were unmarried; one had a male partner and the other, who was secretive and out of touch for months at a time, had never talked about his love life with them.

"Will it be too hot for Molly at the beach?" asked Sandra.

"Oh, no, no," said Anne. "She has family in the jungles of Costa Rica. She loves the heat. The beach is one of her favorite places."

"I'm guessing you've taken her down here already," said Louis.

"Every day we can manage it," said Anne.

"Nine times now," said Bill, glancing at Anne. "I think."

"But who's counting?" said Sandra under her breath.

Louis elbowed her side. She tried to scowl at him but instead had to bite her lip to keep from laughing.

If Anne or Bill had heard her, they gave no sign. Bill was slowing down to park the minivan, a white behemoth purchased with optimism three years earlier in anticipation of a human baby. Louis had asked his sister the previous Christmas if she and Bill were considering adoption, but Anne said they weren't. "If we can't have a baby of our own, we don't want one." After a pause, she'd added, "He'd probably be willing to adopt, but I don't want to." She'd had three miscarriages in four years; she was forty-three and a former heavy smoker, which her doctor thought might be partly responsible for the miscarriages. Bill was forty-six, the same age as Louis. He'd never smoked, but he sometimes joked that he liked smoked meats, which Anne did not find funny.

Louis and Sandra didn't want children, which for reasons that weren't clear to him his sister resented. ("It's because we haven't been through any of the same difficulties she has," Sandra insisted. "If we wanted kids too, she'd feel better." But he didn't think this made sense. "If we wanted kids and went on to have them," he said, "she'd feel even worse, wouldn't she?" "Not necessarily," said Sandra. "It's not logical. Not at all.")

The glare from the sand scraped at Louis's eyes, despite his polarized sunglasses. Sandra had insisted he pack a hat, and he'd also brought her sun hat, a wide-brimmed straw one that made her look girlish and unattainable. She was two years older than Anne but, with her unlined olive skin and trimmer figure, she looked several years younger. Louis had spent the summer with her in Hartford, and they were both still adjusting to his return to Chicago for the start of the school year. She'd been searching for a comparable job in Illinois but hadn't yet found one, despite having made it to the final round of interviews for several. The positions had all gone to men, she'd eventually discovered and been furious over, Louis commiserating in his own disappointment over these hirings. The trend wasn't the same in the history department or elsewhere on campus; most of the new jobs were going to women. Sandra had had a caustic response to this disclosure: "Most men don't want university teaching jobs," she said. "For one, they don't pay very much. No offense to you, Louis, but you know it's true."

Anne was trying to clip the leash to Molly's harness, the monkey shrieking and skittering from her lap to Bill's in her excitement. Bill grabbed the monkey and held her determinedly while Anne attached the leash.

"Can you bring the diaper bag?" Bill asked over his shoulder.

"Sure," said Louis, reaching for it, but Sandra snatched it first and slung it over her shoulder.

Friday afternoon and the beach was festooned with umbrellas and clusters of chairs on which oiled-up, exhausted parents reclined, dazed by the heat, their children scattered around them, digging energetically in the sand or else sobbing over some recent affront. Molly rode into the melee on Bill's shoulders, children's heads turning when they spotted her, their excavations paused.

"A monkey!" several of them cried, before dropping their plastic shovels and running over. The children twirled and danced around Molly and her parents on sandy, sun-browned feet, pointing up at her, their faces transfigured by joy.

Molly stared down at them from her regal height with what looked to Louis like scorn. The monkey blinked and turned to Anne, who stepped closer and put a protective hand on her tiny blond head. In the next second, the monkey sprang from Bill's shoulders onto Anne's head and worked her little hands beneath Anne's sunglasses, covering her eyes in a repeat of what had happened at the house. The kids' laughter at this maneuver grew hysterical. Sandra stood a few feet away, covering her mouth with one hand to muffle her laughter, taking it all in. Louis tried to catch her eye.

"I want to pet the monkey," cried a little girl in a pink swimsuit, her belly a large hard balloon. Louis watched her stare commandingly at Bill and Anne, admiring her a little. She was still years away from self-consciousness and its inconveniences.

A little boy with black hair and a skinny girl in a ruffled blue swimsuit made the same demand. "I love monkeys," said the boy. "Let me pet him!"

"Me too," cried the girl, both arms raised toward Anne and the monkey. "I want to pet him."

"She's a girl," said Anne. "Her name is Molly."

"Molly," said the girl in the ruffled swimsuit. She giggled. "That's my mom's name."

A second little boy asked if he could please touch the monkey's tail.

Louis saw Bill grimace before Sandra spoke up from behind. "Come on, you guys. You have to let them pet the monkey. Why else bring her here?"

Bill turned to Sandra with a harassed look as he tried to free his wife's eyes from the monkey's grip. "Molly is very excitable," he said. "We need to give her time to adjust to her new surroundings." He looked pointedly at the children. "Give us about fifteen minutes. Why don't you go back to your sandcastles for now?"

"You said that the last time we saw you," said the girl in the pink swimsuit. "But you left before you let us pet her."

Sandra laughed in a hard burst.

"I'm sure if we—" said Louis, looking at Bill.

"For God's sake," cried Anne from behind the monkey's hands. "Help me!"

Molly screeched as Bill tried with more force to pry her loose from his wife. When at last he succeeded, the monkey leapt onto his head and was about to clap her hands over his eyes when Bill grabbed them and lifted her squirming hirsute body away from his face. "Molly, no," he snapped. "How many times have we told you not to do that?"

"Does she understand you?" asked one of the little boys.

"Apparently not," said Sandra. "Or else she's decided to ignore them."

"You think this is all very funny," said Anne, her face blanched with fury. "But it's not. This is our life!"

"I was only making a little joke," said Sandra, taken aback. "I'm sorry if I offended you."

"You've been making your little jokes at our expense since you and Louis got here, and they're not funny at all," said Anne. "You can see very well just how difficult this is."

"I think we need to change Molly's diaper," Bill said ominously.

"Then do it," said Anne through gritted teeth. She yanked the diaper bag from Sandra's shoulder and thrust it at her husband. Molly bared her teeth.

"Stop it," said Anne. "You're being very naughty, Molly!"

"Do you think we should go home?" asked Louis.

Bill and his sister both shot him annoyed looks. "I—I just thought it might be a good idea," Louis mumbled.

"We're not going home yet," said Anne. "Molly needs her beach time."

The kids returned to their shovels and pails without another word, cowed by Anne's outburst. One of their mothers had removed her sunglasses and was glaring at Bill, but he hadn't noticed. Anne was ordering him to put down a towel and change the monkey's diaper as he struggled to keep Molly away from his face. "You do it," he said. "You can see very well that I have my hands full right now."

Sandra came up beside Louis and gripped his elbow. "I'm sorry if I offended your sister," she whispered. "But she's going to need a better sense of humor if she expects them to survive this whole thing. Bill too."

The monkey squirmed free of Bill's grip and leapt onto the sand, more children turning to stare at her in electrified amazement. Anne was still holding the leash and ran after Molly in her flight toward the water. Near the shoreline, her sagging diaper fell off and some of the children screamed with laughter. With a cry of distress, Anne jerked the leash to stop Molly and bent down to pick up the diaper before the tide carried it away.

"Calm down, Molly," she said. "You're acting like you've never been here before."

Before Anne could stand up, the monkey jumped onto her back and pressed her hands over Anne's eye sockets again. Louis winced as his sister released a great howl of frustration and dropped the diaper at her feet.

Bill stared down at the sand, his mouth a grim line, before he went over to his wife and picked up the soiled diaper. He glanced at Louis helplessly.

"I'm sorry," said Louis.

Bill didn't reply.

"I think she's overstimulated," said Anne in a strained voice. "She's not used to sharing us with strangers for so long."

On the ride home, Sandra scrolled through email on her phone and Louis fell asleep with his head against the window, his right hand resting on his wife's warm thigh. His neck was stiff by the time Bill turned abruptly into the driveway and jolted him awake.

"What's wrong with you?" cried Anne. Molly chittered from her lap and looked imperiously up at Bill.

"Come on," he said. "I wasn't going that fast."

In the house, Sandra went directly to their room, but Louis lingered in the den, knowing he needed to mention the sheets. Bill muttered something about a shower, and left them alone with the monkey.

"I know what you're thinking," said Anne, from the sofa she'd collapsed onto. Molly was in her playpen, denuding the Mr. Potato Head and tossing the pieces aside.

"What?" asked Louis.

"That we've bitten off more than we can chew."

"I wasn't thinking that," he said.

"I was," she said, morose.

"Do you have to keep her?"

Anne was silent for several seconds. "No, we don't, but I want to," she finally said, her look imploring.

"You're sure?"

She nodded. "I think we can make it work if we're committed."

"Does Bill think so too?"

She leaned her head back against the sofa. "I don't know."

After a moment Louis said, "Don't you think you should ask him?"

Her mascara was smeared beneath her eyes, her lipstick long gone. The monkey's presence had drained her in a way Louis hadn't expected—he was used to her air of aggrieved injury when she was upset, but now she only seemed sad and luckless. "It's only been a few weeks," she said softly. "He's just taking longer to adjust than I am."

"Have you adjusted?"

She nodded. "Yes. She's the light of my life."

Louis had to look away from her beseeching gaze.

"I know it's hard to believe, but most of the time she's very sweet and well-behaved."

"That's good," he said. "I want you to be happy."

Anne started to cry. "But I didn't think this would be so hard." She wiped roughly at her cheeks.

"Are you sure you should keep her? Really sure?" he asked, stricken.

"Yes," she said. "I'm keeping her no matter what."

An hour after midnight, Louis was still awake. Out in the yard, a bird he couldn't identify began singing, another bird answering from farther away. When it was quiet again, he heard the monkey push open the door of her room. Sandra had asked at dinner if they'd thought about keeping her in a cage at night, but Anne said they weren't willing to treat their monkey like a prisoner. Molly would eventually get used to sleeping through the night on her own. No one expected a human baby to sleep for more than a few hours at a time right after coming home from the hospital—why should they expect a baby monkey to be any different?

Louis slipped out of bed, Sandra murmuring and rolling onto her side as he left the room. At the far end of the hall, he could see Molly turning the knob of Bill and Anne's bedroom door, but it didn't open. Anne opened it after a few seconds, her white night-gown phosphorescent in the glow from the hall night-light. Molly leapt into her arms, and Louis, overcome by shame, watched his sister press her face to the monkey's soft head, both she and Molly closing their eyes in ecstatic surrender.

Direct Sunlight

The twins' father had a second family, one he'd kept hidden throughout his life. Even after he died, it was more than fifteen years before the twins and their mother learned of his secret. His two other children were younger than the twins by two and three years, and they had glamorous names, Portia and Diana, whereas the twins' names, Tom and Stephanie, sounded flat and unremarkable to Stephanie's ears. Her half sisters' names made her wonder if their father had loved these girls, and by extension, their mother, Jennifer, more than he'd loved her and Tom and their own mother, Carol.

He'd died when the second tower fell. They were told he was in a stairwell with hundreds of others fleeing for their lives, probably somewhere between floors thirty-five and twenty when he was killed. They hoped his death was instantaneous, but there was no way to know for sure, and very little of his remains were ever recovered—half a library card, his wedding ring, a shoe their mother swore belonged to him. She and Tom were eight when he died, a week into second grade, and they lived in a Park Slope townhouse with a dog and a cat, both dead now too, Portia and Diana innocently living their own parallel lives in Queens.

It was the strangest experience of Stephanie's life—other than the immediate aftermath of her father's death—to learn that not only was he unfaithful to her mother, he had in fact had a whole other identity, one almost mythical in the devious ingenuity it implied, in its cinematic richness and mystery, as Stephanie could not stop resentfully imagining.

They might never have found out, either, but for a conversation Carol overheard at her dermatologist's office. Jennifer was there in the waiting room with her own mother, seated a few chairs away from Carol. It was October 1, Tom and Stephanie's father's birthday, a warm and cloudless day. He would have been fifty-five, and Carol heard Jennifer say his first name, Kent, and go on to tell her mother that each year she had baked him a devil's food cake from scratch and served it with butter pecan ice cream and fresh strawberries.

"That's exactly what I used to make for my husband's birthday," Carol interjected, stunned by the coincidence. "And his name was Kent too."

Jennifer, who had known of Kent's other, more public family, didn't recognize Carol, having only ever seen a photograph of her, and in the intervening years, Carol had changed her hair color and lost weight. (Stephanie imagined that at one time Jennifer must have collected facts and formed very specific ideas about her rival but had doubtless allowed many of them to slip away.)

She kept on talking, oblivious to Carol's identity, mentioning the tragedy of Kent's death, the Irish accent that showed itself when he drank but otherwise was hard to detect—he had moved with his mother to New York from Limerick when he was nine. "He was always ready with a corny joke too," she said. " 'Why did the leprechaun go outside? To sit on the paddy-o.' " She smiled and shook her head. "Terrible, I know, but he always made me laugh."

With these facts darkly aligning in Carol's mind, there was nowhere to go but black, and when she woke up, the receptionist, the dermatologist, and one of his nurses were all standing over her,

Dr. Wing gently repeating her name until she opened her eyes and broke into tears. "Where is she?" Carol sobbed. "I need to know what she knew about us. I need to know how she lived with herself."

It surprised Stephanie that although her mother had no plans to befriend Jennifer, her mother did not react as negatively as Stephanie anticipated when Carol met this other woman in a park near the townhouse where Carol still lived, on a day not long after their unheralded encounter at the dermatologist's office.

Jennifer was embarrassed and contrite, Carol later reported. Apparently, she hadn't expected to have two children with a man who had no plans to marry her, a man who had already fathered two children with the woman he was in fact married to.

The first pregnancy, all right, Carol supposed she could understand—things happened when people had affairs—but the second pregnancy? This couldn't have been an accident, could it? Was either child truly an accident?

"I don't know what I was thinking," Jennifer confessed. "I was only twenty-four when we met. I must have thought that at some point you would leave him or"—she hesitated—"he would leave you." Jennifer couldn't meet Carol's eyes as she spoke these words.

"I started crying then," Carol told Stephanie. "Of course this was what she was hoping for. What on earth did other women hope for if not that? And it wasn't hard to imagine your father leaving us. I was fat and he was so good-looking, women were always ogling him when we were out together."

"Mom, you were never fat," said Stephanie. "You were very pretty too. You still are."

They were on the phone, her mother's voice alternately a whisper and a sob. It was a little after ten in the morning and Stephanie was in her cubicle at the museum fundraising office where she worked in Echo Park. She had lived in California for the last two years and was happy, more or less, until her mother called to inform her that her father was not the blameless man they had always believed him to be. In truth, he was a liar and a cheat of such magnitude it almost defied comprehension.

"I couldn't stop crying," said Carol. "But I knew I had to control myself because what could I do about it? It had happened and your father was responsible and then he left us all to fend for ourselves."

Stephanie sighed but tried not to let her mother hear it. "It's not like he died on purpose," she murmured.

"How can you be so calm?" Her mother sounded genuinely bewildered.

"I'm not that calm, but I'm at work. I have to be quiet," she whispered. "You know there's no privacy here." She was sure her coworkers were eavesdropping, bored in their cubicles and buzzed on coffee and the cheap sugar cookies someone had left in the kitchen, junk food washing up on the countertop next to the microwave with the regularity of the tides.

"You should come home for a few days. Your brother won't even let me talk to him about it."

"I can't come home until Thanksgiving," she said. "I'm sorry, Mom."

"That's almost two months away."

"You can come visit me."

"I'll think about it," her mother said, dispirited. Stephanie knew she was lonely—her mother's boyfriend of the last three years, Chip, an advertising executive, had moved to London for a year to open a new office. Carol had stayed behind, although he'd asked her to come with him. ("What on earth would I do there?" she'd wondered. "Enjoy yourself, maybe?" was Stephanie's reply.)

"Where are Diana and Portia?" she asked her mother now. "Are you going to meet them?"

"I don't know. I suppose I will. Do you want to?"

"I'm not sure." She paused. "I'm guessing Tom doesn't want to."

"Of course not. Your brother wants nothing to do with any of this."

"I'm not surprised."

"He prefers to act like your father never existed."

"That's not true, Mom. He's just not very sentimental."

"That's an understatement," Carol scoffed.

Her brother still lived in New York, where he was in medical school, gradually sleeping his way through the women in his class and the one below it, although he claimed only to be dating around. It didn't surprise her he had no interest in looking into their father's past, as he himself possibly risked repeating it.

And hanging over everything—their father's infidelity, his violent, horrifying death, the existence of two other children bearing his genes—was money. Carol had been awarded more than three million dollars by the administrators of the compensation fund for the victims of September 11. Jennifer too, as it turned out, had admitted to receiving a similar sum from the fund's administrators.

"That man, that lawyer, I spoke with several times," said Carol. "The one who decided how much money to give the victims' families—he knew about her but he never told me."

Over the top of her cubicle, Stephanie saw Dmitri, her boss, poke his head out of his office and look in her direction before he stepped back inside and shut the door. She stared down at her desk, at the assortment of papers, at the blinking cursor on her monitor, her heart beating hard. Dmitri was only five years her senior and looked like a soap star with his blond streaks and broad, muscular chest. Merrill, her roommate, thought it plausible Stephanie would end up in bed with him after the next drunken office party. They were the two youngest people in the office, and Stephanie had had a crush on him for months, but was certain it would be a disastrous move to sleep with him. She wondered if anyone she knew behaved well when confronted with the possibility of sex with someone attractive. Not if they're still breathing, her brother would have said.

"Mom, would you—would you really have wanted to know?" she asked. "Don't you think it would have made Dad's death even harder to deal with?"

"No," her mother said firmly. "I wish I'd known."

Stephanie listened to her mother's long, angry sigh. "I'm sorry," she said quietly. "I have to go. My boss just came out and gave me a look."

"I don't know what to do."

"Go to London and see Chip, or come out here and see me."

"Maybe. I don't know. I love you, sweetie."

"I love you too, Mom."

After they hung up, she sat in a stupor at her desk for several minutes, pretending everything was fine, pretending to go over a list of annual donors who hadn't yet pledged for the coming year. She didn't know how she felt—other than very bad, for her mother especially—about Jennifer with her three-million-dollar widow's fund or her half sisters who had known for a few years that she and Tom existed but had not tried to contact either of them. And how much of the blame resided with Jennifer, really? What did it all actually mean, other than that her father wasn't the man she'd been told he was? That he had led a double life with astonishing skill and seemingly conscienceless daring and likely would have continued to until someone, probably Jennifer herself—tired of her role as his clandestine wife—stepped out from behind the curtain and exposed him for the selfish fraud he was?

That night she couldn't sleep. Her poor mother—it was she who had to pay the full price for her dead husband's duplicity. Although Stephanie was trying to figure out how to live with this revelation too, her father had been dead for eighteen years, almost three times her age when he died. He was now more of an idea than a person to her, and had been for a while. There was also the fact that his death, tasteless as it seemed to acknowledge it, had enriched their family. Her mother had sensibly invested the money given to her by the government, thus guaranteeing her and her children's present and future comfort.

Stephanie wasn't sure what purpose it would serve to meet her half sisters and their mother. She could understand her brother's unwillingness to make nice and bear up or whatever it was they'd be doing if they went to Diana and Portia (those names!) and tried to befriend them. Even if they shared some DNA, it didn't mean they were required to like each other.

A few days passed. Her mother called again while Stephanie was at work, but she dodged the call. When she tried her mother later, she didn't pick up. That same evening, Stephanie's roommate took her to a sensory-deprivation float tank, which nearly caused Stephanie to have a panic attack. She should have known beforehand she wouldn't like the damp, claustrophobic, pitch-black space.

"How did this ever catch on?" she complained as Merrill drove them home. "What the hell is wrong with people?"

Merrill looked over at her. "I don't know. I like it. It relaxes me."

"You also like liverwurst."

"True."

Stephanie stared blearily out the window while Merrill sang with the radio, an Eagles song Stephanie knew the words to but didn't feel like singing. They stopped at the Ralph's a few blocks from their apartment, and Merrill went in to buy Oreos and a bottle of wine while Stephanie waited in the car and looked at her phone. She had only talked to her brother once since the news about Jennifer and their sisters had crashed into their lives a week earlier. But it wasn't a surprise—he was busy with his fourth year of medical school and his various short-term girlfriends. He was going to be someone—this was the aura he cultivated, at any rate.

At home that evening, she and Merrill drank the wine as they watched *Witness*, which Merrill had seen more than a dozen times already. Stephanie didn't want any Oreos. The wine made the cookies taste foul, but Merrill ate several and cried throughout the movie as if it were her life she was witnessing unfurling before her in muted colors and vintage clothes. "I'd still do Harrison Ford," she said when it was over, her eyes streaming tears. "What a babe."

"He's like, eighty now," said Stephanie.

"So? I wouldn't care." Merrill sighed. "I love him."

They were both lonely and sex-starved, but the bars and singles' meetups they'd gone to had left them feeling demoralized by the attention-getting dress code ("Yuppie Slut" was what Merrill called it) that seemed a tacit requirement. They'd watched other women preen and stand with breasts thrust out, giggling at every bland or inane word the men drunkenly aimed their way. And Tinder—no, it simply wasn't possible. Too depressing and pointless. She and Merrill clung to each other and their female friends who were of like mind, although Merrill had been asked out recently by a client at the law firm where she was a paralegal and was thinking she might let him take her to dinner, even if he was slightly cross-eyed and had a laugh that sounded like he was gargling.

Stephanie likewise held on to the possibility of Dmitri, but was afraid to make her feelings known—because what if they did sleep together, and afterward everything went off the rails, which, odds were, they would? Or worse, he rejected her outright?

"And even if he does like me, he can't ask me out," said Stephanie as they were getting ready for bed, Merrill brushing her teeth, Stephanie smearing night cream on her face in their wincingly bright bathroom. "How would he know for sure I wouldn't accuse him of sexual harassment and try to get him fired?"

"You could find another job and ask him out yourself," said Merrill.

Stephanie laughed. "Um, no."

"You don't love your job, so why not look around?"

"I like my job. I don't have to love it, do I?"

"Do you see yourself doing it forever?"

"I don't see myself doing anything forever," said Stephanie. "But I'm not going to quit just so I can ask out my boss who would probably say no anyway."

Merrill spit a mouthful of toothpaste foam into the sink. "I think I'm going to say yes to that Brinkley guy."

"Good. You should."

Merrill looked askance at her. "Don't be sarcastic."

"I'm not. I really do think you should go out with him."

"A free dinner, and he's not bad-looking, even with the walleye."

Stephanie smoothed a few drops of lotion over her neck. "Is it really a walleye?"

"No, it's just a little crooked. I know I've made him sound like a cartoon, but he isn't."

"Go out with him. Who knows, maybe he's great."

"At this point I'd settle for mediocre," Merrill said.

The next morning when Stephanie logged into email, there was a message with the subject line "This is a little awkward . . ." that turned out to be from Portia, the older of her two half sisters.

> *Dear Stephanie,*
>
> *I thought I'd take a risk and write to say I'm sorry for whatever hard feelings this situation with our father has caused you and your/our brother. Pardon the expression, but it's a mindfuck, I know.*
>
> *I live in Chicago and my/our sister Diana lives in Portland (Oregon) where she's in her last year of college. If you ever want to talk or meet, I'd be up for that, but I realize you might not want to. Obviously I don't know how I'd feel if I were you.*
>
> *For what it's worth, our mother (Diana's and mine—I suppose that's clear?) was very glad your mom was willing to meet with her the other day. Diana and I were too.*
>
> *Take care, Portia*

Stephanie glanced up from her computer and found her boss watching her from his office doorway, his face unreadable. He was wearing a silky, slate-blue shirt, her favorite. Was it possible he might be as lonely as she was? She held his gaze until he motioned for her to come into his office.

*

Whenever Joon stayed over, Tom didn't want to get out of bed in the morning. Their schedules didn't match—he had to be at the hospital by seven, but she didn't have class until nine. He'd feel sorry for himself as he left the apartment, Joon waking to kiss him goodbye before she fell back asleep for another hour. She would eat a leisurely breakfast and do all the dishes in the sink before she left for class; she knew how much he appreciated this. She was a nice person, nicer than he was. He didn't know why he wasn't calling her his girlfriend. He wasn't interested in sleeping with anyone else, but that would probably change before too long—it always had in the past.

He had enough on his mind, anyway. He now had to live, until he died, with a major revision to the story about his father. Formerly it was, "Kent Donnelly was a good man who died tragically and much too soon." Now the story was, "He was not a good man. As it turns out, he was a total fucking liar who lived a double life. No, not great that he died so young, but who the hell knows what else he would have gotten up to if he'd lived another forty or fifty years?"

Things were not so pleasant right now, not in Tom's head. He wasn't sleeping very well and his current clinical rotation in geriatrics was much harder than he'd expected—not the facts or the treatments so much as the emotions. Many of the patients he saw were seriously unwell—dangerously overweight or else alarmingly malnourished, some with lungs ruined by years of committed smoking, quite a few with teeth missing or rotted, their hearts under strain, and their bowels—he didn't even want to think about this, but of course he had to. Many of the patients he saw had landed in the hospital after years of neglecting their bodies in such egregious fashion it was miraculous they were still alive.

Yet, when they looked at him, their eyes were often bright and interested and appreciative of his role in their lives as caretaker, as a man with answers. They weren't bad people. Some expressed contrition for what they'd done to themselves. He admired a few of these patients and despaired for most of them. No one, frankly, wanted to grow old, but of course it was better than the alternative. It *was* better than that.

"People want to be healthy, but their behavior is so often at odds with their intentions," his attending physician, Dr. Day, had said to Tom and his white-coated classmates as they trailed after her through the hospital corridors. Most people, Tom had observed, died slowly. They did not die in a cataclysm as his father and three thousand others had on September 11, 2001. Tom could not say for sure which way he'd prefer to go. Both options seemed terrible to him.

He was, admittedly, in something of a state. He had confessed this to Joon but no one else, not to his sister in L.A., nor to his mother a few miles away in Park Slope. His mother seemed always to be calling now, but he could think of nothing to say to her about his father, other than that he was sorry. He'd advised her more than once to try not to think about it, which of course was ridiculous because how could she not? It was a lit sign in her mind that would probably never go dark. His father had cheated, and on such a grand scale it was difficult not to be a little in awe of his Zeus-like machinations.

Joon commiserated with him, but once the shock of the revelation had worn off a little, she'd suggested that he try to think of it as an opportunity. He had two more sisters now, and these girls were as blameless as he was. He should make the best of it, no? Wasn't it actually kind of exciting?

His answer was that one sister was plenty.

The lids of her dark eyes fluttering, Joon had looked at him and said, "Sorry, but you don't get to choose."

"I know," he said, unable to keep a note of aggrievement out of his voice.

"You actually don't get to choose a whole lot if you think about it," she said. "Not the really important things, like who your parents are, or where and when you're born."

"You think I'm not aware of that?" he said.

She shook her head but said nothing else. He knew he was being childish, and that she didn't deserve it, but he was so tired and confused and angry. He was very angry—angrier than his mother or sister seemed to be.

A week passed, then another: mid-October, New York still in the sixties on most days and the leaves were turning picturesquely gold and crimson in the parks and squares. He and Stephanie had just turned twenty-seven. Their birthday was exactly two weeks after their father's. What *had* he been thinking? Why not just screw around, have some fun in the off hours, instead of starting a whole other goddamn family?

Tom went through the motions at the hospital, briskly cheerful and attentive, capable of small talk when required. His classmates and Dr. Day liked him, although there was some jealousy among the former, but Tom didn't worry about it too much—he would rather be a figure of envy than of pity. This struck him as something he might once have heard his father saying, but he was probably making that up. It merely seemed like something his father would say, especially now with family number two having emerged from the fog of the past.

On the Friday after his birthday, Tom was summoned to the nurses' station, where he was told a woman was waiting to talk to him. She had waited all morning and had brought along her knitting and a fat book of sudoku puzzles. There were three orange chairs situated across from the nurses' station, and she and her bulging handbag sat politely waiting for three hours for him to appear in his doctor's coat with his brisk, masculine air of authority.

When he stepped through the doors and was pointed toward an unfamiliar woman, her silver hair held back in a black barrette, a burgundy shawl wreathing her shoulders, he stood looking at her, wondering if someone had made a mistake. He had no idea who she was, but when she looked up at him from her puzzle book, her soft, elderly face radiated warmth and recognition.

His mind labored to form a theory: she couldn't be Jennifer, his father's secret quasi-wife—she looked too old. He moved toward her, bemused, as she dropped her puzzle book onto her chair and stepped toward him, both hands reaching out to him.

"Dr. Donnelly, I'm Iris Hollander," she said shyly. "Jennifer's mother. Your sisters Portia and Diana's grandmother? I'm sorry to surprise you like this, but I couldn't think of another way. Jennifer doesn't know I'm here. The girls don't either. I came all on my own."

Tom felt the blood rush from his chest to his neck and face. His voice cracked as he greeted her, her warm, dry hands gripping his. She looked intently at him, her blue eyes rapt. "You look a lot like your father," she said.

He stared at her, at a loss. Why on earth had she come? What did she want? He didn't know what he felt. "I—I've been told that before," he managed to say.

She was still holding his hands. He knew enough not to pull away. "You must wonder why I'm here," she said.

He nodded. "You're right."

She looked over his shoulder, toward the nurses' station. He could sense their eyes on his back. Of course they were curious. He would be too.

"Do you—" She paused. "Do you have a minute? Maybe we could get a coffee? But this is probably your lunch break and you'll need to eat. I won't keep you long. I promise."

He led her two floors down to the cafeteria. The large, institutionally bland room was filled with people—some of whom he knew or recognized. They smiled at him and nodded, their eyes flitting to Iris before they returned to his face. They had no idea what was happening, likely assuming Iris was a friend or a relative, if they thought anything at all.

There was a long line at the cash registers. He didn't usually take more than fifteen minutes for lunch, and she was right, he did need to eat. He bought a turkey sandwich and two coffees while Iris found a table in a corner near a family of five. By the time he was through the line, he had used twelve minutes of the twenty he'd allotted himself.

As he sat down across from Iris, he felt self-conscious about eating his sandwich in front of her. They looked at each other for a moment before she reached across the table and touched his arm. "You and your sister must be having so many thoughts," she said.

He had no idea what she expected to happen during this meeting—this ambush, he couldn't help but think of it. "Yes, I suppose we are," he said.

"I realize you don't want to hear me defend your father," she said, glancing down at her coffee to which she added cream, the white delicately unspooling across the black surface.

He took a bite of the sandwich, unable to look at her. With his mouth half full, he mumbled, "No, not really."

"He wasn't a bad man," she said. "I think he thought at some point he would be able to introduce your mother to my daughter and you and your sister to your half sisters. I think he thought maybe there'd be a way you would all understand."

"Did he ever say that to you?" he asked, taken aback. "Why would he think we'd understand?"

Iris sipped her coffee, keeping her gaze on him, her expression neutral.

"If you were my mother," said Tom, "would you have wanted to meet the woman your husband had two other children with while pretending you and your kids were his only family?"

"I honestly don't know how I would have responded," she said.

Tom shook his head, incredulous. "You don't?"

"If it meant keeping my family together," she said, her voice trailing off. She smiled tremulously. "I guess I don't . . ."

The family of five at the table next to them stood up, scraping back their chairs, leaving their trays and dirty dishes and utensils where they lay. The youngest, a girl of about ten dressed in red corduroy overalls, looked over at him and Iris blankly before turning to follow her parents and two brothers.

Iris reached for his arm again. "I'm sorry. I can see I've upset you. I didn't mean to. I just—" She faltered. "I didn't want you to be angry with your father."

"I'd stopped thinking about him mostly," he said. "Until we found out. He died a long time ago." He paused. "I was only eight."

Iris looked chastened, and a wave of exhaustion and sadness rose in Tom's chest, more emotion than he'd felt when his mother first told him about Jennifer and his half sisters. "I'm sorry," he said. "I don't mean to be unpleasant, but I hope you understand this has been hard to process. For my mother especially."

She was reaching into her voluminous handbag, pulling something out and presenting it to him. It was an African violet in a small green pot, stiff clear cellophane protecting it. "This is for you," she said, her face sheepish. "I wanted to bring you something. I wanted—"

"Oh," he said. "Thank you."

"It doesn't like direct sunlight. But it does need bright indoor light. The care instructions are on this marker." She touched the plastic tab that had been thrust into the dirt at the base of the plant. The violets were a rich purple. Joon would love it. He could already imagine himself asking her to take it off his hands.

"You probably want to finish your lunch," said Iris.

Tom looked at his watch. Dr. Day would be expecting him and his classmates back in the next five minutes. "I do have to go back to work in few minutes," he said. His sandwich was half-eaten. He wasn't very hungry anymore. Later he would be and he knew he would have to force himself to eat the rest of it before he went back to join the others.

At the door of the cafeteria they said an awkward goodbye, Iris wavering, Tom sensing that she wished to hug him. He leaned in very slightly and she reached up and put her thin arms around his neck. She smelled like lilies and her hair was silky against his cheek.

As he rode up to the third floor in the elevator, wondering if he'd been rude to her, if he should have been more patient, he looked dazedly at his phone. His sister had texted several times, first to say she might quit her job at the museum and work for the guy who was her boss there—he was starting a consulting company for nonprofits and wanted her to leave with him.

I think I'm in love with him, was her second text.

Should I tell him? was her third.

I think I'm going to tell him, was her fourth.

Tom could not make sense of Stephanie's words. He kept thinking of Iris and looking from the potted violet in his left hand to the phone in his right.

If he likes me too, I could stay at my museum job, was her fifth.

Are you on break? I thought you would be by now. Answer me! Oh! Portia emailed me—almost forgot to tell you, was her sixth.

He remembered their father as a smiling man who loved the Mets and the ocean and had taught him and Stephanie how to ride a bike two summers before he was killed. Their mother had saved his business suits for Tom, thinking he would grow into them, but Tom had grown taller than his father, although their feet were the same size. When he left for college, his mother had insisted he take with him the new Nike running shoes his father had bought a few days before he died.

Tom thought her insistence morbid, and he kept the shoes in their box in the back of his small dorm room closet. After a few months, he asked his roommate if he wanted the Nikes, not telling him where they'd come from. He didn't know why he felt ashamed to say whose shoes they really were. He didn't know why he himself didn't want to wear them. His father's feelings, like his mother's, were so easily hurt—this too Tom remembered about him, along with the way his father would crack the bedroom door to look in on him as he drifted off, the TV droning softly down the hall, a feeling of languorous well-being enveloping him as he fell asleep.

In the Park

From: lauren3@lakewalk.net
To: marksanders72@goodmail.com
Sent: Friday, 2 July
Subj: Bananas

Dear Mark,

   Your silence all these months must mean you haven't forgiven me, which I understand, even if it's hard to accept. You once said that if we tried hard enough, we could control our thoughts and feelings, but I didn't see how and still don't, to be honest. I've never been able to control anything, least of all what I think or feel.

   I haven't yet moved out of the house we lived in together, and some nights no man-made sounds smuggle themselves inside, which is the kind of night I remember you liked best—no cars passing on the road, no radio turned up too loud, no planes flying low overhead. Do you still call the sky the "firmament" sometimes, like your lonely, churchgoing mother does? I called her last week to ask about you. Maybe you know this already.

   Most of the time, it's not so hard being out here alone. I go into the city three or four times a week for work, and Elburn is of course only a few miles away, if I need groceries and want to see other people on the off days. I planted squash, eggplants, tomatoes, string beans, basil, carrots, muskmelon, and cucumbers this year, and I pull weeds early in the morning, before the ground is too dried out and the tops break off and leave their roots in the soil. Sometimes I take pictures of the weed piles and email them to friends. I've started naming the piles too. This morning's was Mt. Weedmore. Two days ago it was Williston Weed. The secret to happiness is this, I think: be easily amused.

Do you remember the time not long after we met when we went to the park on Webster Avenue (back when they still had the public pool, which is now just a filthy eyesore full of dead leaves because the city can't afford to maintain it; meanwhile, mysteriously, the mayor keeps putting additions on his mansion. Seven bathrooms and counting!), and you said, "Those birds look like balloons," and I said, "That's because they are balloons"?

The bird balloons were big and silver and owl-shaped, for sale by a man wearing a green apron who was stationed next to the merry-go-round. You were staring up at the cloud of bobbing owls in disbelief. It was one of those times you'd warned me about, I was pretty sure, when you were having trouble sorting out what was happening to you—were you awake or were you dreaming?

"Their skin is so shiny," you said, awed. "Would they be able to fly all the way to the moon? Where are their feathers?"

"Those are balloons, Mark," I said again, softer than the first time.

You were still confused. "But if that guy lets go," you said, "they'll fly away."

The man holding the balloons looked at us and smiled. "You two lovebirds want one?"

"Lovebirds," you said, and laughed as if it was the funniest joke you'd ever heard. I was offended, even if I knew something might be going a little haywire in your brain. As of that afternoon, we were actual lovebirds, whether you wanted to call us that or not. You'd just seen me without my feathers, so to speak.

"Yes," I said. "I'd like one."

"No," you said. "I don't know what kind of food to give owls."

"Rodents," said the balloon man with a laugh, not realizing you were serious. "But these owls don't need to be fed, young man."

I was the one who ended up buying a balloon, not wanting to disappoint him, but you made me release it before we even got back to the car, which made me very sad, though I pretended not to be.

Another day at that park, you bought us ice cream cones (strawberry for me, spumoni for you) sold by the woman who was married to the balloon man. She was also an expert in the art of animal mimicry, monkeys in particular. It was very hot and the clouds looked to you like the faces of some of your high school teachers, you whispered, your mouth close to my ear. I was watching a little boy in a red shirt with a blue whale on the front, water spouting out of its blowhole. He laughed so hard at the ice cream lady's monkey shrieks that he dropped his scoop of pink bubble-gum onto the grass, but instead of crying, he put the ice cream back on his cone and picked off the grit before making quick work of the whole thing.

My thought then was that he would be all right, and whatever he was made of, it was pretty good material. I told you I wanted a little boy just like him, but you pretended not to hear me.

Sometimes I dream about this park with its owls and merry-go-round and dilapidated, abandoned pool. It's like the big city park I saw in a movie about aliens who came to earth disguised as bananas, and whenever someone stooped down to get a look at where they lay in the grass, the banana alien sprang up and poked the unsuspecting guy or girl in the eye. This was all that happened in the entire movie too. For an hour and a half, one rube after another got popped in the eye by a rude banana. I kept thinking there had to be something else going on in their alien brains (if they even had brains)—maybe they were killing their victims by injecting them with a slow-acting poison, but it turned out they weren't killers at all, nor did they want to take over the planet—they only wanted to play practical jokes on dumb people who would all scream, "Oh, my eye!" in various tones of distress and dismay when their eyeballs were attacked.

You might recall that my brother is the one who recommended I see this movie because he thought it was brilliant, the best movie he'd ever seen.

"It's about the absurdity of life," Josh said when I told him that *Go Bananas!* wasn't for me. "Like, how we keep making the same mistakes and not learning from them."

"Well," I said, unconvinced. "Maybe. But it's a different person every time who's trying to pick up the banana. If it were the same person, then maybe I could see your point."

What I'd really wanted to say was, "It must have been made by someone who thought it'd be funny to see how many morons would actually sit through the whole thing."

I knew this would make him angry, though. You of course know firsthand about his terrible temper—remember his meltdown on my birthday a couple of years ago? I think there's still a little frosting encrusted in my parents' living room carpet, and they haven't fixed the paper towel dispenser yet either. They never knew what to do about his rages when we were growing up. If Josh were a different kind of person, I could have pretended to poke him in the eye when we were talking about the banana movie, and we would have laughed about it. The irony is, he doesn't even like bananas. He claims their mushiness makes him gag, even when they're not overripe.

Sometimes at night I stare out the back windows into the yard, no lights on in the room where I'm standing, and it's like I can see into the future, though I know in my head that no one can do that, not really. But I see you there, and you're wearing a banana suit.

Just kidding. I hope that made you laugh a little bit though.

Love, Lauren

*

From: lauren3@lakewalk.net
To: marksanders72@goodmail.com
Sent: Monday, 5 July
Subj: Bananas, Part 2

Hi Mark,

Still trying to figure out how a movie about alien bananas springing up from the grass and poking a bunch of dimwits in the eye got into theaters, especially when the kind of movies these theaters usually show feature mid-level managers getting hammered in Vegas or yet another comic book villain trying to take over the world.

I just realized that for some reason, squirrels and dogs never got poked in the eye in *Go Bananas!*—this being the one interesting thing about that silly movie. The bananas would just lie there and play dead when animals sniffed at them. It was only when the dog owners tried to pick them up that they would come to life and play their prank, accompanied by a soundtrack of crashing cymbals every single time.

If I ever dare to bring up this movie with my brother again, I might also have to ask him why a few of the aliens didn't take the shape of a banana peel. It would have been a lot funnier if some of their victims had slipped on them instead of having their eyes poked.

Okay, yes, maybe I'm obsessed. But like I said the other day, it's impossible for me to control my thoughts (or feelings).

Hope you're well,

Lauren

P.S. I miss you.

*

From: lauren3@lakewalk.net
To: marksanders72@goodmail.com
Sent: Sunday, 11 July
Subj: Velcro

Dear Mark,

Just curious, what are your views on Velcro?

I know you have a fondness for double-sided tape and Post-It notes, but we never discussed Velcro when we were together and this now seems to me to be a sad omission.

You don't need to write back too much if you do reply. I was only wondering what you thought.

I saw the most beautiful fox by the garden yesterday around three in the afternoon. She (he?) was sniffing the tops of the chives—so delicately and adorably, her little nose twitching. When she sensed me staring at her from the sliding door off the kitchen, she met my gaze for a long second before turning and loping back toward the brush line. Her tail! So enormously fluffy. I wished so much that I could touch it.

I think we need a new category: fox people, instead of only dog and cat people. Foxes technically are dogs, aren't they? Or at least are in the same genus? Though of course they're not the same kind of dog as a poodle or a Pomeranian.

One last question, where are you? —L

*

Unsent draft 1
From: lauren3@lakewalk.net
To: marksanders72@goodmail.com
Date: Monday, 12 July
Subj: Earliest days

You were the golden-haired focus of so many of my adolescent longings: junior high varsity basketball player, A student, AP English classmate, future MD. You liked me, you liked me not. We skirted each other for years, two near-strangers afraid to graze hands or shoulders in a narrow hallway.

I wrote lengthy, florid, lovesick entries about you in my diary, scribbled love poems in a separate notebook with a rose on its cover, and slept with my yearbook opened to the page with your photo on my bedside table. My friend Beth had a Ouija board we consulted in her bedroom, giggling with the door locked against Dylan, Beth's older brother, who reeked of cigarettes and contraband beer. At seventeen, Dylan was skinny and unathletic and sparsely bearded, but he'd made it known once with a whispered dare in my ear, when Beth was downstairs in the kitchen checking on the chocolate chip cookies we'd cut off a roll of store-bought dough and thrust into the oven, that he was available for sexual favors if I had the guts to take him up on his offer. I was repulsed but politely tried not to show it. I was saving myself for you, but kept this information to myself too.

The Ouija board had emphatically proclaimed you to be my soulmate. But Beth's soulmate, apparently, was an otter. Or had the spirit that lived in the board meant someone whose name was Otter? This remained in question. Beth was offended and worried by this bizarre prognostication. Could it also mean she'd been an otter in a past life? Or would be in a future one? And why, Beth wanted to know, was the Ouija board so clear on you being destined for me?

It was a momentous day for me, needless to say. I didn't really care that Dylan had made a pass at me; Beth and I could still hear him skulking around in the hall. "What are you doing in there, little girls? Is it lezzy time?" He cackled loudly and banged on the locked door. "Let me in, or I'll huff and I'll puff and I'll blow your Barbie dream house down!"

"Go away, you idiot," Beth shouted. "She doesn't like you! Go whack it in your room like you always do."

"Open the door and I'll do it in yours this time."

"Mom!" Beth screamed. But we all knew Gail Tandy was in the basement smoking a joint with her latest boyfriend. I'd smelled the herbal fug when I arrived. Gail and the boyfriend would probably eat all the cookies on the cooling rack too, if Beth and I didn't get down there soon to rescue a few for ourselves.

What do you think, Mark? Do you wish I hadn't told you these things? Should I be confessing any of this to you?

*

From: lauren3@lakewalk.net
To: marksanders72@goodmail.com
Sent: Thursday, 15 July
Subj: <empty>

Hi again,

Just so you know, along with being a fox person, I could be a giraffe person. Or a kangaroo person. Or a gargoyle person. Or a Rice Krispie bar person. Or a wintergreen Altoids person. (I realize some of those aren't pets.)

Happy birthday, Mark.

I miss you, and on some nights it's hard to sleep because I want to be near you or at least hear your voice, but your mother said you threw out your cell phone and you call her from strangers' phones and rarely check your email and you've been traveling around the country for three months straight now. What about all your patients? Who is taking care of them while you're gone?

Two men have asked me out in the past month. I'm moving on, okay? —L

P.S. I wouldn't tell you that if I thought it would bother you. Well, maybe I would.

*

Unsent draft 2
From: lauren3@lakewalk.net
To: marksanders72@goodmail.com
Date: Saturday, 17 July
Subj: A few more thoughts

M—For a long time I have wanted to tell you some things I never found the courage to when you were here, right in front of me.

You weren't my first and only—or even my seventh or eighth. For a long time, I fell in love very easily. At one point, I even had a crush on your best friend, though he'd always ignored me. I believed at fifteen, sixteen, seventeen, that all future possibilities were already defined by who I was and how I looked, something I later realized was the core narrative for the soap operas endlessly repeating themselves among anyone aged thirteen to twenty-eight. Aside from his prowess as a high school golf team star and his nearly perfect SAT scores, my brother Josh was known for his startling physical beauty. I was pretty too, I could see, pretty enough, but not beautiful like my brother was. People stopped their conversations to stare at him when he entered parties and restaurants and airport security lines. The way women's and some men's faces subtly shifted when they looked at him made me feel both proud of him and embarrassed for them. In general, he was extremely charming, his bad temper reserved for rare occasions; our parents and I were the only ones, Josh claimed, who knew how to draw out his primordial frustrations.

You were handsome too, though not in the aggressively obvious way Josh was. You were also naturally self-effacing, possessing early on an awareness of the absurdity of the conflicts arising between teenagers and the adult world of steady jobs and firm morals and fixed bedtimes. Most kids, needless to say, did not want to become their parents, but of course, twenty-odd years later, there they were, living in homes in similar neighborhoods, raising children with whom they were having the same battles over curfews, video games, and study habits identical to the ones they'd had with their own disheartened, exhausted mothers and fathers.

But you had a rare perspective on all this—even at a young age, you were aware that the comforts of a steady job and money in the bank were sneered at only until it became clear they were the same factors that made one's earliest rebellions possible.

—L

*

From: lauren3@lakewalk.net
To: marksanders72@goodmail.com
Sent: Tuesday, 20 July
Subj: re: Ireland

Dear Mark,

I was so happy to hear from you, and it sounds like you had a good birthday, though I was surprised to learn that you're all the way over in Ireland right now. Exciting!

But I hope you aren't serious about your quest to find a leprechaun. It was hard to read your tone. You are aware they're fictitious creatures? And from what I've heard, if by some miracle they do exist, they're very small and hard to spot, and they aren't interested in making friends with human beings.

Anyway, it's good you exchanged your dollars for euros and pounds (so I guess you're traveling in Northern Ireland too?) before you left Chicago—the interest rates on international transactions are absolutely nuts. When we went to Europe two summers ago, you remember that Visa charged us what ended up being something like a 29 percent interest rate! I couldn't believe they started adding interest as soon as we made a purchase and it didn't stop until we paid the tachycardia-inducing bill a few weeks later. Who makes these stupid laws? The bankers, I'm sure, via their bribed representatives in our esteemed federal government.

Yes, I'm done.

Before I sign off, one thing—remember that leprechauns are known for being tricksters. Keep a firm hand on your wallet. (Hee.)

Yours, Lauren

P.S. Have you ever noticed that in the dark, pine trees look like ogres? Mild-mannered ogres, though. (That's probably an oxymoron.)

*

Unsent draft 3
From: lauren3@lakewalk.net
To: marksanders72@goodmail.com
Date: Wednesday, 21 July
Subj: re: Ireland

Dear Mark,

I stopped myself from saying in yesterday's note that sometimes it feels as if I am barely hanging on. Not long after you left, I canceled the adoption proceedings, as you know, but that didn't bring you home, and by now I'm thinking maybe nothing ever will.

You haven't sent me divorce papers though, and your mother said, when I talked to her last, that you haven't mentioned a divorce to her either. I won't tell her you're searching for leprechauns on Irish soccer pitches, even if it's tempting to do so. But one word of caution: keep an eye out for any bananas in those fields.

You were smart not to go with me to see that movie, although at the time I resented you for your refusal because I'd go to every movie you wanted to see, even the three-hour ones from eastern Europe where everyone walked around scowling and terminally grim. I know those countries have been the victims of an ungodly amount of war, of one madman after another slashing and burning every long-suffering village and villager in his path, but I was at the point where if I'd had to see another one, I would have screamed.

If you come back, I'll bake a pineapple upside-down cake. I'll let you eat Cheetos in bed and watch TV until after midnight and won't ask if you've remembered to brush your teeth. I know I'm not your mother and I'm sorry if sometimes I might have acted as if I were.

Still, that's all a part of it, isn't it—the whole tragicomedy of trying to love another person? No one is perfect, and if I'm being honest here, each person's definition of perfection must change with every passing day. Maybe that's why we're such a lonely, confused, angry species, all of us wanting so much what we can never have, or, if somehow we do manage to get it, it isn't what we thought it would be. And to make matters even worse, all the instant applause we've come to crave—what good is it, really? Here we are posting photos of our dogs dressed as hot peppers and our cats in stovepipe hats and bow ties and the huge dandelion piles we pulled earlier in the day, and now I'm crying and can't really see what I'm typing and I can't think straight either because it's so hard to sleep without you here.

Come home, Mark. Even if it's only for an hour or two to collect your mail and eat a tomato from the garden (they'll be ready before long). I just want to be able to look at your face for a little while, one that I have loved for most of my life, long before you loved me.

Lauren

*

Unsent draft 4
From: lauren3@lakewalk.net
To: marksanders72@goodmail.com
Date: Friday, 23 July
Subj: Journal

I found a small red notebook of yours in the bedroom closet when I was searching for an old bandanna to wear over my hair during my gardening work this morning. I'd never seen this notebook before and figured out pretty quickly that it's a diary from when you were still in college. God help me, I read it. Every word.

Two things I can't stop thinking about: I wasn't mentioned once, despite the fact we exchanged at least a dozen letters during the span of months covered in the diary. Not even on your birthday, when I sent you that huge care package with all those glittery Super Balls and the joke snake in the can, and jumbo-size bags of Blow Pops, Tootsie Rolls, Smarties, Laffy Taffy, and Sixlets. (I remember exactly what they were because those are my favorite cheap candies.)

There was also a homemade card in the box, one I spent a whole week making—I drew a comic strip of you and me at Six Flags, with me projectile-vomiting green stars and blue hearts onto the heads of other riders while we went down the steepest incline on the Eagle roller coaster our senior year, the day after prom. I'm glad I got to go with you to Great America and to prom the night before, though seeing as how it was a gang of eleven of us, I only got one slow dance with you, and having to watch the other girls who also, I'm sure, had big crushes on you dance with you too—well, it was what I imagine it'd be like to stay for the night in one of Dante's circles of hell. From day one, I've had to admit to myself, I've been crazy about you. You were always nice to me but I think for the longest time your feelings for me were only skin-deep. It's okay, because there's nothing to be done about it—we are each only and ever the person we are—but it does hurt.

The other thing I keep thinking about from the diary are the multiple-choice questions you included in a few places, which were very odd. I don't really know what to think about them.

> Of the following, what's the worst, in your opinion?
>
> a. Being stripped naked and having all your body hair shaved off on national television
>
> b. Having to listen to one song (the same one, over and over) for the rest of your life
>
> c. Watching your dog and your parents be pelted with rotten eggs by the guys you liked least in college in a packed football stadium

What was this about? Was it for a performance art class? Or for an assignment on torture? It wasn't clear which answer you'd pick, either; you didn't say anywhere in the diary. For me, it's a tie between a and b, though I'd feel really bad for my parents too. I don't know. Obviously, they're all awful.

*

From: lauren3@lakewalk.net
To: marksanders72@goodmail.com
Sent: Sunday, 25 July
Subj: Home

M—I once admired how you would never take an umbrella from the stand by the door when you left the house unless it was already raining. I always took an umbrella, even when there was only a 10 percent chance of rain that day.

You rarely wanted dessert. For me, it was all but inevitable. We both loved Wednesdays, though; we were each able to discern the coast of the weekend from the prow of Wednesday night.

It was from a large pallet of crumbling bricks that we tried to construct a home together.

*

From: lauren3@lakewalk.net
To: marksanders72@goodmail.com
Sent: Wednesday, 28 July
Subj: All for now

Dear Mark,

Thank you for writing to me again, especially when I know it's difficult for you to see the point, because as you say, you're not the same person you were when we started our life together eight years ago. But that is the whole point, isn't it? People change together—like the landscape on a road trip, or the temperature of bathwater—and although sometimes these changes can be difficult to adapt to, I have wanted nothing more than to take road trips and baths with you and to see you come around to admitting such things as porta-bella mushrooms being a decent substitute for meat, and thinking that long hair on men, but not on women, is unattractive.

This will probably be the last email you receive from me. I realize that my jokes and my naked pleas for your attention are probably becoming oppressive. Your mother and I want to remain friends. One of the worst things about a long-term relationship ending is that it also often summarily ends your relationships with other people who have become important to you too.

Please think about returning home in order to continue practicing medicine. Your patients must all miss you.

Yours, Lauren

P.S. I'm relieved you were kidding about the leprechauns. It was very hard to tell.

House of Paine

The home inspector was fifteen minutes late but didn't apologize when he arrived. Behind his smudged glasses, his dark eyes were furtive, his face closed off. "You ready?" he asked, glancing at Jim, who'd been waiting for him on the porch. "Let's get a move on." His hand was already reaching for the door.

As the inspector brushed past him, Jim thought he smelled alcohol, but the older man didn't seem unsteady. Maybe he'd had a beer at lunch—or maybe it was cheap cologne? Jim said nothing and followed him into the house.

Only a handful of days after Jim and his wife Kathryn moved into their new home, however, water began pouring into the attic during a thunderstorm. The following week, the downstairs toilet stopped working, and three weeks after that, squirrels arrived to colonize the walls, at least one of these creatures always seeming to be awake and patrolling its intramural territory, and Jim began to have obsessive, baleful thoughts about the inspector: of course what he'd smelled on the older man was booze, not Aqua Velva. But he said nothing to Kathryn and didn't know when or if he would because what would this information do other than poison her opinion of him? "Why didn't you say something?" she would have asked, a question to which the sole plausible reply was: "Because you're married to a coward."

No, no, he couldn't tell her. He simply couldn't.

After the squirrels began their occupation, Jim lay awake past midnight nearly every night, listening to their rustlings and what sounded like footraces in the walls. (Why were they always in such a hurry? he wondered, irate and exhausted.) His wife, as a rule a better sleeper than he, slumbered a few inches away, a satin mask over her eyes, her long-fingered hands resting on her stomach. She didn't want to hire an exterminator. She'd insisted they find a wildlife specialist who would humanely trap the squirrels and drive them miles away before setting them free, far enough—ten miles? fifteen? three hundred?—to keep them from coming back. Such a person was hard to locate, although after a few days of searching, they'd found one, but she was booked for the next two and a half weeks. Could they hold on for now? The squirrels weren't likely to do more damage than they already had, the specialist assured them. Kathryn believed her. Jim did not.

The house had a thriving population of spiders too, some of their webs appearing to spring from the house's corners fully formed only a few hours after their predecessors had been cleared away by his or Kathryn's determined sweeping. Before the house on Juniper Street, they'd owned a two-bedroom condo they were able to sell for a small profit that went immediately into the down payment on the Victorian. They would be happier, Jim was now certain, if they'd stayed in their erstwhile condo, despite the sound of their downstairs neighbor's snores through the bedroom floorboards, despite the sweltering summers and the noisy schoolyard across the street where parents routinely screamed obscenities at each other from their cars if they didn't get out of the way fast enough during afternoon pickup. Jim would sometimes catch glimpses of the children riding in these SUVs and minivans—their eyes downcast, their small mouths set in stern lines. They looked sorry and put-upon and older than they should have.

When the roof had developed several leaks during a thunderstorm that pounded the ancient treetops and suffering roofs of the neighborhood for twenty-five minutes, flooding gutters and yards, the squirrels were still a month in the future, and Jim had futilely hoped the leaks would be the worst of what the house had in store for them. They lost most of the attic's contents—Kathryn's old school papers and all her family photo albums, along with the books they didn't have room for on their bookcases. Only their winter coats and sweaters were salvageable.

And then the repair estimates came in: one contractor wanted $30,000 to replace the roof; another $36,000. He and Kathryn had the leaks patched instead, this bill setting them back $1,800, the roofer predicting there'd be more leaks when the next big storm arrived. Jim said they'd take their chances. He felt like a fool and a victim; he also resented the roofer's certainty that more grief and expense were inevitable.

The following week, two outlets in the living room stopped working. An electrician was summoned and stood shaking his head sorrowfully as he delivered this fresh bit of bad news—the problem was extensive; it was, in fact, a whole series of problems, and a complete rewiring of the first floor's circuitry, $8,000 plus materials, was needed.

"That's a bargain," the electrician promised. Jim stared at this sunburned stranger with his large, dark mustache and gold signet ring, feeling his own face drain of blood, worrying he might break into tears.

"That's not a bargain," Kathryn said when she returned home from work later in the day. "That's highway robbery. We'll just have to get by without those outlets for now."

This did not seem like such a good idea to Jim. The electrician had warned him they ran the risk of an electrical fire if anything short-circuited, but Kathryn also shook her head over this information and said, "He's trying to scare us into coughing up money he knows we don't have."

The squirrels, by comparison, seemed the least of their troubles, although Jim's insomnia was making it impossible for him to work for more than a few groggy hours at a time, and whenever he tried to nap during what seemed to be a quiet period in the interlopers' schedules, one squirrel would inevitably spring into action, and if Jim pounded on the plaster in an attempt to stun the creature into silence, other squirrels would rise up in outraged solidarity and a whole cacophonous idiot circus would immediately launch into another unscheduled performance.

More than once, he had shouted at the squirrels until he was hoarse, furious with himself for having ignored the inspector's drunkenness. The Victorian, despite its beautiful facade and the lushness of its trees and flowerbeds, was an unmitigated fiasco. Mercifully, Kathryn was never home to witness these meltdowns, being safely four miles away at the performing arts high school where she'd taught English for the past seven years and was now the head of the department. Jim worked at home as a web designer, or had worked at home before they'd bought the House of Usher and he'd begun to lose his mind.

And yet another quasi-crisis was looming—his in-laws were due for an inaugural visit before Judy, the squirrel whisperer, was scheduled to appear and lure the squirrels out of the walls. Her plan was to drive them to a wildlife preserve in McHenry County, an hour away. Jim had his doubts about whether she would actually take them there, but other than following her like a low-rent PI, he knew he'd have to trust her.

Her online testimonials were extremely favorable, but their relentless effusiveness made him suspicious:

Judy is AMAZING!!! —Melissa L.

I have her in my phone's primary contacts! She's essential.
—Beatrice G. (Where in the world did this client live?
  he wondered. In the middle of a forest?)

Best pest control professional I've ever met. —Harold S.

Reading through Judy's online encomium, he felt a headache forming and turned off the computer. His wife loved the house, despite its many costly problems—she would believe anything in order to save it, he realized.

And now his in-laws would soon descend upon them, Kathryn insisting they come despite the faulty outlets, the squirrels, the cobwebs, the tenuous situation with the roof, the laboring dehumidifier in the basement. Kathryn was sleeping fine with her mask and early-morning yoga. Jim couldn't take sleeping pills—something in his brain chemistry caused him to have nightmares if he resorted to them.

He couldn't figure out how Kathryn had made what appeared to him to be a complete reversal since they'd moved into the house—her home-buying anxiety having been offloaded onto him, as if some underhanded magic had occurred. She was no longer cross-examining him about the soundness of their 401(k)s, their meager stock portfolio, how much they could expect their monthly income to be when they retired, which probably wouldn't be possible for another thirty years, when they were in their seventies, considering the mortgage they were now carrying. He wondered if her sanguine moods were due to pregnancy, or if she was taking antidepressants, but when he asked, she stared at him, nonplussed, and shook her head. "No, I'm not pregnant. I'm not on Prozac either. Why would you think that?"

"Haven't you noticed our new house is a train wreck?"

"No, it's not," she said, affronted. "It's just growing pains. We're getting used to it and it's getting used to us."

"This house is not getting used to us," he said. "This house is self-destructing. It's had enough."

"It has good bones," she said stubbornly. "It'll be around for at least another fifty years."

"Yeah, as an abandoned house and neighborhood eyesore," he said.

It was the dinner hour and he was standing over a pot of boiling linguini, the steam searing his face. Kathryn was slicing tomatoes for a salad while the squirrels were again doing something noisy in the walls—shredding the insulation or fucking each other senseless, or maybe they were chewing through more wiring. If the squirrels electrocuted themselves, there'd be no need to hire Judy, it occurred to Jim, but the house would be uninhabitable for weeks while their corpses rotted in the walls, the stench permeating every room.

"It's not that bad," she said. "You're overreacting. Once we get the squirrels evacuated, everything will be fine. We'll have the outlets fixed too. We just need to get another estimate. I'm sure it's not as bad as that guy said."

How would you know? he almost barked. He looked at her but didn't reply.

"It'll be okay," she said firmly, glancing over at him. "I promise."

"If you say so," he mumbled. How long would they have to stay in this house before they could move? Were they trapped indefinitely? Because it certainly felt like it. There was no way, for one, they'd be able to sell it for anything close to what they'd paid for it with the repairs it now needed. He'd thought about suing the housing inspector, but the idea enervated him, and there was certainly no guarantee they'd win.

Kathryn finished the tomatoes and put the salad bowl on the table, her curls brushing her shoulders. He didn't know why she wasn't more upset, but it probably had something to do with her ability to sleep through the night. "Stop worrying so much. You're making yourself sick. We're here, and this is our home now. We'll get through it," she said.

"I hope so," he said. He tried to catch her eye, but she didn't look at him.

When Kathryn's parents flew in from Fort Myers the following Friday, a storm was tailing them, one that swiftly blew through town but not before the gauge in the backyard registered nearly an inch and a half of rainfall. The roof did not cave in on their heads, but Jim went up the attic ladder to check for new leaks after the storm moved on. Marty, his father-in-law, insisted on helping him. He looked exhausted from the trip, the bags under his eyes a deep violet, nearly the same color as those under Jim's, but he wouldn't be deterred. He stood in the hallway yawning and gripping the ladder on both sides as Jim climbed up.

"You really don't have to do that," said Jim. The heavy ladder—one of the few things in the house that didn't seem on the verge of collapse—was firmly attached to the attic's trap door.

"Oh, I don't mind. I'd go up there myself, but Kathryn's mother would never let me hear the end of it."

"I really am okay by myself."

"No, no, no," said Marty. "It's the least I can do."

Downstairs, Jim could hear laughter as he shone the flashlight in the attic's corners and swept it across the insulation before shining it on the floor's rough wooden planks. He was so relieved not to find evidence of water or other damage he almost told his father-in-law he loved him, words he and Marty had never exchanged in the ten years they'd known each other. Kathryn told her parents and siblings she loved them whenever they ended a phone conversation, and she'd once said it to a Pizza Hut employee after putting in an order, which Jim still teased her about. "I'm tired!" she'd said with an embarrassed chuckle. "But I do love pizza."

"Find anything?" Marty called from below while Jim climbed down the ladder and silently thanked the house for not adding another item to his list of miseries.

"No, but I really was expecting the worst."

"Of course you were," said Marty with a caustic chuckle. "I'll never move again if I have anything to say about it. All the rigmarole with the buying and selling and then surprise! You just bought a lemon."

"Oh god," said Jim, his stomach tightening. "Tell me about it."

"It'll get better," said Marty. "This is a nice house. A few quirks, of course, but what place doesn't have them?"

When Jim didn't reply, he said, "Let's make popcorn. With butter. Elizabeth said I could have some."

"That sounds good," said Jim.

"No margarine. I'd rather eat it plain. That stuff is ghastly."

"We have butter. We might even have some of that dried cheese stuff to sprinkle on top if you want that too."

"Oh yes," exclaimed Marty. "Let's lay it on thick."

In the hall's sepulchral light, he and his father-in-law smiled at each other, Marty's sagging cheeks covered in silvery red stubble, the fringe of his remaining hair trimmed neatly above his ears. Jim had always liked him. Marty was one of the most amiable people he knew, in spite of having raised five children and endured five overlapping adolescences.

The squirrels started up in the walls while they were popping the corn. The creatures were often activated by the scent of cooking food, Jim had noticed shortly after the invasion. Kathryn had warned her parents about their unwelcome housemates before they flew in from Florida, adding that she and Jim were waiting for the squirrel specialist's appointment the following Wednesday. Her mother was worried about disease—what if one of the squirrels managed to find its way out of the wall and bite someone? Most likely it would have rabies, because why else would it bite a human?

Kathryn told her she was being preposterous—there was no danger of a squirrel, rabid or otherwise, biting anyone during their visit. As far as Kathryn could tell, the squirrels were happy where they were and most likely had a portal that led outside, which the squirrel woman claimed she'd be able to locate, and after the squirrels were all evacuated, Jim could board it up. He was already worrying about how Judy would know if she'd removed all the squirrels. Did she have a special device, like a stud sensor but for squirrels? (In his recent experience, stud sensors were the carpentry equivalent of snake oil—he'd had to drill five holes in the living room wall before he found the damn stud.)

He also planned to challenge her if she too showed up drunk. He'd certainly learned his lesson.

The squirrels, he suspected, had infiltrated the house through the attic, but the roof repairman claimed none of the leaks was large enough for anything other than an insect to crawl through. This hadn't reassured Jim; it had made him feel worse—he was more afraid of a spider biting him than a squirrel, but he kept this information to himself.

Earlier in the day, he'd spotted a pristine cobweb in the upper corner of one of the guest room windows, a blueberry-sized spider holding court near its center. When he went back with a broom a few minutes later, the spider was nowhere to be seen but the web was still intact, so perfect it seemed the aesthetic ideal of a cobweb. He swatted at it anyway and fled the room, hoping the spider had not rappelled down from wherever it was lurking and landed in his hair.

Before the popcorn was ready, he checked the guest room again for new webs and the absent spider. Marty was in the den, waiting for his snack, and Elizabeth and Kathryn were still in the kitchen, bickering about how much butter to melt. "And how on earth," he could hear his mother-in-law saying, "have you lived with those things in your walls for almost two entire weeks? Are you and Jim completely crazy?"

"We refuse to kill them, Mom," said Kathryn. "They don't deserve to die just because they found their way into our walls. They're innocent creatures. Not a mean bone in their bodies."

Elizabeth snorted. "That's beside the point, dear. They don't belong in the house. They're terribly destructive. If they get out—"

"They're not going to get out, Mom," said Kathryn, exasperated.
"We'll see."

"They're not going to get out," Kathryn repeated. "They're just not."

There was no spider, nor any new cobwebs, in the guest room. He hoped it had permanently checked out of the House of Paine, but he doubted it. From what he'd observed, the wildlife population continued to significantly outnumber the human population in their ailing abode, and he wasn't confident this would ever change.

In the morning, when Kathryn and her mother went to the farmers' market that materialized in front of the library on Saturday mornings throughout the summer, Jim confessed to his father-in-law over breakfast that he thought their housing inspector was drunk.

Marty blinked as if dust had been tossed in his eyes. "Did you say anything to him?" he finally asked.

Jim shook his head.

He held Jim's gaze for several seconds. "Did Kathryn smell alcohol on him too?"

"I don't think she did."

"You mean you didn't ask her?" Marty was incredulous.

"She was already so nervous, and I thought I might be imagining it anyway. Like maybe the inspector was only wearing strong cologne."

"That's one way of looking at it," said Marty wryly.

He glanced sheepishly at his father-in-law, wishing he'd kept his mouth shut. He was so deeply tired. Even after resorting to three Advil PM the previous night, he'd only managed to sleep for a few hours. The squirrels were quiet for once too, but his mind limped through its usual obstacle course of worries and self-recrimination.

"You could sue the man," said Marty. "Have you thought about that?"

"I have."

Marty nodded. "You might look into it."

"Okay," said Jim gloomily. Maybe he would look into it. The friend who'd recommended the inspector claimed not to have had any problems—his new house was fine! In fact, it was terrific—he and his wife had never been happier. Toward this friend, Jim now felt the boiling rage of the maliciously duped.

"For your own peace of mind," said Marty, sensing Jim's ambivalence. "Just make a few calls. I understand why you didn't want to alarm Kathryn at the time, but it's clear to me this situation is eating at you, as it should be, frankly."

"She loves this house, warts and all."

"Women are tougher than men," said Marty. "I know when some guys say that they don't mean it, but I do."

"I'll look into it," said Jim. "I want to see what the squirrel woman says first."

"One bit of good news is that we slept fine last night." Marty drained his coffee mug and helped himself to a second cup. "Elizabeth, for all her grousing and whatnot, fell asleep before I did."

Jim's phone dinged with a text. It was in his shirt pocket, a bad habit, but he had trouble staying away from it and in the last year had fully surrendered to it.

It was from Kathryn. *The squirrel woman can come today! She just called.*

When is she coming?

In an hour or 2!

He knew he should have felt elated but mostly what he felt was discouraged.

"What is it?" asked Marty, dropping two sugar cubes into his coffee.

"The squirrel whisperer," he said. "She's coming this morning."

"At least it's not termites. They're all but impossible to get rid of. We almost didn't move to Fort Myers when Elizabeth started googling them. It got a little nuts, but the pull of our grandchildren proved stronger than any insect threat."

The youngest of Kathryn's four siblings had ended up in Miami after college, marrying a Florida native and producing three children in five years. Only one of Kathryn's other siblings had kids, but he lived in Manhattan, a city their mother didn't like to visit—too noisy, too expensive, too self-important. Jim loved Manhattan and it was there where he and Kathryn often vacationed, to the staunch disapproval of his mother-in-law. Once or twice a year they flew to Fort Myers, too, which Kathryn liked more than he did. He was fair-skinned and burned easily. He couldn't swim very well, and the threat of sharks, farfetched as it was, kept him from wading more than a few yards into the Gulf. He was an indoor person, principally, a trait it had taken him years to admit to.

Judy Benson, the squirrel specialist, was a slender, smiling woman in her sixties with a kind face and a gray crewcut. She wore a clover-green windbreaker, olive Bermuda shorts, and red Nikes, and had a flitting way of moving that reminded Jim of the small brown birds nesting on his parents' porch before they'd moved to a condo like his in-laws', theirs in the hilly desert outside of Tucson instead of a few miles from the ocean. Judy was carrying a scuffed black violin case and a large blue duffel. "Are the squirrels getting a recital?" Jim joked.

Judy turned her gray eyes on him and nodded. "Yes, in fact, they are," she said.

"Like the pied piper and the rats in the children's story?" asked Kathryn.

Judy shook her head. "No, not at all."

"Oh," said Kathryn haltingly. "I was just kidding."

He was relieved her parents weren't there too; they'd set out for an outlet mall almost as soon as Kathryn and her mother returned from the farmers' market. Marty would probably have had the good manners to save his insults for after Judy's departure, but about Elizabeth he wasn't so sure.

"I know you have your doubts," said Judy. "Everyone does at first, but please don't worry. This is an open-and-shut case, based on what you've told me."

She set the violin and the duffel next to the kitchen table and went immediately out to the yard, Jim on her heels, Kathryn a few steps behind.

"I always start with an inspection of the roofline," Judy informed them before nimbly climbing up and down a ladder several times to peer under the eaves. It was a humid day, the sky dense with low-hanging clouds. Jim felt sweat trickling down his sides as he monitored Judy's progress from the lawn.

"Ah ha," she at last crowed from her position at the top of the ladder. "I'm sure this is where they got in. The gap is small but it's big enough for a determined squirrel." She pointed under an eave near their westernmost bedroom window. "Ah ha!"

Kathryn looked up, shading her eyes. "I don't see anything."

"I don't either," said Jim, squinting into the darkened reaches of the eaves.

"It's here," said Judy, tapping something Jim still couldn't see. "It'll need to be boarded up, but let's get the squirrels out first. I'm going to have to saw a hole in your wall after I locate the area where they're likely nesting."

"You didn't tell us you'd need to saw into anything," said Jim, his voice rising in alarm.

Kathryn gripped his arm hard at the elbow. "Let her do her work," she whispered. "You want the squirrels out, don't you?"

"Yes, but I wish someone had told me about this earlier." He pulled his arm free and stalked into the house. The squirrels were scratching and scrabbling as he took the stairs two at a time up to his office where he googled the housing inspector's name for what was probably the fiftieth time. The same tired links came up—the inspector's Facebook and LinkedIn pages, his business address and website and Craigslist ad. He changed the search parameters to show only posts that had gone up in the last week.

5 days ago: "Buehl Home Inspectors to Open New Location on September 15"

3 days ago: "Buehl Home Inspectors Welcomes New Receptionist"

2 days ago: "Man in critical condition after two-car collision on I-290"

The URL led to a *Chicago Tribune* article: "Carl Buehl, 59, of Downers Grove, sustained serious injuries in a car crash on westbound I-290. The collision occurred shortly before midnight on July 10," the article reported. The inspector's karma, it appeared, had finally caught up with him, but Jim couldn't tell what he felt about this news—schadenfreude? Guilt? Certainly not pleasure.

> Buehl's van collided with a passenger car driven by Miguel and Ellie Rodriguez when Buehl attempted to merge onto I-290 and lost control of his vehicle. Soon after, all three were taken to the Loyola University Medical Center in Maywood where doctors performed emergency cranial surgery on Buehl. He is believed to have gone into cardiac arrest before colliding with the Rodriguezes' vehicle.
> The couple sustained no serious injuries but were kept overnight for observation at the hospital.

Jim read the article a second time before going back downstairs, where he trailed Judy and Kathryn as they moved around the house. The squirrel specialist had her violin out of its case, and with her free hand thumped the wall above the baseboard in the hallway off the kitchen. Her blue duffel lay at her feet, and a stainless steel crate, one big enough for a medium-sized dog, was positioned next to it.

"I think they're nesting near here," she said. "But I'll get them to come out, wherever they are."

"What are you doing with that violin?" asked Jim.

"I'm going to play it for them," she said. "It's my signature. It soothes them. It's always easier for me to get them out of the wall if I've played for them first."

"I don't know about this," he said, glancing uneasily at Kathryn. "I don't want them running around loose in the house."

Judy shook her head. "Don't worry about that. I'll catch them as soon as they come out of the wall." She smiled reassuringly. "But I need you and Kathryn to go into the next room right now. It's best if I don't have an audience, other than our squirrel friends."

"You're amazing," said Kathryn, her face glowing. "Just like I've heard."

The older woman laughed. "I wouldn't say that. At least not until your squirrels are safely in this crate."

"How are you planning to get them in there?" said Jim. "Won't they be able to escape whenever you open the door to put a new one inside?"

Judy regarded him, annoyance briefly darkening her face. "I've done this dozens of times, Mr. Paine. I use blankets. They're in the duffel with my saw." She gestured toward the duffel with her chin. "Now just please try to relax and let me do my work."

"He's sleep-deprived," said Kathryn.

"And cash poor," said Jim wryly. "If I had more money, I'd be happy enough to sleep at night."

Judy gave him a quizzical look but said nothing.

"Come on," said Kathryn, taking his arm. "Let's go."

From the kitchen, they heard Judy start to play "Greensleeves." The squirrels, possibly sensing upheaval, had been silent for the last several minutes, but not long after she started playing, Jim heard them again. A few minutes later, Judy set aside her violin and started up her electric saw. He was clenching his jaw, he realized; his whole body was clenched. Kathryn giggled, avoiding his eyes across the table. He put his head in his hands and felt the whole of his life reduced to the size of a dust mote.

When Judy was done with the saw, she resumed playing. This time it was "The Devil Went Down to Georgia."

"Come on, my friends. Come on now," they heard Judy say in a coaxing voice.

A few seconds later, in the same tone, she said, "All right, my friends. Here we go."

Jim could feel his blood pressure spiking; he wanted very badly to go into the hallway. A horrifying thought arrived: there might be a litter of half-grown squirrels, old enough to fend for themselves, hiding somewhere in the airless darkness. He looked at his wife, who smiled back at him. He said nothing. To voice his fear might cause it to come true.

Finally, years, decades later, Judy appeared in the kitchen, her face flushed. "All done," she said. "Only the trip out to McHenry to release them and we're all set."

Kathryn jumped up from the table and surprised them both with a hug. "I can't believe it." She started laughing. "You really got them? I can't believe it."

"I did," said Judy, clearly pleased. "I got them."

Jim slipped into the hallway and there they were, three full-sized squirrels, their suspicious brown eyes all trained on him before they began frantically climbing the walls of the cage, trapped and angry and anxious in Judy's metal crate. "Are you sure there aren't any others?" he asked.

"I'm about ninety-five percent sure," said Judy. "But call me immediately if you hear any others. I'll come back and remove them at no charge, of course."

"What about the hole in our wall?" he asked. It was a relatively neat square with sides of about five inches.

"You'll need to patch it in about two days. If there are any other squirrels in your walls, that'll give them a chance to emerge. But I suggest you board up the hole under your eaves today."

Jim glanced at Kathryn. "You and Dad will make quick work of it," she said.

"But this wall repair is going to be a big job," he said.

"Yes," said Kathryn. "But she got the squirrels. Let's enjoy the moment, okay?"

He looked at the squirrels in the cage again. "You little bastards," he breathed. "You owe me two hundred and fifty hours of lost sleep."

Judy nodded. "That's over now," she said. "It's over, Mr. Paine."

It seemed she was right. They heard no more squirrels in the walls, nor did any remaining fugitives emerge from the hole in the hallway over the next two days to vandalize their home. The squirrel whisperer had performed something of a miracle, as her previous clients had alleged she would do, and Jim finally slept through the night for the first time in several weeks. Marty and Elizabeth were initially aghast at the hole she'd left behind, but they both admitted it was a small price to pay for the removal of a trio of destructive and fast-breeding wild creatures.

Marty helped Jim with the eaves repair, holding the ladder for him again while Jim covered the small gap between the house and the roof's overhang with a thick piece of plywood, pounding in twelve nails, three on each side. The patch was going nowhere, and no new squirrel intruders, unless they were wielding a crowbar, would be able to pry it loose.

When they were finished, Jim told him the home inspector had been in a car crash. "He's in the ICU," he added. "I don't think I'm going to try to sue him."

Marty looked at him, his face unreadable. "That's a shame."

Jim hesitated. "The accident or the lawsuit?"

"Both," said Marty. "But I think you've turned a corner with the house. Just attend to what needs to be attended to and hope for the best. Elizabeth and I can help you out a bit if you need it."

He could feel his face coloring. "I wouldn't want to—"

Marty shook his head. "Don't worry, Jim. We'd be happy to help. Elizabeth feels exactly the same."

"That's very kind of you."

"Well, shit happens. And I'd say you've had more than your share lately."

"I wish I could disagree," said Jim.

The day after his in-laws went back to Florida, he told Kathryn he'd smelled alcohol on the home inspector's breath. They were in bed for the night, but Kathryn sat up and turned on her reading lamp. "What?" She stared at him in dismay. "Why didn't you say anything?"

"I was hoping I was wrong."

She sighed and shook her head. He was surprised she didn't look more angry. "I wish you'd told me," she said quietly.

"I do too. I'm sorry."

"I probably would still have wanted to buy this place," she said. "I'd already convinced myself that no matter what he found, we had to live here."

"I didn't feel the same," said Jim.

"I know you didn't."

Outside a car passed, music blaring from its windows.

"We have insurance," she said. "We should use it."

"I'm almost certain none of the problems we've had are covered."

"But we need to make sure." She settled back into the bed but left the lamp on, her gaze still on him. "I bet the roof would be covered."

"I doubt it. They'll call it natural wear and tear. We need a tree to fall on it. Then maybe it'll be covered."

She was silent for a long moment. "I wish you'd told me about the inspector. We could have gotten a different one."

"You're right." He hesitated. "I'm really sorry."

"At least it's better now, with the squirrels gone." She turned onto her side. "I need to go to sleep. Let's not dwell on it. We're not moving. I don't want to. Not for a long time."

"No."

"Good," she said. "Because I won't do it."

She clicked off the lamp and was asleep within a few minutes, but he knew it would be a while before he calmed down enough to drift off. The house felt alive around him, its walls and stairways exhaling their stealthy breaths. Why had he and Kathryn felt they needed this particular assemblage of plaster and wood and glass? It seemed a foolhardy move, hubristic and reckless, to buy such a large old house and believe they could bring it to heel.

They'd bought it anyway, as others had done with similarly crumbling houses everywhere. No one was going to stop doing it, either. "It's what adults do," he could hear his mother-in-law saying, one of her favorite expressions.

It was, yes. It certainly was.

The Petting Zoo

The one photo Dana found online of Marc Lillès showed a graying, arrestingly handsome man whose tentative smile did not reveal his teeth. He'd smoked half a pack of Gitanes a day when she knew him and had made no pretense of quitting; she suspected it was vanity rather than reticence that kept him from displaying for the unnamed photographer his yellowed incisors.

They'd met when she was twenty-three, he two years older, during the hottest Chicago summer on record, the same year hundreds of people died during two spectacular July heat waves, the city officials at pains to dispose of so many decaying bodies in the overflowing morgues, many of the dead the solitary elderly with no next of kin coming forward to claim them and offer a proper burial or cremation rite. As floodwaters more frequently did, the heat overwhelmed the ailing urban infrastructure: the power grid stuttered, the asphalt buckled on the congested highways, and cars stalled in traffic jams from overtaxed radiators. Children, those intrepid or unparented enough to be outdoors, were shooed out of the parks by police officers hoping to stave off heat exhaustion and dehydration.

In the evenings after work, Dana walked with Marc through the leafy streets of Lincoln Park to the second-floor apartment he shared with three other young Frenchmen, he subdued by the extreme heat and humidity, she by a dire, witless love for him she was certain he didn't feel for her. He was leaving soon, in any case, returning to the northern suburbs of Paris where his aging parents awaited him, as did whatever career he found to immerse himself in (briefly, there was the threat of a job in South Africa, but it led quickly to nothing) after his internship at the French Trade Commission ended—a few weeks more, and that would be all. She was leaving the city too, several weeks after his exodus, for graduate school in another state.

On the nights they spent apart, she recorded thousands of words in a journal she doubted she'd ever want to reread—its hopeful, obsessive cataloguing of the hours she spent with him unpleasant for her to review even so close to their passage. Her roommate, Angela, a high school friend who was finishing a nursing degree and dating a corporate attorney she would marry two years later and go on to have three children with, was off carousing with him most of that summer, trying on the disguise of lawyer's wife and finding she liked how it looked.

Angela never met Marc, and Dana later wondered if her roommate thought she'd made him up out of jealousy over the doting attorney, a man a dozen years Angela's senior who, when Dana was introduced to him a month after her roommate started seeing him, still looked shocked that his young, pretty girlfriend, taller than he was by two inches, had agreed to have sex with him and continued to agree to it.

It was a stray question from Angela over a late-summer lunch with her and her oldest child, a slender, confident girl named Hannah, that triggered Dana's long-dormant curiosity about Marc, his role in her life having turned out to be a minor one, which for a while had surprised no one but herself.

"Are you Facebook friends with that French guy you dated when we were still living on Jackson?" Angela asked, glancing up at Dana as she poured a package of sweetener into her iced tea.

Dana shook her head. "I haven't talked to him in twenty years," she said. "What made you think of him?"

"Hannah's going to Paris over spring break with her French class. Isn't that where he lives?"

"Lucky you," said Dana, smiling at Hannah, who was extracting the anchovy from her Caesar salad and entombing it in her napkin. "I'm not sure if he still lives there," she said to Angela.

"Hannah," said Angela. "Stop that. You'll get dressing on your sleeve."

"I haven't been to France since my honeymoon," said Dana. "I should try to get Tim to go back, but he always wants to go skiing on our vacations."

"You could go to the Alps," said Hannah. "Or Tim could go there while you're in Paris."

"Didn't your French boyfriend want to start a petting zoo?" asked Angela, her large blue eyes oddly blank, as if the question and what she was actually thinking weren't the same thing.

Dana laughed. "A petting zoo? No, not that I know of. I've never dated a guy who wanted to start a petting zoo."

Angela stared at her for a moment. "You haven't?" she asked, her eyes more focused now. "I thought for sure you did."

"You're thinking of Joyce, Mom," said Hannah.

Angela looked at her daughter. "Joyce?"

"Yes, Mom. Your college roommate."

"I think Marc went into something with computers," said Dana. "That's the last I heard."

"Don't you want to know what he's up to now? Haven't you googled him?" asked Angela.

"No." Dana sipped from her water glass. "It's funny you were thinking about him. I don't, not very often. I don't even know if he's married."

"But you were so nuts about him!" She glanced at her daughter. "He was all Dana talked about that last summer we lived together. The same summer I met your father."

"You certainly had better luck with Sid than I did with Marc," said Dana.

Angela made a face. "Yes, and three demanding kids later—"

"Oh, Mom. Dad told me you wanted four and he's the one who said you had to stop at three."

"Your father is a terrible gossip," said Angela. "See what you're missing by not having kids, Dana?"

Dana had told Tim very little about Marc. There'd never seemed a reason to—as an impressionable, inexperienced girl of twenty-three, she'd been briefly, ardently in love with a man from another country, dated him for a few weeks, and then she'd lost him. It was an old, vaguely sad story. Time and circumstance had intervened, and before long, other men materialized to occupy her bed and imagination, and before the end of the same year, her life had veered off in a different direction from the one she'd hoped for during their shared summer of murderous heat very near the end of the previous century.

Tim, her husband of eight years, was the same age as Marc, and both men (if Marc retained the preference) liked to go to bed earlier than she did, and both men had large, bony feet. Neither could tolerate big dogs, friendly or otherwise, either, but beyond that, she didn't know what the two men had in common other than their association with her.

The night after the lunch with Angela and her daughter, Dana lay awake listening to Tim's breathing, the large, masculine slab of him taking up more than half the bed and radiating so much heat that she needed only a thin blanket to sleep beneath. She loved him and did not doubt he loved her too. He was kind and suffered when others weren't kind; upon meeting him, she'd sensed that he would know how to take care of her, and she hadn't been wrong. His hulking, sheltering presence still calmed and reassured her. He was, she'd recognized after their first date, back in the verdant pastures of their early thirties, who she'd been waiting for.

It was Marc's almost feline beauty, not his warm, redolent maleness, that had initially charged toward her at full gallop, sword extended, though he would never have characterized their first encounter in this way. It was possible he hadn't noticed her at all that morning, but the sight of him on the elevator in the building where they both worked, his office seven floors above hers, had summoned in her chest a roiling, physical discomfort she couldn't recall having felt more than once or twice before. The kind of beauty Marc possessed was hard on other people, Dana later realized, because it was difficult to ignore, and therefore both suspect and intrusive. His finely wrought nose and cheekbones and long-lashed dark eyes made other men anxious or confused or jealous, whereas women felt both cowed by him and avid for his good opinion and sexual interest.

Two days passed after the lunch with Angela before Dana went to her computer to search for Marc online. Tim was at the gym playing basketball with college friends who were known to bloody each other's lips and stab at each other's eyeballs on the scuffed, echoing court when the game became hotly serious, which was every week, more or less. Her husband would return home with a limp on some nights, though mysteriously, the injury often disappeared by the following morning, as if she had dreamt it or else he was some species of cyborg capable of repairing itself. Nearly every week Dana wished aloud that he wouldn't go, fearing a forlorn call from the emergency room, but so far it hadn't happened and Tim insisted it wouldn't.

Marc had not been especially athletic but he'd liked dancing in clubs and had walked everywhere, eschewing cabs and buses because Chicago with its vast, unruly grid of streets and parks, the lake hemming them all in on one side, charmed and stirred him.

His neighborhood was also full of beautiful former sorority girls he liked looking at and having stare back at him, some of them open-mouthed and giggling as Marc glanced down at them, as if from a kingly height.

And here he was on Facebook, as Angela was certain he would be. *Beau gosse*, some admirer had written in the comments under his profile picture, the only photo Dana had found of him anywhere. *Handsome boy*. Yes, he still was. Before she could think better of it, she sent him a friend request, the blood rushing in her ears, both shame and bravado in her veins. She shut off her computer and fled the room, as if fleeing an exploding bomb.

When Tim returned from the gym half an hour later, Dana was standing by the kitchen sink, peering blindly out the window, a bowl of Cheerios going soggy in her hand. His skin was still pink from his exertions and the excitement of masculine competition; he was wearing silky, knee-length black basketball shorts and a red, sweat-stained Bulls T-shirt, the front of which bore a vast dark patch, evidence of the previous two hours' battles.

Out of habit, she asked, "Did you have a good time?"

He lowered his head to kiss her. "Yes," he said. "I played pretty well tonight."

She nodded. "But of course." He smelled like hot rubber and laundry soap and she put her arms around him, not caring that he was coated in sweat. What was she doing, mucking through her past when she was happy with the present, with her lanky, earnest husband and the life they'd made for themselves? At least she thought she was happy. It was probably nothing other than idle curiosity, brought on by Angela, who seemed always, out of boredom or mischief—Dana was never sure which—to be stirring one pot or another.

Truly, was there anything wrong with being curious about Marc Lillès, who had once been almost absurdly important to her? Why was the past always being held up as if it were a stained sheet, belittled and pointed to as an era filled with bad judgment and emotional excess?

Her lips were moving and Tim was staring at her. "Why do you look like that?" he asked.

"Like what?" she said, feeling her face turn hot.

"Like you're doing math in your head."

"That is what I'm doing," she said. "I'm trying to figure out how much to spend on you for Christmas—$12.15 or $12.35?"

"Ha ha. I hope it'll be at least $12.50. I want the cotton socks this year, not the polyester ones." His expression was still scrutinizing. "What were you really thinking about?"

"An ex-boyfriend," she said, surprising herself, but Tim's expression didn't change.

"Poor slob," he said. "I'm sure he still rues the day you dumped him for me."

She laughed. "I'm sure he does."

She hadn't spoken to Marc or exchanged letters with him in nearly twenty years. After he'd gone back to France, she'd seen him one other time, when he returned to Chicago for a visit the following year, but she'd had classes to attend and was teaching by that point too; she'd only been able to drive in from Cincinnati to spend one afternoon with him, which they spent walking around Marc's old neighborhood, her heart pained by nostalgia for their old, fleeting intimacy and her previous certainty that the night would end with them naked together in his tussled bed.

Tim left the kitchen to take a shower, stripping off his T-shirt as he disappeared into the hall. "Tell him he has to arm-wrestle me first if he wants to see you again," he called.

"There's no danger of that," she said. "He lives in Paris."

"I'm getting in the shower," Tim yelled from deeper in the hallway. "Is there any spaghetti left from last night?"

"There's stir-fry," she yelled back. "I made some while you were at the gym."

"Did you say filet mignon? Excellent. My lucky night."

He knew she hadn't said that. "It's tofu and broccoli," she said, not bothering to raise her voice. "Your favorite."

Three days passed without Marc accepting her friend request. She knew there was no reason to be disappointed or annoyed by this, but she was. Two more days passed, then another.

She didn't understand why he wasn't responding—his silence, her sixth sense informed her, was not due to the fact he hadn't seen her request. His lack of a response implied that either he had forgotten her entirely and didn't accept requests from strangers, or else she had offended him in some unfathomable way in the twenty-one years since their liaison. She'd always assumed, in any case, that she'd made very little impression on him, that she was one woman of many whom he'd passed the time with since his beautiful mid-twenties and now, in his still-beautiful mid-forties, if his Facebook photo was to be believed. Though of course it was also possible he was leading such a full and meaningful life that he had almost no time for frivolities such as social media and distant exes.

Tim wasn't on Facebook, another one of his admirable qualities. "Why would I want to look at pictures of other people's dirty bathtubs?" he'd asked the last time she'd badgered him about joining.

"What are you talking about?" she'd asked, baffled.

"Didn't I see you looking at a picture of someone's bathtub not long ago? Jeff's or someone's?"

"Oh, those were before and after pictures," she said. "Jeff bought some new cleanser he thinks everyone should try."

"Your brother needs to find a real hobby," said Tim.

"You can be the one to tell him that the next time you see him."

On the twelfth day, Marc at last responded to her friend request, and less than an hour later, he sent a message. It was after 11 P.M. and Tim was already asleep; in Paris, however, it was early morning. She wondered if Marc had been up all night or if he was routinely awake before 6 A.M.

Hello Dana,

It's good to hear from you—a friendly voice from my past.

From your photo, you look like you haven't aged at all—maybe this is because you've never smoked (or have you started since I saw you last?).

I see from your profile that you are still in Chicago and are married. I was married too, but am divorced now. She wanted to live in the country; I did not. She wanted two cars, I only wanted one.

There were other complications that I won't bore you with. Some other time, maybe.

I am happy to know you are out there and remember me. I hope you are feeling good in all ways.

M

"What do you think he meant by that last line?" Angela asked after Dana called and read her the message. "It sounds a little risqué. Was he good in bed?"

"He wasn't bad," said Dana.

"So, he wasn't good. Not really."

"I honestly don't remember."

Angela laughed. "If you don't remember, it means he wasn't. You don't forget the good ones. I used to think sex was the be-all and end-all until I met my husband."

Dana snorted. "I hope you haven't told him that."

"There are more important things than sex. You know that by now," said Angela, no trace of irony in her voice. "I got tired of dating men with no money who always wanted to split the check and have me loan them twenty dollars to fill their gas tank. The sex was good with Sid because he was rich. Money is the most effective aphrodisiac, I figured out pretty fast."

"I haven't written Marc back yet," said Dana. "I really don't know what to say."

"Tell him you're happily married and see if he replies. Then you'll know what his intentions are."

"I'm sure he doesn't have any intentions. He's in Paris, for one."

"Don't be so naive," said Angela. "He could have intentions even if he lived on Mars."

"We only went out for a few weeks, and it was so long ago."

"But you were madly in love with him and I'm sure he knew it. I wouldn't underestimate the nostalgia factor. For him or you."

"There's nothing there," said Dana firmly. "Only curiosity."

"Which killed the cat."

"You're the one who told me to get in touch with him! But now you're warning me off." She paused. "Nothing's going to happen. Nothing at all."

"Good," said Angela. "Then everything's fine."

"You're a nutcase, Angela."

She didn't respond to his message until two days later, her attention derailed by a thunderstorm that struck the evening after Marc's note. High winds uprooted a neighbor's maple tree and knocked down power lines before the tree fell on Tim's backyard vegetable garden, squashing most of the tomatoes in their wire cages, the prickly cucumber vines, and the string beans. It also flattened the chrysanthemums that marked the garden's perimeter (a disappointingly ineffective rabbit deterrent, as it turned out), his once-pristine and thriving garden now a forlorn and messy bed of mud and crushed greenery.

Tim was out of town when it happened, having left that morning for a few days in Cleveland where he was working on a story about a fair-trade chocolate company for the weekly show he produced for Chicago's public radio station. "I'm sure the Reynoldses have homeowners' insurance," he said wearily when she called with the bad news. "We'll probably need to have some sod put down too. Take a few pictures of the damage and send them to me. God, all that work for nothing."

"A couple of the tomato plants survived," she said. "But every-thing else is pretty much gone."

"Did Harold at least say he was sorry?"

"It was Rhea I talked to."

"So, no, no one said they're sorry."

"Nope."

"What a surprise," he said, even more dispirited now. "I'll deal with them when I get home. Don't talk to them again until I get back. I want our insurance companies to handle this."

The Reynoldses were quiet, unfriendly, longtime residents of Winnemac Street; they never attended the July block party or the Christmas cookie exchange. They locked their doors and kept their porch light off on Halloween, but they did mow their lawn and promptly removed any litter that appeared on their front walk or the strip of grass near the street. They had no bark-ing dogs and their house always looked freshly painted; their gutters were also cleaned each spring. If nothing else, they could not be accused of bringing down the value of the neighboring properties. Dana was grateful that Tim would handle the maple tree crash. Rhea and Harold made her nervous with their grim, thin-lipped faces and suspicious, measuring gazes. What had hap-pened to them, she sometimes wondered, to make them who they were?

"Hurry back," she said. "I love you."

"Love you too," said Tim gruffly. "Why did we ever move out of our condo?"

"You wanted a garden," she said.

"Yeah, I know. The joke's on me, obviously."

"We can plant another one," she said.

"I suppose we can." He sighed. "Maybe. We'll see."

She wrote back to Marc the next morning from her office in the attic, the cavernous but stuffy room's one window overlooking the ruined garden where she spied on two squirrels foraging among the broken vines and leaves as she sipped coffee and tried to decide what to say.

Dear Marc,

Thanks for accepting my friend request. Yes, it's true, I'm still in Chicago. I'm managing the Cubs, who are again on track for the World Series this season. (Kidding, but not about the World Series, believe it or not!)

Actually, I write training manuals for an insurance company—extremely boring, but it pays well and I get to work from home.

I'm sorry about your marriage not working out. It sounds like the end was stressful (but I suppose divorce isn't usually a fun thing). Your Facebook profile says you're an information systems analyst. What is that?

As far as my husband and cars are concerned, we agreed that we should each have one, which could be one reason why we're still together. ;)

Best, Dana

She could see that her message was read within minutes after its receipt, but he didn't reply that afternoon or evening. It didn't matter one whit if he ever wrote back, she told herself, and she wasn't at all sure why she'd bothered to contact him in the first place. Had Tim ever dabbled in risky online behavior during their marriage? She very much doubted he had, at least not with the women he'd dated seriously before they met—one had become a born-again Christian and wasn't online at all, another only dated women now, and a third was living in an ashram in India and had taken a vow of silence, which Tim said he couldn't believe because she had talked more than any other person he knew.

Dana lay awake in their king-size bed for a long time that night, listening to the wind in the remaining maples and the few cars that passed in the street, her sixth sense telling her she was making a mistake by reaching into her past to summon a man with whom things had ended inconclusively. She hadn't fallen out of love with him and he hadn't dumped her for someone else. It had ended because they'd both lacked imagination—his job in Chicago had run its course, and the expectation was always that he would return to France. She'd gotten into graduate school and since the spring had been planning to move to Ohio in August.

The next morning, she called Angela and confessed that she'd made a mistake by getting in touch with Marc. "I should have let sleeping dogs lie."

"Then unfriend him," said Angela. "He'll survive."

"I can't do that."

"Why? You just said you should let sleeping—"

"I know, I know, but it seems so harsh. I don't want to hurt his feelings."

"Dana," said Angela flatly. "Let me tell you something. I know I gave you a hard time the other day, but it was only because of the mood I was in. I've been married twice as long as you have, so trust me on this. From what I can see, your marriage is a big, solid rock and Marc is only a little bit of water lapping at its edges. You're not doing anything wrong. Haven't you flirted with anyone else before now? Tim isn't going to divorce you if he finds out you've exchanged a couple of emails with an ex."

"I did tell Tim that we were in touch," said Dana. "Sort of."

"You're a little bored," said Angela. "That's normal. The human condition."

"Have you been in touch with one of your exes lately?"

Angela laughed. "My youngest is four. When would I have time?"

"So, I guess you haven't."

She laughed again. "No, I wouldn't say that. I exchanged a few sexts with Jim Hinton a couple of years ago, when he was going through his divorce. You remember him, don't you?"

"Jim Hinton from high school, the guy you lost your virginity to?"

"The one and only."

"You didn't tell me you sexted with him."

"Because it wasn't a big deal. I hardly thought about it. I know Sid hasn't always been an angel. Life is long," she said. "Even if it doesn't feel that way."

Tim returned from Cleveland the following evening, dark circles under his eyes from three back-to-back eighteen-hour days, which was often the routine when he traveled for work. For dinner, Dana baked two potatoes and grilled a steak for him, something she hadn't done in several years.

He was flabbergasted when he saw her heading to the patio with the T-bone. "What the hell has gotten into you?" he said, peering at her closely. "Are you feeling okay?"

She froze, realizing her error—she was acting like a guilt-stricken wife. "You deserve it," she said weakly. "I'm so sorry about the garden. I hope Harold and Rhea won't be hard to deal with."

"That's what insurance is for. The tree is theirs, so at least that isn't in dispute." He'd gone out to the backyard twice to inspect the carnage in the first half hour he was home, his expression shading from disbelief to bereaved resignation.

"I have a confession to make," he said over dinner, his steak half-eaten, its juices an oily dark pink against the white plate.

She blinked at the pieces of marinated seitan and broccoli florets that sat next to her baked potato. Her heart was pounding so hard she wondered if Tim could see it through the fabric of her blouse.

"I had a steak last night too," he said with a look of feigned contrition.

She laughed in a hard, exultant burst. "That's okay. You probably didn't have time for lunch."

"Or breakfast."

"I thought you looked a little skinnier," she said.

He nodded. "I had to go to the next notch on my belt this morning. I'm so glad to be home, dead garden or not."

"I'm glad you are too, sweetie."

While she was rinsing their dinner plates in the kitchen, he came up behind her and put his arms around her, crossing them over her breasts; she could smell the steak and the beer he'd drunk at dinner on his breath. "Why don't we leave those for later," he said, his lips at her ear. It had been almost two weeks since the last time, not so unusual, but one of the longer stretches in recent months.

She turned in his embrace, pulling off her dishwashing gloves. "How about right over there," she said, tilting her head toward the table on the other side of the room.

"Well," he said, his grin sly. "It really is my lucky night."

She took his hand and led him to the table, pushing their dinner napkins and the dolphin-shaped salt-and-pepper shakers they'd bought on their honeymoon in St. Lucia off to the side. She bent over, her hands gripping the table's far edge as he lifted her skirt and unbuckled his belt.

It was over fast, both of them panting and a little dazed when they were done. "Jesus," he breathed. "I really needed that."

He had an eyelash on his right cheek. She touched her fingertip to it before instructing him to make a wish.

"I wish the garden hadn't been ruined," he said, blowing on the eyelash.

"You're not supposed to tell me your wish!"

He lowered his head and kissed her. "How else can I be sure the wish fairy heard me?"

Later she realized that with the kitchen lights on and the maple tree gone, Harold and Rhea would have seen them if they'd been looking over at her and Tim's house from their living room.

Marc had sent her a message while she and Tim were laboring in the kitchen.

Dana, hello again,

 I have been in San Francisco on business the last six days,
but I will be passing through Chicago tomorrow. Do you have
time to meet for coffee? Please forgive the short notice.
—Marc Lillès

PS Your husband is welcome to join us too.

She didn't write back until the morning, and half hoped it
would be too late, that he would already be airborne or else have
made other plans.

Hi Marc,

 How much time do you have? I'm about thirty minutes
from O'Hare and I think I could probably get out there for a
quick coffee. Or are you staying somewhere overnight?
—Dana

He replied within five minutes:

I decided to stay in your city for three days. I will be at the
Hilton near the Field Museum, a small vacation before I
return to Paris. I haven't been to Chicago in seven years. Are
you able to meet me at 5 or 5:30 p.m.? I could come to you
too. Just let me know. —M

She recognized him immediately; he had not gotten uglier in the
years since she'd last seen him, that was for certain. If anything, he
was even more striking. The hotel was a cacophonous welter of people checking in at the crowded reception, talking showily on their
sleek phones, laughing with each other in animated groups, already
well into happy hour, the ennui of the workday sloughed off.

Marc was sitting alone on a wide beige sofa in the lounge con-
nected to the reception area, his dark hair shot through with silver,
his head bent over a hardbound book he held in one hand, his long

fingers splayed across its back, its title obscured. She approached him warily, wondering if he would be disappointed when he saw her. She could feel her chest constricting as she moved closer, struck suddenly with the crazed thought that she should turn around and run right back to her car, parked expensively only a few minutes ago in the hotel's garage. Tim knew where she was, though; she hadn't lied to him, and he'd rewarded her by not appearing jealous.

Marc looked up from his book, glancing around the large, airy space until his eyes found her, and then they held her, unblinking, his own expression very serious, as if he were about to share news of an unexpected misfortune. He stood up, the book still in his hand—something by Michael Lewis, the author's name in large block letters on the spine, Dana registering this fact as if it was a warning: Lewis was Tim's favorite author.

She could feel her face arranging itself into a tremulous smile, tears, embarrassingly, springing to her eyes—for her much younger self? (Twenty-three! Almost impossible now to imagine herself so young, waking up each morning in an invincible body with a love-addled head on its shoulders.) Or for Marc, for having lost him only a month and a half after first being singled out by him?

He took a few tentative steps toward her. His light blue shirt and gray pants fit him perfectly, his black hair still thick, the same as it had been the last time she'd seen him. Tim was starting to lose his. Angela had ordered her to take Marc's picture—several, if she could manage it. She didn't know how she'd be able to do it without making a fool of herself, but she would take the pictures, of course she would. She'd have a drink or two and then she'd do it.

Without saying a word, he stepped forward and kissed her. She could smell his lemony cologne as he pressed his warm, foreign lips to her face. She moved back and smiled up at him, heat rising from her neck. Everything—her ears, her cheeks, her chest—all of it was burning.

"Well," she said idiotically. "Here you are."

He nodded. "And here you are." He reached for her hand and squeezed it once. "I have been wondering how you are."

"The same, I mean—" She paused. "I've been wondering how you are too."

"I knew you were on Facebook, but I wasn't sure if you'd want to hear from me. It made me happy when you got in touch."

"But you didn't accept my friend request for a more than a week," she blurted.

He laughed and shook his head. "I don't always check to see what is there. You aren't the first person to say this to me."

"You don't have your account linked to your email?"

He shook his head. "My ex-wife spent too much time on Facebook. I didn't want to do the same."

"My husband isn't on it at all."

Marc smiled. "And so you are still married to him."

"Yes," she said, smiling too.

He motioned toward the sofa. She sat down primly, flipping her hair behind her. It was loose around her shoulders, which it rarely was, but Tim hadn't been there to see it when she left the house. He would have guessed, if he hadn't already, that her meeting with Marc was something more than a casual outing.

He motioned to a passing server and looked at Dana. "Would you like a glass of wine?"

"The house pinot noir would be good," she said, glancing up at the server who was blond and long-legged and not far beyond college age. His suntanned, fine-boned face revealed nothing about his interior state.

"Whatever you would like," said Marc, who was drinking red wine too, his glass almost empty. "I'll have another," he said to the server, raising his glass. "The Meiomi pinot."

After the server left, Marc turned on her the full heat of his gaze, the clamor of nearby laughter and piped-in rock music making her feel disoriented, almost disembodied. A river of intention flowed all around them—here was a vast room filled with people who wanted to be touched, to be taken somewhere and undressed. Marc presumably wanted the same thing. She couldn't say she didn't want it too.

"You haven't changed very much," he murmured, raising his chin, tilting it slightly as he spoke, a mannerism she remembered. His knees were angled toward her bare ones, her taut, hairless skin glowing in the lamplight. She was wearing a fitted khaki skirt and a black V-neck blouse, two of the more flattering items in her closet. She'd stayed the same trim size she'd been when they'd met, and would show off her legs a little if the occasion merited it.

"You haven't either," she said.

He shook his head. "Oh no, I have," he said. "I'm much more cynical now."

She laughed and looked around for their server, certain she'd feel more at ease with a glass in her hand.

The wine did help her feel less self-conscious when it arrived a few minutes later, her chest growing warmer with each sip. She leaned toward Marc as she relaxed, and could see his face turning rosy from his second, and before long, third glass of wine. She had a second glass but turned down a third, despite his gentle bullying before their impassive server. She stared up at him, giddy. "Are you married?" she asked. "What's your name?"

Surprise briefly transformed his features. "Alex," he said. "No." He pursed his lips, suppressing a smile. "No, I'm not married."

"Don't do it," said Marc. "You don't have to."

"No, you don't," Dana agreed. "But we did."

Alex regarded them. "You're a very handsome couple."

"We're not married to each other," she said.

"Oh, I just meant—" said Alex, reddening.

"We were a couple once," said Marc. "But she broke my heart."

Dana smacked his upper arm, which, startlingly, was solid muscle. She put her hand back and groped his warm bicep through his sleeve. "Goodness," she said. "You must work out a lot."

The server had already drifted away when she looked up again a moment later. "I didn't break your heart," she said. "It was the other way around. I would have gone to France with you if you'd asked me to."

There was a measured pause. "You were leaving for graduate school. You wouldn't have come with me."

"No, I would have, but you didn't ask." In that instant, she believed it to be true.

"You didn't ask *me*," he insisted.

"I couldn't have! You were the one in charge."

"No, I wasn't. I had no idea what I was doing."

"Hindsight is twenty-twenty," she said.

"What is that?"

"You don't know that expression?"

"No, I don't think so."

"It means you can see the mistakes of the past clearly because—" She paused. Her voice was echoing inside her head; she realized she would probably need to wait at least an hour before she'd be able to drive home. "Because they're behind you."

"Can I see you again tomorrow?" he asked. Two of his finger-tips rested on her knee. She glanced down, but he didn't move his hand.

"I don't—God, it's—" She looked at him helplessly.

"Say yes," he said.

"A tree fell on our garden the other day and my husband—" she said, the words coming out in a nonsensical rush. "He's very upset, and there's so much to do. I don't think I can, Marc."

"Are you sure?" he said, looking at her closely, a half-smile on his lips. His beauty loomed before her, a separate, sentient creature that gazed at her intently.

Who was his ex-wife? she wondered. Was she as beautiful as he was? "I shouldn't," she said quietly.

"But you could," he said.

She shook her head. "No, I can't."

He shifted an inch or two away but kept his fingertips on her knee. "You are very loyal, Dana," he said, solemn. "Is your husband?"

She bristled. "Yes, he is."

Marc's expression was unreadable, his eyes clear, no haze of drunkenness detectable. He nodded and withdrew his hand.

"I envy him," he finally said. "If I hadn't had to return to Paris so soon after we started our adventure—" He glanced at a nearby table where four women and one man were seated close together, shoulders touching, all of them younger than Marc and herself. What exactly was she doing here? "Who knows what might have happened," he said, tapping her knee once. "You should probably eat something. I'll order appetizers."

"No, no, I'm all right," she said. "I'm not hungry."

"You'll get a headache if you don't eat anything."

"You remember that?" she asked, surprised.

"Of course. I remember a lot of things."

"Why didn't you ever call or write me after that day I drove in from Cincinnati to see you?"

He wavered, glancing again at the table of women with their lone man with his elaborate dark sideburns and violet silk tie. "Because you'd already moved on," said Marc. "I could tell as soon as I saw you."

"But I hadn't," she said. "Not really. I was still in love with you."

"You were already seeing someone else, you told me."

"I was, but it wasn't important."

He shook his head. "And now you're married and it is important."

She said nothing.

"You love your husband."

"Yes," she said. "I do. He's a good person."

"I'm happy for you," said Marc. "He's probably wondering where you are right now."

"He knows I'm here." Two hours had passed, however, not including her drive downtown from the north side of the city. Tim probably would be wondering if she was on her way home yet. "But I should text him, I suppose."

Marc nodded and looked away, searching for their server again.

Tim had sent her a text forty-eight minutes earlier. *Will you be back in time for dinner?*

His words stared up at her innocently. It was a little after seven now. *Probably not*, she typed. *Had 2 glasses of wine & should wait a bit before driving home. Back by 8:15–30, I think.*

She put her phone under her thigh, waiting for the throb of Tim's reply, but it didn't come.

Marc ordered edamame and spring rolls, and Dana worried they would be slow to arrive. She was feeling more sober now, but knew it would be wise to wait another half hour before leaving. Marc reached for her hand, and she let him hold it, telling herself she would never see him again after tonight. He would vanish back into his life across the Atlantic, into a new relationship, his glamour and the torch he supposedly still carried for her disappearing with him. Would it be such a terrible thing to go up to his room, just once, and this night would be all, forever?

What if Tim had cheated on her? Because it wasn't impossible; he traveled for work nearly every month and met interesting strangers, some of them doubtless attractive, women there was little risk he'd encounter again. But it was she he returned home to every night—this was what was real, not some imagined trespass her own guilty conscience had summoned.

She could probably let Marc kiss her goodbye. One kiss from another man after so many years of kissing Tim and no one else—it wasn't so reprehensible, was it?

This was what she told herself in the car an hour later as she drove home through the rainy, humid streets to her husband who, just before she'd let Marc kiss her in the parking lot next to her car, had finally replied to her text with a surly-seeming thumbs-up.

She had wrapped her arms around Marc, breathed in the scent of red wine and soy sauce and cologne, allowed him to pull her close and hold her hard. She kissed him for several minutes, wondering if she should relent, go with him wordlessly into the elevator and be ferried up to his room and thrown onto the bed after he'd stripped off all her clothes and his.

But Tim would find out. Somehow he would, and she wouldn't be able to live with herself, even if he didn't leave her. She knew this as she kissed Marc, who had once been the burning, bright focus of so many of her hopes, of her youth and the idea of herself as a woman who could transcend her ordinary upbringing to marry a glamorous Frenchman, become someone different from the person everyone else assumed she was, who, she knew, she still was. But this wasn't so bad, was it? She and Tim had been happy, were happy.

The streetlights that led her to Lake Shore Drive glowed distantly, smeared yellow by sooty rainfall. She was almost certain Marc would call her tomorrow and ask to see her again. She could picture him stepping out of the shower, a white towel around his waist as he murmured his request into the phone, *Come back here. Now. Yes?* She would have to say no. Tim needed her; he should not have to face their neighbors and the ruined garden alone. He was, in a way she had never believed herself to be, an innocent. Possibly, above all else, she had fallen in love with him because of this innocence.

Mega Millions

All his life there was only just enough money, but at fifty-seven, he suddenly had too much.

It was not the first time Sam, Glenn's boss, had suggested he and several others who worked on the wire-harness line at the Speed Queen washer and dryer factory pool their cash and buy four hundred Mega Millions tickets, but it was the first time Glenn had gone in on the buy. He'd never before frittered away money on the lottery, but Sam had caught him in a foolish moment. There was also the fact he had a few more dollars in his pocket than usual because he and his wife Bernadette had decided not to go on vacation this year—not even down to the Dells for a long weekend of overeating and window-shopping. Instead Glenn had promised to clean out the backyard storage shed and paint the kitchen during his week off in August, two tedious chores he was supposed to have done the previous summer but had evaded with wheedling and small bribes.

The night of the drawing, as heat lightning lacerated the sky to the west, they won a sum so preposterous Glenn initially felt nothing but confusion, his stunned mind laboring to understand that $528 million could be something other than a hyperbolic abstraction. Only eight people would share all that money. No other ticket buyers anywhere in the world had chosen the same numbers, as it turned out. So much money made in an instant, and all he'd done was play a game requiring no skill!

Bernadette was even more stunned than he was, and happier. She had always been a generous person, baking two cakes for everyone's birthday, buying too many gifts, giving away more than half the vegetables in the garden to the neighbors each year. In the week and a half following the arrival of the first installment of their big win—Glenn had insisted on the annual disbursement rather than the lump sum, of which the tax man would have taken 50 percent upfront—his wife sent hundred-dollar donations to every charity that had ever sent her a sheet of address labels, a pack of flimsy greeting cards, or an ugly reusable bag. The solicitation letters kept coming, the requested amount always increasing: *Could you give $150 this time, Mrs. Ballard, for the starving children in country X? For confused whales being led off course by ship sonar? Do you know just how hard it is out there for owls? For monkeys kidnapped from their natural habitats? For people with chronic eczema?* She wrote so many checks they soon ran out, but she immediately ordered more and paid the fee for expedited delivery.

Everyone appeared to be in dire need, and before the Mega Millions bus picked him up and drove him straight into a mountain-sized heap of dollar bills, Glenn hadn't realized the extent of this neediness. His three sons and their families certainly had a multitude of pressing needs of their own. His youngest son, Jeff, twenty-three and already a father of two, had approached Bernadette with a shopping list containing an eye-popping number of apparently essential luxury goods. Without them, his family would doubtless cease to function, and Bernadette was happy to oblige, taking Jeff and Junie, his wife and the mother of his children, on a two-day shopping orgy.

Jeff and Junie's list, penned by Junie:

Blu-Ray player

Wii

Subaru Forester

Swing set

MixMaster

Fiesta Ware (12 place settings, please! ☺)

Blend-Tec blender

Sub-Zero fridge

Duxiana bed

Rastar Bentley GTC battery-powered 12V (for Mickey—
a child's car, not the adult version)

All-Clad pans (set of 8)

Timberland boots (4 pairs—one for each of us!)

Maclaren Grand Tour LX stroller

4- or 5-bedroom house w/2- (or 3-) car garage and
in-ground swimming pool (dream big, right? ;))

25 sessions with a personal trainer (Junie)

Family gym membership for 24 Hour Fitness

Wüsthof Classic knives (7-piece set)

72-inch plasma screen TV

Dania leather sectional sofa (rush delivery)

Glenn's other two sons were a little more tempered in their
requests, but he was sure that before long they would find out
what Jeff and Junie were getting their hands on, courtesy of Bernadette's wallet, which was always open for business. Jim, their
oldest, and his wife Candace had one child, an eleven-year-old girl
named Rachel who bossed her parents around as if she were the

First Lady instead of a small-town child of modest intelligence and means. Lately, when she tried to boss around Glenn, he started repeating everything she said back to her, which she and her mother didn't find funny, but his son seemed to get a kick out of. Bernadette wasn't amused either, and scolded Glenn for teasing Rachel, who she said would probably grow up to hate men, especially old men. "Good," said Glenn. "She needs to be wary. Some of them are up to no good."

The first thing Jim asked for was a college savings account for Rachel, which Bernadette set up in the same week the lottery money arrived, starting it with a $60,000 deposit. When she called to tell Jim the fund was now alive and earning interest, he patched in Candace and together they asked if Bernadette and Glenn would help them put a down payment on a new house. The two-bedroom, one-and-a half-bath ranch they'd been making do with for the last twelve years was too small, and if they had to spend another year in it, well, they didn't know if their marriage or their sanity would survive.

"Of course I told them we'll help," Bernadette told Glenn after the call ended. "I said we could probably just buy the house for them outright."

"I really wish you hadn't told them that," he said. "What if they ask for one of those big houses in Green Lake that rich people from Illinois use as their summer homes?"

"What if they do?" she asked. "We're now as rich as they are, Glenn. Richer, I bet." She laughed. "We should buy one of those houses for ourselves. We could have a summer home."

"We live six miles from Green Lake," he exclaimed. "You don't buy your summer home one town over."

"Who says? We can do whatever we want."

"We can do some of the things we want," he said.

"I'm not talking about breaking the law. I just want to live it up. I think we deserve that. The gods are smiling on us, Glenn. You could at least do them the courtesy of smiling back."

Their middle son, Justin, wasn't asking for a new house or car or a set of fancy European knives. Unlike his brothers, he wasn't married and raising children; he'd always been close-mouthed about his private life. It was Bernadette, not Justin himself, who'd told Glenn that he preferred to date men, and Glenn had spoken to Justin about this only once—a stilted conversation with Glenn saying he accepted his son for who he was. Justin had taken this in stoically before he said, "Thanks, Dad," though he sounded more disappointed than thankful or relieved. He lived in Chicago with his boyfriend Rob, who had never come up to Ripon to meet Glenn and Bernadette.

Glenn himself had only been down to Illinois twice to visit Justin since he'd graduated from tech school in Milwaukee and begun his work as an X-ray technician, both of these Chicago visits in the pre-Rob era. Rob taught Spanish language classes at a private high school in the Lincoln Park neighborhood of the city—his full name was Roberto Gimenez, and in his teens he had moved to the U.S. from some city in Mexico Glenn had never heard of, San Miguel de something or other. "De Allende," Bernadette always added, wondering why he could never remember it himself.

Via Fed-Ex, she'd sent Justin a check for $50,000 the day after their money came in, and more than a month and a half later, Justin still had not troubled himself to drive home to thank them in person, though he did call his mother regularly, and she had since sent two other checks, one for $30,000 and the other for $25,000. Glenn was certain she was already thinking about sending a fourth check when he moved most of the money into a new account he didn't give her or any of their sons access to.

She'd already spent nearly half a million dollars, more than a third of their first disbursement, in less than two months. At her current headlong rate, she'd have it all frittered away before Christmas and he'd have to go back to work at Speed Queen, if they'd even take him back, until the next annuity payment arrived in August. Their health insurance premiums alone, now that they were off of Speed Queen insurance, were over $1,600 a month.

He knew he had to tell her he'd cut off her access to the lottery money before she wrote more checks to relatives, charities, her church friends, and former coworkers. He'd left a hundred thousand dollars in the joint account at the credit union, which ordinarily would have covered close to a year and a half's worth of bills and other expenses, with something left over for one or two budget vacations. They'd lived frugally all their lives, and although he knew Bernadette loved giving gifts, he hadn't known how many she was interested in giving until recently.

He told her over breakfast the day after he moved the funds to a money market account only he had access to. She was sipping coffee and looking at the *Oshkosh Northwestern*. When his words registered, she set down the paper and stared across the table at him.

"I'm glad you're having a good time buying everyone gifts, but you're overspending," he said. "We have to live on this money too, and I don't get another payout until next August."

"We have plenty to go around," she said. "Don't be such a miser."

He looked at her in disbelief. "I'm being a miser? I've been letting you do whatever you want up until today."

"You're a miser, Glenn," she said. "If you'd taken the lump sum instead of the annuity, we wouldn't be arguing about this in the first place because we'd have a lot more money in the bank right now."

"That's exactly why I chose the annuity. At the rate you're going, it would all be spent by the end of the year." He was almost shouting, something he'd never done before winning the lottery. "I left a hundred thousand in our joint account. That's more spending money than we've ever had in our lives."

She turned her back and fixed her gaze on the television on the other side of the kitchen, which was tuned to an old episode of *Let's Make a Deal*. He'd sprung for premium cable a few weeks ago and they now had over three hundred channels, but he found himself watching the same ones as always. "It's not fair, and you know that," she said flatly.

"You can get by on a hundred thousand," he said. Again, he had to quell the urge to shout. "That's more money than we made in a year when we were both working full-time. If you need more than that before next August, you can ask for it. I'll cover all our expenses out of the funds in the new account. I'd say that's more than fair."

She shook her head, her eyes glassy with tears. "I can't believe you. You're being so selfish. We've always shared everything equally."

"Yes, we have, but now you're spending every penny, and at this rate, there won't be anything left for me."

"I'll tell our sons that their father is cutting them off because he's being a miser." Her breath was coming in short gasps.

"You tell them that, Bernadette," he said before he left her in the kitchen, tears on her cheeks, and stomped outside, climbed into his truck, and drove to Green Lake, where he'd lately taken to going for an afternoon cup of coffee at a café and souvenir shop run by the daughter of one of their neighbors.

He and Bernadette had gotten iPhones when the money came in (their sons insisting on it—what if there was an emergency!— their own or someone else's in the family? Now they could afford smart phones, so no more excuses), and as he drank his large cup of monkish decaf, he checked the balances on the accounts he shared with his wife. Their checking account showed a new thirty thousand dollar withdrawal, their savings account a twenty-five thousand debit. There was now $53,244.16 total in their joint accounts; the previous day, when he'd transferred the money to the protected account, the two balances had totaled $109,503.93.

He called the bank and asked if they had a record of these withdrawals being turned into cashier's checks or else being funneled into some other account, maybe one Bernadette had set up in her own name, just to spite him. Lonnie, the personal banker who'd answered his call, told him he'd have to come into the bank in order for that information to be disclosed, which further infuriated

Glenn. "I'm sorry, but it's a safeguard for our customers," she said politely. "I'm sure it's you, Mr. Ballard, but it's best if you come into the bank. Is there anything else I can help you with?"

"No," he said, and hung up without saying goodbye.

He called Jim, his oldest, and when his son picked up with a too-enthusiastic greeting, Glenn gruffly asked, "Have you talked to your mother today?"

"No," said Jim, immediately wary. "Is something wrong?"

"We had a little disagreement."

"Are you okay?"

"We're fine," he said.

"I was planning to call today because the automatic deposit you guys set up for our monthly stipend didn't go through. The routing number might be wrong on your end. Or maybe it just takes a little longer because it's the first time?"

Glenn was standing on the sidewalk next to his truck—the same one he'd had for the last nine years; he hadn't replaced it yet because it still ran well and he'd replaced the tires only five months ago. Bernadette and his sons were baffled by his stoic attitude toward all the money he'd won, but he saw no reason to plow through it at the same speed his wife was. He'd never been the person who leapt headlong into the lake. When everyone else was cannonballing off the end of the dock, he'd always held back and observed. He couldn't help his watchful nature. It was who he'd always been.

He'd parked across the street from Susie's Coffee & Curiosities, in front of Green Lake Realty and Moonstone, a small jewelry store owned by a gemologist from somewhere in the Upper Peninsula. He'd stepped out of the café when he called the bank, not wanting the four people sitting at the round mosaic-topped tables to overhear him. The sky was clear and the temperature in the low eighties, despite it being late September. Indian summer, he'd heard people call it all his life. It was an expression that made him happy, but Justin had told him years ago, when he was still in high school, that he shouldn't use it.

"How much did she say we're giving you each month?" he asked. This was the first he'd heard of it.

Jim hesitated. "She said three thousand."

Glenn closed his eyes. If Jim was getting these monthly handouts on top of the other gifts, Justin and Jeff likely were too. "If you want to know the truth, your mother and I are still working out our finances. You probably know she's been spending a lot lately. I've had to put the brakes on this a bit, and she isn't happy."

"I didn't know," he said. "I thought—"

"I shouldn't have said anything."

"Are you sure you're okay, Dad?"

"Yes. We're just getting used to all this. It's been—" His shirt was sticking to his back. It was too hot for September. "A learning experience."

"If you can't do three grand a month, we'd understand."

"We're okay," he said. "But I think we're going to set up trusts for you and your brothers. I don't want your mother to have access to so much cash. Between you and me, and I mean this, Jim, keep this between you and me—she's already spent more than a third of our first annuity and as you know, it's only about a month and a half since we got it."

"She's spent how much already?"

"Over half a million dollars."

"That's a lot." He was silent for a second. "But didn't you win over sixty million?"

"Yes, but you know I didn't opt for the lump sum. And there are a lot of taxes. The annuity isn't as much as you'd think. That sixty million is spread out over thirty years. After taxes, it works out to about 1.3 million. I have them take 25 percent for taxes right from the get-go, but this doesn't mean there won't be more taxes to pay for the year. It depends on how many expenses we can claim."

"You have an accountant now, right?"

"Not yet, but I'll get one."

"You need an accountant to work out a budget for you and Mom. Then she'd have someone outside the family telling her how much she can spend, instead of you trying to do it."

"I suppose that would be a good idea."

Before they hung up, Jim said, "Mom was telling me she thought there'd be a way for Candace or me to quit work. Maybe even both of us. But if you guys are planning to set up a trust, we'd have to rethink this."

Glenn looked up at the sky and quietly exhaled. "Give us a little more time to figure things out before you or Candace quit your jobs."

"Jeff said he was quitting his job."

"Jesus Christ," said Glenn.

"I think he and Mom talked about it yesterday. She didn't tell you?"

"No." He looked across the street, into the café's windows. A woman and a man were looking back at him, the woman's bright red hair piled on top of her head, the man young and bald with tattoos on his arms and neck. Glenn turned away.

"He hasn't quit yet, as far as I know," Jim added hastily.

Glenn rubbed his forehead hard, the skin clammy. "Jeff should not under any circumstances quit his job. He knows we didn't take the lump sum, doesn't he?"

"I think he knows."

"I'd better call him."

"It's slow here right now," said Jim. "I could call him."

Glenn could feel a headache approaching, a steady, soft pounding starting behind his eyeballs. "Okay, but tell him I'll call him later."

"I'm sorry, Dad."

"Things should calm down soon," said Glenn. "With a little luck. If I have any left."

"You guys are golden," said Jim. "Just tell Mom to chill out."

"You tell her to chill out," said Glenn. "Maybe she'll listen to you. And promise me you won't quit your job, even if it's only to hold on to your health insurance. Your mother and I pay a fortune for ours."

"Okay, Dad. Just try to stay calm," said Jim. "We'll work it out."

"I hope you're right."

"Me too," said Jim with a weak laugh.

It was after five o'clock when Glenn returned from Green Lake. The exterior of their three-bedroom house had been given a fresh coat of yellow paint the previous week by a high school friend of Jeff's who ran a painting and carpentry business with his older brother. The week before that, all the bedroom and living room windows had been replaced, each one now with ultraviolet light–deflecting film embedded in the glass. These two improvements were Glenn's only splurges since he'd received the first annuity. Bernadette wanted to move into a bigger house and had been looking all over Fond du Lac and Green Lake counties, but so far she hadn't found anything Glenn liked more than where they already lived. This too had caused a rift between them.

It wasn't that he didn't enjoy having so much money now at his disposal. He'd treated himself to a fancy haircut at Miriam's Hair and Nails—his first professional cut ($45 for a haircut that had taken less than twenty minutes!) in more than a decade. Bernadette usually gave him a monthly cut at home, her stylist skills having been honed on the boys while they were growing up. He'd also bought a pair of Nike running shoes—four ounces each, which felt lighter even than the thick cotton socks he'd worn with his steel-toed boots, each boot two pounds, compulsory gear for every Speed Queen worker on the floor. He'd purchased memberships for Bernadette and himself to the 24 Hour Fitness a mile and a half from their house too; everyone he'd talked to in the Mega Millions group seemed to be trying to drop a few pounds and upgrade their wardrobes and hairstyles, and Sam Raymond, his now-former boss, was also upgrading towns, having bought a fancy house down in Milwaukee where he was moving in two weeks.

Since the big win, it was the desire for escape and new experiences that Glenn found himself beset by more than by a manic urge to acquire. His former coworker and fellow lottery winner Curt Shukowski had had a brief taste of this kind of freedom—six days of it in his RV before his wife, who hadn't gone with him and had been struggling ever since their son, a Marine, was killed in Iraq several years earlier, started throwing the contents of their house into the street and had to be hauled in to the police station where she was held until Curt was able to return. At the time of the police chief's phone call, Curt was camped out by the ocean, not far from Savannah. He drove all day and through the night to make it back to Ripon in less than twenty-four hours.

Before Curt had left on his ill-starred trip, he'd told Glenn he hoped it would be the first of many, and that night Glenn started looking online at RVs like Curt's—a Gulf Stream 5210, which was a smaller and lighter model than many of the gas guzzlers that crowded Wisconsin's and other state highways in the summer. Bernadette said she'd be happy to try motor-homing, especially if Glenn was willing to go west to visit some of the national parks. When the boys were little, they'd made one trip to the Grand Canyon that had thoroughly exhausted them and their credit cards. Car trouble had added another thousand to their expenses.

Bernadette's car wasn't in the driveway or the garage when Glenn pulled in after his coffee in Green Lake. She'd traded in her six-year-old Ford Focus for an orange sherbet Volkswagen Beetle—useless on the icy roads during a Midwestern winter, he was sure, but she couldn't be dissuaded. "We can buy another car with four-wheel drive later this year," she said.

At six, she still wasn't home. At seven thirty, he called her cell but voice mail picked up on the first ring. A few minutes later he texted: *Where are you? Are you okay?*

She didn't respond. A little before eight, he got back into his truck and drove around town for a while. He didn't spot her car at any of the strip malls, or at the Pick 'n Save or Save-a-Lot stores, Save-a-Lot having taken over the building where the Piggly Wiggly had operated for many years. She wasn't at the Country Kitchen, Pizza Hut, or Walgreens, or at the park where she sometimes went for speed walks with two friends she'd known since grade school, Marcia Fitzsimmons and Helen Baker. He called them too, but they hadn't seen Bernadette all day.

Finally, at ten o'clock, his son Justin called from his and Rob's apartment in Chicago. "Mom's here with me," he said, his phone voice always startling Glenn with its deepness. Neither of his other two sons or Glenn himself had a voice like that.

"She's in Chicago?" he asked. Dumb question, he realized too late.

"Yes," said Justin patiently.

"She didn't tell me she was going to see you. Did you know?"

"No," said Justin. "She just showed up. She's sleeping now. She didn't want me to call you."

"She's mad at me," he said. "She probably told you."

"She said you'd been arguing. I'm sorry, Dad. You must have been worried when you couldn't find her."

"I can't believe she drove all that way by herself. Did she bring an overnight bag?"

"She has a suitcase with her."

"A big one?"

His son hesitated. "Pretty big."

Glenn had gone down to the basement earlier to see if any of their luggage was missing, but their four suitcases were in the same place as always. Her closet and dresser drawers hadn't been raided either. She'd probably bought clothes and a new suitcase before arriving at Justin's place. "Do you think I need to come down there tonight?" he asked.

"Probably not a good idea," said Justin. "I think she needs a little space right now."

This sounded ominous but he didn't want to get into it all right now. "Then I guess I'll call back tomorrow. Maybe she'll talk to me then."

"She wants to get a massage in the morning," said Justin. "Robby and I both go to a guy we really like. She wants to try him."

He wondered where his son and his boyfriend went for this service that Glenn had always thought too intimate and invasive. To some back alley where the shirtless masseuses all had oiled-up muscles and were covered in tattoos? He didn't know where these images came from—TV, he suspected. "Your mother's never had a massage before, as far as I know," he finally said.

"I'm not sure if Marcel will be able to fit her in on such short notice, but we'll find out in the morning."

"Is Marcel American?"

"Dutch."

"I see." The thought of his wife disrobing for a stranger in some private, dimly lit room, a stranger who would then work Bernadette over for what Glenn guessed would be quite a lot of money—what separated this activity from prostitution? He didn't want to think about it.

"I'd better go, Dad. I should get to bed. I have to be at work at seven tomorrow."

"What about your mother's massage?"

"Robby's going to take her."

"I guess she needs to find a way to relax," he said, trying to sound agreeable.

There was a pause before Justin said, "Thanks for the money you guys have been giving me. It helps a lot. I'm sorry I haven't come up to see you yet. Mom said you were hoping I would."

"It'd be nice to meet Robby one of these days too."

"He and Mom have hit it off."

"Everyone loves your mother. Especially lately," said Glenn, unable to keep the sarcasm out of his voice.

"I'm sure it's been pretty trippy for you since you won."

"That's one way of saying it. Stressful is another."

He went to bed around eleven thirty but couldn't sleep and twice got up to look at his phone, which had rapidly become an addiction, exactly what he'd complained for years would be the case, watching people of all ages staring down at the small, glowing screens when they were supposed to be crossing the street or having dinner with their families. Bernadette still had not called or texted him back, nor had she sent an email. He checked his bank accounts online and was relieved to see that she hadn't made any other withdrawals since the two big ones following the afternoon's argument about his decision to move the bulk of their remaining money to a restricted account.

Seeing the large balance in this new account both thrilled and disturbed him. He wanted to find a reason why he and the seven others, only eight people among the many millions who had undoubtedly bought tickets, had been so fortunate.

But of course there was no logic to it. There was no logic to anything when it came to luck, good or bad. He'd had a decent job with a pension, insurance benefits, and union protection. He'd liked his coworkers and was a good wire-harness maker, efficient and quick and reliable. Sam had always praised his work, and Glenn would return home most days feeling competent and valued. Now what was he doing? Arguing with his wife over their good fortune, adding stress and ill will to their previously happy marriage because his wife had turned into someone he hardly recognized.

But he couldn't think of anyone who would pause for more than a second before agreeing to have a $66 million cash bomb dropped on their life, and he knew the other workers at Speed Queen now looked at him and Sam and the other winners with envy, and in some cases, open hostility—William Cline, the plant's general manager, especially. He had to replace eight full-time employees, one of them a foreman—no surprise he was far from pleased. When Glenn crossed paths with him in the parking lot a few days before his final shift, the big boss, as Cline was called around the plant, had stopped directly in front of him as Glenn was making his way to his car and said, "Be careful what you wish for, for you will surely receive it." Then he smirked and shook his head and continued on his way, leaving Glenn feeling more than a little unnerved.

At home, he'd repeated Cline's words to Bernadette, who rolled her eyes and said it was only sour grapes—he was riven by jealousy. Despite his big boss's salary, Cline wanted more, more, more, and was very angry he didn't have millions of lottery dollars heading toward his own bank account. The rumor was that he and some of the other upper-level managers had also bought a pile of lottery tickets, but between all of them, they'd only managed to match a few numbers on a handful of tickets. Jim later told Glenn that what Cline had said in the parking lot was a Chinese proverb. "Well, wherever it came from," said Bernadette, "Mr. Cline can eat his mean little heart out."

Other people Glenn encountered in town—at the post office, at Ace Hardware, at Kwik Trip—people he'd known for much of his life, were looking at him differently, with curiosity and sometimes, like William Cline, with envy that verged on animosity. Bernadette claimed not to notice any ill will, and when Glenn called her on her Pollyanna attitude, she was dismissive. "I don't have to see it," she said. "And you don't either. You can choose how you feel, Glenn. You can."

He wondered if she would say this now, if she would get on the phone down in Chicago and claim she was no longer angry with him, that she'd decided to be happy again and all was forgiven. Because of course it was so easy once you put your mind to it. At the time he'd wondered if she was right, but now he knew it was bullshit.

At four in the morning he still hadn't fallen asleep. Head pounding again, he got out of bed and went into the kitchen. There was so much food in the fridge, Bernadette having stocked up earlier in the week. He stared at the cartons of eggs and orange juice, the loaves of expensive bakery bread, aware of his good fortune. He wondered if his wife was awake in their son's guest room, if she would ever look at him again with love. The air around him was stale and humid. Outside the birds were waking up in their tiny, perfect nests, chirping shrilly into the waning night. He could do anything he wanted to, go anywhere in the world. Nothing was holding him back other than his own cowardice—he needed only to pack a bag and step out of the house. He could almost admire Bernadette now for leaving so abruptly. He wouldn't have to leave a note either.

Ma'am?

"I only need two minutes of your time."

Beginning at age six, when she was first allowed to answer the clunky rotary phone on the wall in her family's cluttered kitchen, Tess had heard these words emerge from the mouths of hundreds of fast-talking salespeople. Some were calling to sell life insurance policies or poisons to make the lawn greener; others accosted her outside of Las Vegas time-share offices or in front of mall kiosks festooned with mobile phones and sunglasses—for decades now she'd been enduring strident pleas to take out her wallet and hand over her money—to a stranger, no less! To make matters more absurd, not once had she wanted what anyone was selling.

The landscape of her life—of everyone's life, she had to think— was thronged with desperate characters begging you to buy things you didn't need. She'd been raised to ignore their pitches and was both surprised and distressed when her brother David called to say their frugal father had just bought a pygmy horse named Peanut Sundae Pie and was using the garage as a stable and the quarter-acre backyard as a pasture.

A week earlier, he'd purchased a derelict school bus and had told David his plan was to transform it into a camper by installing bunk beds, a shower, and a galley kitchen. It presently filled his entire driveway and neighbors had begun to knock on his door to demand he remove the hulking orange eyesore from the neighborhood, or else they would be forced to call the cops. The bus's bumper protruded a couple of inches over the sidewalk, which the neighbors claimed was illegal.

"You have to come help me," said David, his voice strained on the other end of the line. "Dad doesn't care what I think. He's been calling me Shaggy again too. I'm almost bald now but he won't stop."

"You're not bald," she said. "Are you?" She hadn't seen him in six months, not since Christmas.

"Can you come?"

"You should try rosemary oil."

He ignored this. "Can you come or what?"

She was in her study, looking out the window into her neighbor's backyard. Mrs. Penina, whose husband had his own house a mile and a half away, was picking lettuce in her small vegetable patch. Her cat, a tabby named Harry, was skulking in the bushes behind her, as he often was. Tess disliked her neighbor's laxness: she let the cat go after birds. Tess rarely saw Mr. Penina, who was at least ten years younger than his wife and didn't like the cat either—Tess had once heard them arguing over Harry, who was allowed to sleep with them because he'd spend the night clawing at the bedroom door if locked out.

"Yes," said Tess. "I'll come."

"Last week he bought three stars in some galaxy with a number for a name too," said her brother. "Some con man saying he was with NASA called and told Dad he could name the stars whatever he wanted if he bought them."

She saw Harry dart from beneath the bushes around the side of house. Mrs. Penina didn't appear to notice. "Dad's never cared about space before, has he?" she asked.

"Not that I know of," said David.

"I'll be there tonight," she said. "Is the horse nice, at least?"

"She's old. She needs to be on one of those farms for retired circus animals, or whatever they are. I think she's lonely. She looks sad."

"The poor thing."

"He's been sleeping out in the garage with her."

"Is he afraid someone will steal her?" Outside, Mrs. Penina stumbled on her way back into the house and upended the bowl of lettuces. She glared at the greens for a moment before she began snatching them up.

"I think it's a compromise," he said. "He'd probably let her sleep in the house, but there's not enough room."

"This isn't normal, even for Dad."

"No. It's not."

Their father wasn't wealthy. He lived on a government pension and social security checks. His house was small and full of undusted surfaces and old, crunchy carpet. Tess had offered more than once to pay to have it replaced, but he'd declined. "Who do I need to impress? Save your money," he'd said, querulous.

Their mother had died twenty years earlier and Tess's father had never recovered. As if in full retreat from his once-happy life, he'd sold the house Tess and her brother had grown up in less than a year after their mother's death and had moved into a glum, drafty bungalow with north-facing windows that rattled and whistled throughout the winter. David called it the hovel, sometimes within earshot of their father.

Her brother had his own problems, but Tess tried not to instigate arguments. She was the older child, the peacekeeper, her mother had called her, fondly, most of the time. At forty-one, her brother made a small, hangdog living doing food deliveries and renting out half his house, having lost a much better job at a furniture company that had gone under a year earlier, after its owner was arrested for embezzlement. He had no girlfriend Tess knew of, but he did have an estranged daughter, Jenny, born when he was a sophomore in college. Jenny was presently in her third year at Cal Poly, and lived with her mother and stepfather in Los Osos, a coastal town fifteen minutes from San Luis Obispo and Cal Poly. Tess had visited twice while Jenny was growing up and had advised David to move to California, but he'd refused, claiming he'd been shut out of his daughter's life by her mother and stepfather. Now that Jenny was an adult, however, Tess thought she could decide for herself whether to let David back in, but her brother's resentment and stubbornness appeared to be keeping him from doing anything other than sulking where his daughter was concerned.

And now, despite his relative youth, David was living like an embittered old man, and their father, an actual old man, was living like an eccentric. Tess could imagine what they said about her: a goody-two-shoes control freak who should have married the first man who asked but didn't, and when a second man asked, she said yes but he ended up dumping her.

This was inaccurate—it was she who'd kept putting off the wedding—she had wanted to live with Jason, her second fiancé, indefinitely, but wasn't sure when she'd be ready to get married, to him or anyone else. She'd later regretted the breakup, but by the time she realized she'd made a mistake, he'd moved on. In the three years since they'd broken up, she'd dated a few men inconclusively, and for the last year and a half had sworn off dating altogether and dedicated her free time to getting into shape and running a marathon. She'd also been promoted at the law firm where she practiced tax law, her salary nearly doubling, but she'd stopped liking her job years ago. She didn't know what she wanted to do with her life other than spend it running and traveling to places where she wanted to run.

Her friends thought if she were married and had kids she'd have less time to brood, but from what she'd observed, her friends were more miserable than she was. ("The doctor said all three of my kids need Ritalin." "My husband keeps having affairs but I signed a fucking prenup!" "I should have finished medical school but I was twenty-five and stupid and got married and pregnant instead.") She wasn't unhappy, but she didn't know what exactly she felt half the time, or what she wanted most. ("Silence," her married friends would say. "And uninterrupted sleep. No fucking bouncy castle birthday parties either—someone always ends up with a black eye and chipped tooth.") One Saturday morning earlier in the year, she'd gotten into her car and driven three hours to Madison, where she'd gone to college, but when she got there, after an abject hour on State Street, she'd turned around and gone right back to Illinois. She knew no one in Madison anymore, and so many of the places where she used to go had disappeared. It felt like a foreign country.

Her brother and father lived in Indianapolis, David near the airport on the south side, their father thirty minutes due north. She lived thirty-five miles outside of Chicago in Lake Bluff, and could make the drive in four hours if traffic cooperated. She did not call to alert her father she was coming—she knew he would tell her not to—the drive was too long and traffic would be onerous, and why did she want to sit in his house with him, even for a day, and pretend she wasn't bored? Her tacit role was to ignore his protests, and his was to act the widower curmudgeon and claim he didn't wish to inconvenience her, but she knew he didn't mind her visits, whether he admitted it or not.

It was after dark when she turned onto his street. From the corner, she could already see the school bus looming in the driveway, its sun-bleached orange paint glowing dully under a streetlight. Her father's aging beige Corolla was parked along the curb, doubtless now its permanent parking spot (another source of outrage for his neighbors, probably). She doubted the bus was drivable, and on top of that, a tiny horse now purportedly lived in the garage. Her father had made some questionable purchases in the last few years, but they had been limited to very heavy pieces of damaged

Shaker furniture and boxes of moldy books from flea markets and garage sales. To her knowledge, the horse, the bus, and the three stars in Galaxy 60048 were by far the most inscrutable, possibly insane, purchases her father had ever made.

David was supposed to be there when she arrived, but she didn't see his car. The school bus, at least, looked better than she'd expected—no visible dents or rust on the body, the tires properly inflated. She thought she smelled hay and manure as she climbed out of her car and tugged her bag out of the backseat. The air on her skin was warm and a little humid, a half-moon looming overhead. The solstice was only a few days away. This time of year, thunderstorms roamed the area, but tonight the sky was clear.

She heard someone start singing in an uneven masculine voice—her father, she realized with a start. He was behind the closed garage door, serenading the horse. She left her bag on the front stoop and squeezed into the narrow gap between the bus and the garage. The hay and manure smells were stronger here—until now, she'd irrationally been hoping her brother was wrong about the tiny horse. She pressed her ear to the cool steel plank of the door, involuntarily holding her breath.

Now that I've lost everything to you, you say you want to start something new . . . Her father, whom she hadn't heard sing anything but the birthday song in over twenty years, was rasping out a Cat Stevens song to Peanut Sundae Pie.

She could picture him with his arm around the horse's neck, his cheek pressed to her muzzle as he crooned to her. Tess wondered fleetingly if the horse was annoyed or afraid, but perhaps Peanut Sundae Pie liked the attention—she might have been used to being neglected.

Tess stood wedged between the garage door and the bus, waiting for her father to finish the song, but on its heels he began another, "Morning Has Broken." She didn't remember him or her mother ever playing Cat Stevens records when she and David were children. And where the hell was her brother?

"Dad?" she said, knocking softly. She pictured the horse's long, doleful face as her father sang to it, its tail hanging limply between its flanks.

The singing stopped.

She strained to detect signs of movement on the other side of the door but no sounds reached her ears. "It's Tess, Dad. Can I come in?"

"What are you doing here?" His irritation was plain.

"I wanted to see you," she said.

"David called you, didn't he."

"Yes," she said reluctantly. "He's been a little worried about you."

"Because he thinks I'm spending all my money and there won't be any left for him when I croak."

"Dad. David's not like that."

There was a distinct pause. "He might not have admitted it to you," he said, "but I'm sure that's what he's thinking."

"Can I meet your horse?"

"It's her bedtime."

"I won't keep her up much longer. Can I come in?" Tess gripped the garage door handle and tried to lift it, but it didn't rise in its usual loose-jointed way. "Will you let me in?"

She thought she heard her father sigh before he said in a low voice, "You want to meet your sister, Peewee? Do you?"

To Tess he said, "Come around to the side door. Peanut gets upset when I raise the big door. It's too late now to get her riled up."

Tess did as he asked but found the trash and recycling bins in the way of the smaller side door. The bins had previously been stored inside the garage; she knew the raccoons that lived in the nearby woods would discover them soon, if they hadn't already.

Warm, barn-like air rushed toward her when she opened the side door, the old smells of motor oil, lawn fertilizer, and deteriorating rubber less detectable now. It was dim in Peanut Sundae Pie's ersatz stable, the only light source a floor lamp Tess recognized from her father's living room, one bulb of three switched on. He and his pygmy horse peered at her from where they stood next to the ancient, scarred workbench, two small hay bales balanced on top of it. Her father's tools still loomed on the pegboard above the bench, but the garage's previous occupants—the lawn mower, the yard tools, her father's car, the raccoon-attracting garbage cans—had either been exiled outside or herded into the corner opposite the lamp. The rusted brown wheelbarrow Tess and her brother had played with as kids had been enlisted to serve as a grain trough. A red drywall bucket next to it held what Tess assumed was the horse's water.

A few yards farther on in the gloom, spread out next to the garage's primary door that could only be raised by hand—her father refused to install an electric opener, certain it would break down and trap his car inside—she spotted a large plaid dog bed. She'd never heard of a horse sleeping on a cushion, but perhaps million-dollar racehorses did. Most of what she knew about horses came from the movies *The Black Stallion* and *The Horse Whisperer*: don't startle them and don't walk behind them. If you want them to like you, give them sugar cubes and carrots and other crunchy treats. The thought of her solitary father driving to the giant pet supply store a few miles away to buy his new horse a dog bed made tears prick her eyes.

Peanut Sundae Pie was about the same height as a Great Dane, but stockier. Her coat was newsprint-gray, her fetlocks almost black. She peered at Tess with brown, mournful eyes, Tess's father's expression mirroring his horse's. He needed a haircut, a thorough shave, and a bath. His clothes needed washing too.

"Can I pet her?" asked Tess shyly.

Her father looked at the horse. "What do you think, Peewee? Should I let her pet you?"

The horse averted her gaze. Tess stepped forward and gently stroked Peanut's mane and the soft pelt at the base of her ears. She nickered and tilted her head toward Tess's father.

"Peewee's had a hard day," he said, patting her neck, the horseflesh beneath his hand quivering. "I had the vet here this afternoon. He said she's in pretty good shape, but she needed a couple of shots."

"Can I have a hug, Dad?" asked Tess, moving closer. Peanut inched backward, jostling the drywall bucket. The transformation of the garage into a horse barn seemed at best provisional, at worst inhumane. What her father needed to do was find a stable and lease a stall to ensure his horse had proper care and regular exercise, but she doubted he could afford it. She also had a hunch it was illegal to keep a barnyard animal in a residential neighborhood. An ordinance permitting people to keep chickens in backyard coops had been voted down in the last local election—her father, ironically, having voted against it.

He submitted to a hug, barely, his body rigid, his face rough against her cheek. He was thinner than he'd been during her most recent visit, over Easter weekend. "Are you eating enough?" she asked, trying to catch his eye. "You're skinnier than you were in April."

"I'm the same as always," he said brusquely.

He wasn't, but she didn't bother to contradict him. Behind her, the side door opened. David, finally.

"Bedtime for Bonzo?" said David with feigned cheerfulness. He shut the door and made his way over to Peanut, who shifted closer to their father, one of her hooves nearly landing on his left foot.

"Hey, Sis," said David, holding out his arms to Tess as if she were a child.

She smelled beer on his breath as she hugged him. Like their father, he needed a haircut—he didn't appear to be going bald, despite what he'd said on the phone.

"Hey you," she said.

Annoyed by the intrusion, their father turned with a scowl toward the workbench and wrestled a sleeping bag roll out from behind the hay bales.

"Dad," she said. "You're not really going to sleep in here, are you? It can't be comfortable. And what if Peanut steps on you in the night?"

"Hasn't happened yet," he said.

She glanced at David, whose eyes were raised to the ceiling—he was doing a breathing exercise, she assumed, the same one he'd told her a few weeks earlier was keeping him off of blood pressure medication. "You've only had her for three days, right?" she said.

Her father continued to scowl, his brown, bloodshot eyes moving from her face to Peanut's before he looked at Tess again. "What exactly are you doing here?"

"What do you think she's doing here?" said David. "You won't listen to me."

"I don't need to listen to you or your sister, but you two do need to listen to me and stop worrying and gossiping about what I'm doing."

"Who sold you the horse?" asked Tess.

Her father turned away. "I'm not sending her back. They'll make glue out of her."

She looked at David, who was again gazing up at the ceiling, doing his breath work, or more likely trying not to roll his eyes. "Do they still do that?" she asked.

"Of course they do," said her father. "Glue and dog food. That's her fate if I don't take care of her."

"What about the school bus?" said David. "Were they going to turn that into dog food too?"

Their father stooped down and started unrolling his sleeping bag on the floor beneath the workbench. "Have you eaten dinner, Tess?" he asked over his shoulder.

"I had a sandwich in the car," she said. She'd also had two Hostess Snoballs from the gas station in Merrillville and what she hoped was decaffeinated coffee, but she wasn't at all tired—someone had likely mixed up the carafes.

"There's some leftover spaghetti in the fridge if you want it. It's only a few days old. You might as well eat if you're planning to stay the night."

"Is there enough for me?" asked David.

Their father grimaced.

"Is there?" David repeated.

Tess touched her brother's arm. "I'm not hungry. You can have it."

"You need to eat, Tess," said their father. "You're the one who's too skinny."

That wasn't true, but she didn't bother to argue. She was thin, yes, but entirely fit. Her doctor had said at her last checkup that she might be overexercising, but to her mind, too much exercise was better than too many Snoballs. What she probably needed was a boyfriend, not more miles or more food, but unless she forced herself to try the dating apps, she didn't see it happening. Her father and brother were lonely hearts too. Of the few women her father had had dinner with after losing his wife, he'd said, "They're not your mother. She was the only one for me." Tess wished he'd talk to a therapist, but she'd stopped suggesting it several years ago when he locked her out of the house and refused for an hour to let her back inside. She would have driven back to Illinois, but her suitcase and car keys were up in her old bedroom.

There was enough spaghetti for both of them, but it didn't smell right. David prepared himself a plate anyway while Tess loaded the dirty dishes in the sink and on the table into the dishwasher, which also smelled off—who knew how long since her father had last used it. She programmed it for the longest cleaning cycle and added extra soap. The bag of trash under the sink needed to be taken out too, but she suspected if she stowed it in the can out-side the garage, raccoons would doubtless arrive in the night to ransack it, and Peanut Sundae Pie would hear them and grow frightened and probably step on her benefactor's head. He was semi-protected beneath the workbench, but this wasn't the most reassuring thought—she really wished he wasn't such a stubborn old grouch.

David ate at the table as Tess tidied up and fretted silently over the fact her visit already bore the earmarks of a fool's errand. She hadn't yet had the will to bring up the school bus or the NASA stars, but it seemed best to wait until the morning to get into a full-fledged argument with her father.

"You sure you don't want any of this?" asked David, motioning to the red-lidded Tupperware container in front of him.

"I'm sure," she said, scrubbing hard at a crust of burnt meat on her father's one good frying pan. "You might want to stop after one helping. It doesn't smell very fresh."

"I'll be fine. I have the stomach of a goat," he said, patting his belly, which she'd noticed in the garage was beginning to hang over his belt.

"Have you talked to Dad again about getting rid of his land-line?" she said. "The last time I mentioned it, he wouldn't consider it, but I'm sure it's only a matter of time before someone manages to steal even more of his money."

"I doubt there's much left to steal, but I'll talk to him again."

"We need to get him back in the house tonight."

"Not going to happen," he said, spooling more spaghetti around his fork. "But go ahead and try. You know he never listens to me."

Tess set the frying pan in the sink and filled it with soap and hot water. It would need to soak overnight, the crust unresponsive to her scouring. "That horse might step on his head," she said.

David forked a meatball out of the Tupperware and dropped it onto his plate. "Dad's going to do whatever he wants. You know that."

"You need to go out there with me. I drove down here because I thought we were going to work on him together."

He bit into the meatball. "You're lucky you don't live as close to him as I do," he said, chewing.

"You don't see him that often," she scoffed.

"I see him more than you do."

He and her father were so much alike it was almost farcical. "Too bad you never see your daughter," she said, regretting the words as soon as they were out of her mouth.

He jerked forward in his chair, almost knocking over his water glass. "Don't start with that," he said. "I've offered to go see her, but she's not interested. And she's perfectly capable of getting on a plane and coming to see me too. I've told her I'll pay for her ticket. But has she done it? No."

"You have to go to her. Make an effort and she'll be a lot more likely to make one for you."

"You don't know what you're talking about, as usual."

She shut off the tap and stalked outside to the garage, where she discovered her father had locked the side door. "Dad?" she said, knocking softly. "Can you let me in?"

He didn't reply. She pressed her ear to the door but heard nothing on the other side. She knocked harder. "Dad? Are you in there?"

"I was asleep," came his muffled reply. "Go back in the house and go to bed. I'll see you in the morning."

"Please open the door." She pictured him huddled under the workbench, the hay bales looming above, a restive horse with its stony hooves a few inches from his unprotected head. Maybe she could convince him to sleep in a helmet.

No, of course he wouldn't agree to that, and she didn't have one, anyway. She wasn't sure if people could even sleep in helmets, unless they were sitting upright? "Your horse will be fine," she said. "Come sleep in the house."

"Her name is Peanut Sundae Pie," he said wearily.

"Peanut Sundae Pie will be fine. She's not a baby. She doesn't need to be monitored all night." A wave of desperation rose in her chest. Her father was losing it, or perhaps had already lost it. She knew she needed to see this for what it was—before he was unfit to care for himself, let alone an aging horse. And who knew if someone in the neighborhood was a PETA member and on the verge of reporting him for animal cruelty. She knocked a third time. "Please come out, Dad. Please." She was crying now, her voice shaking a little.

"I told you, I'm sleeping in here," he said, his voice rising. "Leave us in peace."

An owl's spectral hoot came from somewhere nearby. She'd heard owls on previous visits as she lay sleepless in the guest room's lumpy bed or while she and her father played rummy or Yahtzee after dinner. There were still hundreds of trees in the neighborhood, one of its few charms, along with the nearby Monon Trail where she'd gone running on her last few visits.

"We could play some cards. It isn't that late yet."

"Go to bed, Tess," he said. "And don't send your goddamn brother out here to harass me, either."

Her heart was beating hard, as much from outrage now as worry. She thought of her mother's gradual disappearance from bone cancer, her father less and less like himself as the disease progressed—he'd been funny, mischievous, reliably jocular during her childhood, but after her mother's death, he'd lost interest in almost everything, including, it felt to Tess most of time, her and her brother's lives. Friends who'd also lost a parent prematurely had warned her that the surviving parent sometimes forgot the children were suffering too, so absorbed were they in their own grief and loneliness.

In the kitchen, her brother was still at the table, the Tupperware container in front of him now empty. "I probably shouldn't have eaten all that," he said, noticing her wet cheeks. "Why are you crying?"

"Why do you think?" she said snappishly.

"If that's how you want to play it, fine."

She raised her eyes to the ceiling, doubting he got the reference. "I'm exhausted, David. I drove four hours here after working a full day, and Dad's sleeping in the fucking garage with a horse. I haven't had much to eat all day, and—"

"You could have eaten," he said. "You just didn't want to."

She looked at his sad, stubbly face, biting back a retort, before she went upstairs to the guest room where earlier she'd deposited her wheelie bag, thinking at the time there might still be a chance to turn things around. The room was stuffy and more crowded than on her Easter visit, with its crumbling cardboard boxes and grocery bags erupting with old clothes and other motley junk her father had promised in April he'd donate to the Goodwill or else haul out to the curb for the trash collectors.

The bed had the same unwashed sheets on it as at Easter. She ripped them off and trudged back downstairs to the cobweb-strewn laundry room off the kitchen. David hadn't moved from the table, but his gaze had migrated from the Tupperware container to his phone.

"Call your daughter," said Tess. "If she doesn't pick up, leave a message telling her you miss her and want to see her."

"Sure, boss. Whatever you say."

The sheets she'd pulled off the guest bed were gray-white from laundering with non-whites. She wrangled them into the machine, poured in a capful of detergent and another of bleach. It was after ten and by the time they were washed and dried, it would be close to midnight, but she doubted she'd be able to sleep much anyway. In the kitchen, she heard David murmuring to himself. Across the street, a dog barked at some invisible disturbance.

She felt the beginnings of a headache and tried to ward it off by loosening her shoulders, knowing she'd been hunching them as she drove. In the corner by the washer she noticed large, gray tufts of lint and two expired dryer sheets. She missed her house in Lake Bluff, her comfortable bed, the homemade banana bread she'd forgotten to grab on her way out the door. The phone on the wall in the kitchen started ringing. "Were you expecting a call from anyone?" she asked, passing her brother on her way to the phone.

He shook his head. "Don't answer it."

She ignored him and grabbed the handset. "Yes?" she barked. Their father didn't have an answering machine. Whoever it was, she supposed, might keep calling if she didn't pick up.

The man on the other end of the line released a startled laugh. "I wasn't expecting a lady. Is Ken home?"

"Who is this?"

The man hesitated. "Is he there? He's sort of expecting my call."

"At ten fifteen?" She looked at David who mouthed, You want me to take it? She shook her head. "Who is this?" she repeated.

"His friend Chuck."

"He doesn't have any friends named Chuck as far as I know."

"I'm a new friend," Chuck said gamely.

"You can call back tomorrow at a more reasonable hour. My father's already in bed for the night."

"You're his daughter?" he said, wariness creeping into his voice. "I didn't know he had one. Just a son, I thought."

"How long have you been friends? My brother's here with me. You can talk to all three of us tomorrow. I'm going to hang up now."

"Ma'am, wait," he said. "Your dad and I run a vending machine business together. I really need to talk to him tonight. Our service truck broke down and—"

"A vending machine business," she said flatly. "Great." She covered the handset and looked at David. "Do you know anything about Dad starting a vending machine business with some guy named Chuck?"

David stared at her. "This is the first I've heard of it."

"Ma'am?" said Chuck. "I really do need to talk to your dad."

"How much do you need?" said Tess.

"Pardon?"

"You're calling because you need money, right? How much?"

Chuck cleared his throat. For a second, she almost pitied him. "The mechanic's estimate was a thousand dollars, but it might be a little more," he said, chastened. "I won't know until the morning, but I was hoping to come over and have your dad write me a check. That way I can pay the guy and get back on our route and fill the machines before noon. The rest area up by—"

"He's sleeping," she said. "With his horse. Have you met his horse yet?"

He laughed a little. "I didn't know he had a horse too."

"As of three days ago. She's living in the garage. Her name is Peanut Sundae Pie."

Chuck was silent for a few seconds before he said, "Well, doesn't that just take the cake." He had a mild southern Indiana accent. Unaccountably, Tess found herself wondering if he had sandy blond hair and wore cowboy boots like Robert Redford's character in *The Electric Horseman*. She still had a crush on Robert Redford.

"Are you some kind of grifter, Chuck?" she said. "Because lately my father appears to be the victim of multiple people selling him things of questionable origin and quality."

"I'm not a grifter, ma'am. You can google me, Chuck Wendell, W-E-N-D-E-L-L, and our vending machine business, Chuck-a-Block Vending. Your dad and I met when I was calling bingo over at the Elks Club a few months back. Real nice guy. He won the blackout jackpot that night. Five hundred bucks. Did he tell you about that? What a night."

No, he hadn't told her. "Please call back in the morning," said Tess. "I have to go now."

"Ma'am, hold on, I—"

She hung up and looked at her brother. "Jesus Christ."

"You sure it wasn't that NASA guy again?" he said. "How much did he want?"

"It wasn't the NASA guy. This guy, who claims he met Dad at the Elks Club, wants a thousand dollars to fix his van."

The phone rang again. She let it ring five times, willing it to stop, before she pulled it off the wall and yanked its cord from the jack.

"Don't forget to plug it back in tomorrow morning," said David.

"Are you staying here tonight? If this guy shows up, I don't want to be here by myself."

He nodded. "My tenant's mom is visiting from Florida. She turns the TV up so damn loud I can hear it in my bedroom."

"You could ask her to lower the volume."

"No, not worth getting into it. My tenant's a pain in the ass, but he pays his rent on time."

Chuck did not show up in the night to try to strong-arm a thousand dollars out of her father. She would have heard him if he had—as she'd known would happen, she'd lain awake until very late, wishing she were at home in her own bed where, on most days, she had fewer conflicting feelings to manage. Here in her father's cramped house, old resentments and insecurities always slipped out of the cellar where she'd tried but failed to bury them.

She slept at most four hours. Before turning off the light, she'd googled Chuck and wasn't surprised to find him, but his presence on the internet didn't mean he wasn't a criminal. She knew scammers were increasingly savvy about using fake websites and burner phones to rob their victims, and although his website looked professional enough, if she'd spent a few hours learning HTML on YouTube or wherever the deadbeats were learning their trade these days, she too could start bilking innocents and dummies of their hard-earned money.

A little after six, she was awake and glaring up at the ceiling, wondering if David and their father had managed to sleep any better than she had. Through the open window, she heard her father's voice, followed by a soft whinny. She drew back the blankets and went over to the window that overlooked the backyard. There he was, at the edge of the patio, wearing a filthy Butler University sweatshirt and a pair of baggy blue jeans, feeding Peanut Sundae Pie from a small burlap sack. He patted her neck as she snorted and chewed, Tess's father happier than she'd seen him look in years. The horse kept taking mouthfuls from the bag, its rubbery lips and jaws working mechanically, her father watching and cooing. She had the sense then that if someone were to take the horse away, it would kill him.

She shut the curtains and went back to bed. A few minutes later, she heard him and the horse move back into the garage through the side door. There were no sounds of activity in the house, and outside she heard nothing other than birdcalls and the surf-like whoosh of morning traffic on 91st Street, a few blocks away.

Her brother still hadn't stirred a half hour later, after she'd showered and dressed and started the coffeepot. She went out to the garage and knocked. This time the door wasn't locked, and she opened it without waiting for her father's reply. The smell of horse-flesh and hay was stronger than the previous night. She hoped her father wasn't leaving Peanut's manure lying about. She took a furtive glance around but did not spot any droppings. Under the bare bulb dangling overhead, her father was brushing Peanut, the old horse submitting stoically to the grooming.

"Good morning," said Tess. "Did you sleep all right?"

"Just fine," he said curtly.

"I'm making coffee. Do you want any? I could scramble some eggs for you if you're hungry."

He didn't look up from the horse. "There aren't any eggs, unless you brought some with you."

Tess watched him work on Peanut for a moment before she said, "Someone named Chuck called last night. He wanted a thousand dollars to fix his van. He said you and he are running some sort of vending machine business together."

Her father kept his eyes on Peanut's flank as he moved the brush over it.

"What's going on, Dad?" she said.

"Nothing's going on," he said gruffly.

"A vending machine business?"

He finally looked at her, the bags under his eyes purple. She knew he'd lied about sleeping well. "Why are you needling me? What's this really about?"

"They're going to make you move the horse," she said. "She needs a pasture and a proper barn. People will complain if they haven't already and someone from the city will come and take her. And your school bus—they're going to make you move that too."

He turned his back and stooped down to brush Peanut's belly. "That's a good girl," he murmured. "Just stay calm now." The horse shifted backwards. "I know, I know," he said. "I'll be careful."

Tess held her tongue until he started on Peanut's mane. "Please don't give this Chuck guy any money," she said. "If he owns the van, he should be paying for the repairs. What's your share of the profits supposed to be?"

"Are you my business manager now?" he said.

"I'm trying to look out for you."

"You and your brother need to stop jumping to half-baked conclusions. Chuck's a good guy. I trust him."

"How much did the NASA stars set you back?"

He let out a harsh laugh and shook his head. "I might buy a couple more. They weren't expensive. Now go back in the house and drink your coffee."

"What about the bus? What are your plans for it?"

"I suppose I'll fix it up and travel around the country, kidnapping little boys and girls along the way."

"That's not funny," she said.

The exhaustion and unhappiness on her father's face knifed through her. "What are you planning to do with the rest of your life, Tess?" he said. "Stay in a job you don't like and continue to live alone in your little old lady house until you die? Why didn't you marry that boy back in your twenties and have a couple of kids when you had the chance? Or that Jason fellow? I liked him. Why did you let him go too?" His cheeks were turning ruddy as he spoke, Peanut restive behind him, her ears twitching. "What's wrong with you and your brother? My one grandchild lives on the other side of the country and doesn't even know who the hell I am." He glared at the floor. "Stop worrying about me. Everything will be fine if you and David live your own lives and stop fretting so much about how I live mine."

"What's wrong with David and me?" she said, her voice catching. "What do you think's wrong with us?"

He was shaking his head, a bitter half-smile on his lips. "If I only knew."

There was a knock at the side door. "Who is it now?" her father said angrily.

A man Tess didn't recognize opened the door a few inches. He was short and bearded and dark-haired. He had on a red windbreaker and faded black jeans, the knees almost white. "Sorry to interrupt," he said sheepishly.

"Come on in, Chuck," said her father.

Chuck stepped tentatively into the garage. "So, that's your horse? She's a beauty, Ken." He looked at Tess. "Are you the lady I spoke with last night? Ken's daughter?"

"Yes," she said. "I'm Tess."

Her father set the brush on the workbench and went over to shake Chuck's hand. Peanut started pulling mouthfuls of hay from one of the bales with her big, discolored teeth. They all gazed at the horse. "Looks like she's got a hearty appetite," said Chuck.

Her father nodded. "She likes a good snack. The man who sold her to me said appetite is always a good indication of a horse's health."

"Is he a veterinarian?" said Tess.

Her father ignored her and looked at Chuck. "What brings you here this morning?"

Chuck glanced uneasily at Tess. "The van's at the garage." He faltered before blurting, "I need some help paying the mechanic, but we'll make it back soon. You can bet on that."

"What's wrong now?" her father asked, frowning. "Didn't we just put new brakes on it?"

"Dad," she said. "Don't—"

"Go in the house, Tess," he said. "You're making Peanut Sundae Pie uneasy."

Chuck laughed. "That's her name?"

Her father nodded before he turned to Tess. "Go in the house."

"No," she said, wishing her brother were with them, even if his usefulness was debatable. "I'm not leaving, and you shouldn't be giving your money to one con man after another."

"I'm not a con man," said Chuck, more forlorn than offended.

"How do I know that?" she said.

"Go in the house. Now," her father roared.

"No," she said, staring him down.

He moved abruptly forward and slapped her. "Do as I say. I'm still your father."

She stared at him, her hand on her stinging cheek. "I'm not so sure," she said. "I thought you gave up on parenting when Mom died."

He drew back and collided with Peanut Sundae Pie, who reared her head up from the hay bale and knocked him in the eye. "God-damn it," he said, elbowing the horse again as he covered his injured eye.

"Be careful," cried Tess.

"I'm all right, Jesus." He put his hand on the horse's neck. "You're okay, Peewee," he murmured. "No one's going to hurt you."

"Chuck, please go," said Tess. "My father doesn't have a thousand dollars to spare."

"Don't speak for me. Give me a minute, Chuck, and I'll go in and get my checkbook."

"Thank you," said Chuck, avoiding Tess's eyes. "I wouldn't ask if I didn't really need it."

"I know that," said her father.

"Dad," she said helplessly.

Her father ignored her, his eyes obstinately on his horse.

"I'm not trying to con anyone," said Chuck. "I swear on my mother's grave."

"You don't need to worry about me," her father said, finally looking at her. "If things get bad, I'll just drive my school bus over the nearest bridge."

"Ken," said Chuck with a pained laugh. "You're scaring your daughter."

She could see he wasn't a bad person. Possibly he was a real friend to her father, and maybe their business would thrive, but she doubted it, and she also knew you didn't have to be a bad person to make a mess of everything.

"Tess can handle it," said her father. "She's always been tougher than her brother."

She wondered if this was his way of apologizing for slapping her. "I don't think that's true," she said.

"Go in the house and have your coffee and get your brother up. I bet he's still in bed."

"Are you going to keep that bus?" Chuck asked as Tess left the garage. "I know someone who might want to buy it."

"You think they'd give me a good price?" she heard her father say as she closed the side door and went back into the house, her stomach in a tight ball.

David was awake now, the radio on the counter next to the empty cookie jar tuned to local sports news. He sat at the table eating cornflakes, the sugar bowl unlidded next to him. "They're stale, but they're not that stale," he said, spooning milk and cereal into his mouth. He was wearing a rumpled Colts T-shirt and a pair of raggedy gray sweatpants he'd had since high school. "You want some? At least the milk isn't sour."

"No thanks."

"What's up?" he said.

"I have no idea."

He took another mouthful of cereal. "I called my daughter last night," he said. "She didn't answer."

She looked at him in surprise. "Did you leave a message?"

He shook his head.

"Call her again and leave a message."

"Maybe."

"Just do it," she said. "We could go see her together."

He wouldn't meet her eye but she saw his jaw unclenching. "That's not a bad idea," he mumbled.

She poured herself some coffee and wondered if it was too soon to go back to Illinois.

David looked up at her, spoon hovering above his bowl. "Is Dad okay?"

"I don't know," she said. "He slapped me." Her cheek throbbed at the memory.

"What?" He dropped his spoon into the cereal, splashing his T-shirt.

"I don't think he's done that since I was in grade school."

"Did you slap him back?"

"Don't be ridiculous," she said. She sipped her coffee, bitter and very hot. "He might sell the school bus."

"He just got it."

"I know, but it sounded like he might. That guy's here. The one who wants money to repair his van."

"Do you want me to go out there and beat him up?"

"Stop making a joke of everything." She took another sip. "He doesn't seem like a crook."

"We'll see," said David, unconvinced. "Are you okay?"

"I'm all right, but I think I'm going back to Lake Bluff this morning. Dad doesn't want me here and I can't help him right now if he won't let me."

A few seconds passed before her brother said, "Do you think I'm a fuck-up?" His face was open and boyish and worried. She remembered him asking a similar question not long before he left for college, their mother's health already beginning to fail, but no one knowing yet what her symptoms meant. "What if I'm not smart enough?" he'd asked, plaintive. "Maybe I shouldn't go." At the time, he was tan and fit from a summer of mowing lawns for a landscaping company owned by one of their mother's high school friends. He was learning to play guitar and trying with some success to grow a beard. Girls were taking notice of him and he couldn't believe his luck.

"You're just lonely," she said. "So is Dad."

"Aren't you?"

Peanut Sundae Pie's lugubrious gaze rose up in her thoughts. "I suppose I am," she said.

David shifted in his chair, the milk splash rippling on his shirt-front. "I don't know what to do about it."

She touched his shoulder. He put his hand on top of hers, holding it there.

"At least you have friends," he said. "More than I do."

"You have friends too, but you should call them instead of sitting here complaining about never hearing from them," she said.

He exhaled. "You're right."

"I'm going to go pack," she said, gently extricating her hand from beneath his.

"Do you think Jenny really does want to see me?" he asked as she turned toward the hall.

"Of course she does," said Tess.

Several minutes later, she heard their father come in from the garage with Chuck, both of them laughing. She heard Chuck greet David, followed by a pause before more laughter reached her ears. She didn't think it would last, this quasi-détente or half-hearted madness or whatever it was. Her father might spend all his money and have to move in with her or David, and for a while they would all be miserable, more miserable than they were now. The horse would have to be given away, probably soon, unless her father moved to some shack in the country or found a stable he could afford. Maybe Chuck knew someone. Maybe their vending machine business would make them rich.

Much more likely was that she would have to pay for a stable. It was she who would have to come to everyone's rescue, which she realized had become her role in the family years ago but until now, no one, including herself, had been willing to acknowledge it, probably because she wasn't very good at it. Her father would soon have to accept her help anyway, whether he liked it or not. She would never let him slap her again, either—next time she would see it coming. He was a bully, but she was stronger than he was, and they both knew she had been for a long time.

Dear Kelly Bloom

Colin's original plan was to graduate from college at twenty-two, as most of his high school friends managed to do, but he was twenty-eight when he received his diploma, and during job interviews, he blamed family upheaval and inadequate financial aid for the six-year delay. He suspected that his potential employers knew laziness and poor judgment were the true reasons.

After more than four months of anxious searching, he was offered a position at the *Herald-Gazette*, a newspaper over a century old and on its last quivering leg. The real estate market had just collapsed, the war in Iraq continued with no end in sight, and the big banks were in serious trouble. Colin had written for his college paper and graduated with a journalism degree, but instead of a reporter job, he was offered a position as an editorial assistant, which he accepted, having no other options. The salary was laughably small, $29,000 a year, no bonuses in sight. If he didn't go to the movies or eat in restaurants more than once or twice a month, he would manage, just barely, to pay his rent, put groceries in his cupboard, and send in the monthly minimum on his student loan payments.

As he soon discovered, it was a job that required more than forty hours a week, but Chicago and its environs were hemorrhaging jobs at a rate faster than anyone wanted to admit.

Before the end of his second month at the *Gazette*, Colin was told by Laurie Cramer, the staff writer who did most of the movie, concert, and theater reviews and who was also the paper's primary fact-checker, that he wore his misery too openly. "You need to hide it better," she said. "Or else learn to make a joke out of it."

She smiled, her bicuspids longer than her incisors. He guessed that she was in her early fifties, about the same age as his mother, but Laurie was thinner and funnier and harsher than his exhausted mother was. Laurie wore her dark brown hair piled on the crown of her head and favored black eyeliner, along with dramatic scarlet lipstick, which by noon she had usually chewed down to a residual ring. She spent large swaths of most afternoons striding around the newsroom, her lips pursed or silently moving as she worked out copy in her head.

"Lately, my whole life feels like a joke," said Colin, trying but failing to smile convincingly.

She hovered over his cubicle, scrutinizing him. He could hear his heartbeat in his ears. Had he made some awful rookie error, as his overworked predecessor had once done, typing President Osama instead of Obama on one of the letters he'd prepared for his boss, Preston Dryden III?

"How good are you at giving advice?" Laurie finally asked.

"I'm not sure," he said, wondering who on the other side of his cubicle's walls was paying attention to their conversation. From what he could tell, everyone at the paper eavesdropped; with more cubicles by far than offices with doors, it was hard not to. "Probably not very good. Look where I ended up." He tried to laugh, but the sound stayed in his throat.

She leaned her trim body against his cubicle's flimsy outer wall. It shuddered briefly, Colin's calendar of the city skyline and the giraffe photo an ex-girlfriend had given him swaying on their pushpins.

A fluorescent light flickered overhead. The newsroom bulbs often seemed on the verge of dying; a man in maintenance grays, clipboard in one hand, showed up from time to time to glower at the offending bulb before leaving again without replacing it.

"I'm sure you're as good as anyone else in this dump," she said. "I want you to answer these questions and email them back to me by six today." She handed him a torn half-sheet of copier paper with three barely legible lines scrawled in blue ballpoint.

"All right," said Colin. "I'll see what I can do."

"I think you're the one, so don't disappoint me," she said. She gave him a look more comical than fierce, before going back to her desk, which was inside an office that included a door, one with a lock, and no window for the inquisitive to peer through.

Preston Dryden III and Laurie were rumored to be having an affair, but whether or not this was true, Colin didn't care. He wanted only to report to work every day, do a capable job, and avoid conflict. During his first month at the *Gazette*, he missed the quiet of the library where he'd worked during his last year of college, the orderly rows of the books he'd shelved, the hours spent alone in the carrel he favored on the library's poorly heated top floor, his little steel-frame chair and pen-gouged table situated under a humming, dust-spewing vent. Here he had leaned drowsily over his notes and dog-eared textbooks, trudging his way toward respectability.

The questions Laurie sent weren't as challenging as he'd expected, but he also wasn't sure if he knew how to answer them properly:

> 1) What would you do if you caught your best friend stealing from your wallet?
>
> 2) What would you do if you stumbled across your married mother out with another man?
>
> 3) What should you do about your neighbor whose dog keeps leaving messes in your front yard?

You want me to answer these questions in earnest, right? he emailed Laurie. *No sarcasm, I'm guessing.*

Right, be serious. These folks are fragile.

Okay, great, he replied.

BE great, yes, she winged back at him within seconds. *What else could you possibly want to be?*

He had other work to do; there was always other work to do. He hadn't known when he'd accepted the job that he was being hired to work essentially as a factotum, albeit one with the slightly more respectable title of editorial assistant. After he typed up some of the letters Preston Dryden III scratched out each day onto a yellow legal pad (his boss thinking, Colin assumed, that it conferred on him a certain glamorous stature to be handing off business correspondence to his underpaid assistant instead of sending emails to his business contacts like everyone else did), Colin tried to answer Laurie's questions.

> *Hi, Laurie—*
>
> *Here they are. Rough drafts, probably pretty awful. Just curious—why do you want me to do this? —Colin*
>
> **Best friend stealing from wallet:** *Assuming it has never happened before, offer to loan the friend some money. Avoid accusing/embarrassing/yelling at him. If it has happened before, it's probably time to find a new best friend. If he's stealing from you because he has a drug problem, then you might need to give him the number to the nearest rehab clinic, or maybe you could drive him there.*
>
> **Mother stepping out:** *Don't jump to conclusions unless the man with her is holding her hand, fondling her knee, and/ or kissing her. Maybe you know (and she does too) that your father (or stepfather) has been stepping out on her, and it*

appears what's happening here is quid pro quo. It's probably best, in any case, to let them work out this situation on their own, because for one, you're hoping not to be disinherited.

Bad neighbor: *One thing you might do is lie in wait and use your phone to film the dog, through a parted curtain in your front room, doing its business in your yard. Show the clip to the cops later that day to see if they'll issue your neighbor a fine. They might think you're a little odd to spend your time filming a defecating dog, but, well, they've seen worse.*

Dear Colin: Ha. I love it. You've got an edge. I wanted you to answer these questions because it's fun, no? More soon. —L

The following morning, Laurie called him into her office and shut the door after he sat down on the chair facing her paper-littered desk. Five blue coffee cups with the newspaper's name in red printed on their sides, none of them clean, sat on top of the stacks of papers. "Congratulations, Colin," said Laurie, smiling, her lipstick still intact. "You're our new Ann Landers. But this must stay a secret. You can't tell your family, your girlfriend, your shrink, anyone."

He nodded, wondering how he'd have time to do this new job on top of everything else. Were they expecting him to cut his already truncated lunch hour down to ten minutes, or worse, to eat at his desk? As it was, he didn't risk taking more than twenty minutes. Being a stoner college dropout, a salesman at Circuit City before it went belly up, a Starbucks barista, a Jiffy Lube grease monkey (which he had been very bad at, the jiffy part of the proceedings always hamstringing him), a bartender at Hooters (briefly and ineptly)—most of these jobs had paid better, included the occasional willing and sexy female customer or coworker, and had taken up fewer of his waking hours. Now, he had thirty thousand in college debt, a gloomy apartment with bad plumbing, no time for a girlfriend, and fraternity brothers from his first unsuccessful stint at college who were now mostly sober, buttoned-up attorneys and doctors, probably already pulling down a hundred grand or more a year.

But his new Ann Landers duties did not turn out to be as much of a grind as he'd expected. His own column (and very first—he could hardly believe it had happened and wished he could tell someone about it), *Help Me Help You*, which he was writing under the alias Kelly Bloom, earned him an extra $150 a week. A windfall, in truth, and he was relieved and grateful. The extra one-fifty a week, however, was a better deal for the *Gazette*, Laurie told him in confidence, than subscribing to one of the famous syndicated advice columns.

The extra money meant Colin could send his sister Charlotte twenty dollars every week or two for baby formula—not cigarettes or weed, he hoped, though with her, he couldn't be sure. She had a new baby girl, just six weeks old, from her second deadbeat husband, who had dumped her, and a son from her first. The money also meant he could subscribe to cable and pick up the check when he took his mother out to dinner twice a month. Previously, she'd had to pay or else make him dinner (hamburgers or spaghetti, his habitual requests) at her house. She wanted him to live there with her, but he had moved out to finish college two years earlier and had not wanted to move back in after graduating.

In any case, Charlotte had moved into their mother's house with her two kids a week and a half earlier. There was no way Colin would ever move home again now unless he was being wheeled in on a gurney, paralyzed from the neck down after being hit by a bus while rushing across the street to buy a morning coffee, as had happened recently to an accountant, already on crutches from a skiing accident, who worked in the *Gazette*'s sales office.

His mother noticed the new *Gazette* column right after its first week in print and mentioned it to Colin when they met for dinner at a diner near her house, which was also near O'Hare, planes roaring overhead at regular intervals. He caught himself clenching his jaw several times during the meal, something he had done through most of his adolescence, the relentless overhead noise having likely hindered his brain's proper functioning. He wondered if this was one of the reasons he hadn't been able to concentrate on his homework during the two years he'd spent flunking out of Intro to Philosophy and European History in his late teens. His roommate's Jamaican-grown pot stash and the booze-drenched, near-nightly parties hadn't helped either.

"I googled this Kelly Bloom person," his mother said. "But all that came up was a singer, a garden supply store, and some girls on Facebook who looked like cheerleaders or swimsuit salesgirls."

"I'm glad you use Google," said Colin. "That's great, Mom."

"I've been using it as long as you have," she said. "I do know how to do things online. Don't be condescending."

"I'm not being condescending." He stared fixedly at the menu, unwilling to fight with her. He was tired; Kelly Bloom and the *Gazette* had all but taken over his life.

"Well, your sister seems to think I was born yesterday."

He looked up from his menu, into his mother's tired, suddenly tear-bright eyes. She had dyed her graying auburn hair strawberry blond recently and it suited her. She had also started walking three miles every morning, before she went to work at the high school where she maintained the guidance counselors' schedules, answered the phones in the advising office, and helped orient students who transferred in after the school year had begun. It had been a while, at least a few years, since he'd seen her looking so well. He wasn't sure how she managed this now, with his sister and her children underfoot. "I wish Charlotte had somewhere else to live," he said. "If I had more space at my—"

His mother swatted away his words. "Don't bother saying it. There's no way you'd be able to live with her and her kids without the two of you murdering each other by week's end."

"I don't think it'd be that bad. I'd be at work most of the time anyway."

"Do you want her to move in with you?"

"No, but I wish I could help more." He wondered why he was being so dishonest. Guilt. Of course that was it. Kelly Bloom needed to stare dishonesty straight in its ashen face.

"Don't even pretend you'd be willing to let her live with you. It would never work anyway. Not unless you suddenly won the lottery, bought a big house, and hired a nanny *and* a maid. Your sister is a wreck, Colin. Even more so than usual."

"I'm sure she's very upset about Tag."

"That man," his mother said flatly. "I knew he was bad news from day one, but Charlotte would rather drive her car off a cliff than listen to advice from me." She paused. "She did drive her car off a cliff, I guess you could say, by marrying that bum and letting him impregnate her."

"I think Charlotte will be smarter about the next guy." He didn't think this at all, in truth, and his mother knew it. His sister had been choosing the wrong man since she was thirteen, the year she let Mike Baumgartner, a boy who lived two doors down, climb in through her bedroom window late one night. Mike had gone to school the next day to report to everyone in great detail what they had done while her mother and pothead older brother were sleeping down the hall.

His mother shook her head. "She won't. Not unless she has a near-death experience or a lobotomy."

"Maybe you should ask her to move out, Mom. You sound really stressed."

"I'm going to write to that Kelly Bloom person and see if she gives me the time of day. Do you think she answers any letters besides the ones they print?"

"I don't know," said Colin warily. "I kind of doubt it." He did not answer letters other than those they printed, and if Laurie ever started asking him to, he would for sure have no time for his other work.

"Maybe she'd make an exception for me," his mother said hopefully.

"Maybe, but I wouldn't count on it."

"If I write a letter with an important or interesting enough problem, she'd answer it, wouldn't she?" she asked, dogged. "She probably doesn't have the final say about what they publish. You've said there are a lot of people involved in what gets in the paper and what gets left out."

"That's true, but Mom, really, I wouldn't put money on it. I'm sure Kelly Bloom gets dozens of letters every week. Probably every day."

Letters, in fact, were already flooding in—both handwritten notes and emails. Laurie read through the problem harvest, as she called Kelly Bloom's daily haul of plaintive letters, some of them unintelligible or illegible or plainly ineligible for publication because they were too sexually graphic or bizarre to print. "We'll leave the filthy ones for Dan Savage," said Laurie. "He can handle the perverts. He's very good at it. Our Kelly is more wholesome, don't you think?" She seemed to be leering at him as she said this.

"I guess so," he said, looking down at his desk.

"Why are you blushing?" she cried. "You're not in grade school anymore. Do you only go to PG movies, Colin?"

"No," he said. "I own *Basic Instinct*."

"Wow, that's an old one, Colin," Laurie said, laughing. "How about *9½ Weeks*? You got that one too?"

Colin tried to laugh. "No, but maybe you have a copy you could lend me?"

Something on the other side of the room caught Laurie's eye, and without another word, she went back to her office and shut the door. He could feel his coworkers stirring nearby in their cubicles. He wondered if he was being hazed. Did Laurie do this to every recent hire, or was she flirting with him? He doubted it—he wasn't worldly or ironic enough for her. He imagined her with a handsome gray-haired man in an expensive, rumpled dress shirt, silk tie loose around his sun-baked neck. He would speak three languages and be able to identify the best ales and ports on the menu. He would also once have been a war correspondent and still have shrapnel in his shoulder and thigh. But whatever she really thought of him, Colin knew that Laurie had done him a big favor by giving him the column.

The server was ignoring him and his mother. They had been sitting for ten minutes and nothing other than water had appeared, and that from another server. Colin wanted to go home and sleep for the next three days, but it was winter and the steam radiators in his studio apartment hissed like feral cats at unpredictable hours, which sometimes caused him to wake in the middle of the night with a dangerously leaping pulse. "You need to do yoga," Alissa, his most recent ex-girlfriend, had insisted. "Or aromatherapy. Try it, Colin. I'm right about this." He hadn't tried either. He wasn't going to burn some strongly scented candle in his apartment. Any new girl he brought there would smell it and probably think he was trying to mask the smell of unwashed clothes.

"Let's go somewhere else," said Colin. "This is bullshit."

His mother was already on her feet. "Let's go home. I have hot dogs," she said. "But they're vegetarian. That's the only kind Charlotte will eat now. She might be eating half a bag of Oreos every day, but she's given up meat."

"That's a surprise," he said. His sister had never previously encountered a hamburger she couldn't inhale in four bites.

His mother nodded. "Makes it even more fun for me to cook for her. She's not letting the kids eat meat, either."

"I'm sure the baby wouldn't be eating meat yet anyway."

"That's true. Thank God I don't have to cook for her too."

The house was in breathtaking disarray when they arrived. Charlotte was staring at a rerun of *Seinfeld* on the living room television set, her infant daughter nursing at her breast, bright maroon throw pillows strewn at her flip-flopped feet, along with orange peels, two apple cores, several sippy cups, a dozen unopened juice boxes, and a handful of miniature boxes of Raisin Bran. Channing, Charlotte's three-year-old son, was running around naked from the waist down, his face streaked with someone's burgundy lipstick, his grandmother's it turned out, Colin's mother gasping when she found the capless stick smashed down to a nub in a seam between two of the sofa cushions. The sofa was only a year old and had been purchased with a settlement from a car accident two years earlier. A teenager with only a learner's permit had sideswiped Colin's mother's car, his parents later pleading to pay her out of pocket for the repairs instead of filing an insurance claim. Mrs. Bennett had hired a former student to pound out the dents in her car and used the rest of the unofficial settlement to buy new clothes and the fancy sofa.

"Charlotte," his mother said, trying hard not to shout. "What on earth is going on here? Why is Channing playing with my lipstick?"

Charlotte peered blearily at Colin and their mother, blinking as if bringing them into focus. "What?" she said. She was pretty, her eyes a deep blue, her brown hair long and luxuriously thick, but she had grown plump and sluggish with the second pregnancy. Her absent second husband, Tag, had already moved in with another woman; Charlotte had declared to Colin and their mother many times during her and Tag's courtship that he was the love of her life. But she had said the same thing about Harry, her first slacker husband. Colin thought her too hopeful and naive; their mother thought her obscenely foolish. Her own husband, Colin and Charlotte's father, had also left her for another woman and had later moved from Chicago to Seattle. At the time, Colin was eight, Charlotte six. Mrs. Bennett had not remarried, and this fact, Colin had come to realize, was a point of pride for her, but also a source of private disappointment.

"My house is a pigsty," his mother cried. "Why are all these cups and cereal boxes out of the cupboard?"

"Channing did it. I couldn't stop him," Charlotte said wearily, guiding the baby, who had become dislodged from her nipple, back to where she belonged. Colin averted his eyes, his sister's pale, bare breast gleaming and globular beneath her baby's busy mouth. He could picture Laurie Cramer shrieking with laughter and he blushed. He was always blushing now. He hoped his mother and sister wouldn't notice.

"You need to set boundaries with him, Charlotte, effective immediately," their mother said direly. "Otherwise he'll grow up to be a hellion and never listen to a thing you say."

"Like us," said Charlotte.

"Yes, exactly," said Mrs. Bennett.

"We're not that bad," said Colin.

His mother snorted.

"What?" said Charlotte, offended. "Why are you always coming down on us? At least we're not alcoholics or drug dealers."

"At least you're not shoplifting or sniffing glue or stealing old ladies' purses either," said their mother.

Charlotte gave her a sullen look. "Ha ha."

"You could have turned out better," said Mrs. Bennett, staring at her daughter.

"Mom, come on," said Colin. "We're still young."

"Colin," she said, turning her exasperated, weary gaze on him. "In case you haven't noticed, Charlotte is twenty-six and already has two failed marriages and two children by two different men."

His sister stood up abruptly from the sofa, jarring the nursing baby, who started to cry in hiccupping gasps. "This is bullshit," said Charlotte. "You have no sympathy for what I've been going through, Mom. You're the one who's the piece of work." She stalked out of the room, her T-shirt hiked up, gray sweatpants straining across her broadened backside. Colin watched her retreat, both sorry and embarrassed.

"Bullshit!" Channing parroted, chasing after his mother, giggling maniacally.

Down the hall, Charlotte slammed her bedroom door but had to reopen it a second later when Channing started pounding on it, keening for her.

Mrs. Bennett said nothing and went into the hall; Colin followed, accidentally kicking one of the juice boxes. Without turning her head, she said, "Pick that up, please." He bent over and collected the box, a smiling apple emblazoned on its side.

His mother had stopped on the kitchen's threshold, her face pinched with weariness and disappointment. "I'm not going to be able to live like this for much longer. Something has to change," she said portentously. All of the pots and pans had been pulled out of the lower cupboard and tossed about the room. Channing had also gotten to the paper dinner napkins on the kitchen table, ripped them up, and strewn the shreds like confetti. "I go out for an hour and this is what I come home to?" She turned toward Colin. "She's been here two weeks. It feels like twenty years."

"Mom," he said softly. "I know it's hard, but you're being pretty harsh. She really has gotten a raw deal. Tag is an asshole, but for a while, he didn't seem that bad."

She stared at him, her gaze fierce. "That might be the case, but your sister is old enough to clean up her own messes, Colin. More than old enough. I should never have let her move back in with me." She paused, looking sad and harassed. "It'd be nice if someone gave me a break for once, instead of it always being the other way around."

After he'd returned to his overheated apartment with its gurgling plumbing and hissing radiators, the knot in his stomach beginning to loosen, he knew a letter would soon arrive for Kelly Bloom, one penned by his despairing mother. He hoped Laurie would weed it out before he had a chance to see it, but he suspected his karma was bad enough that the letter would likely reach his desk with a note attached in Laurie's scrawl: *This one's GOOD*, which was her code for "You're answering it."

He was right. Six days later, the letter he'd been dreading landed on his desk. Laurie had not attached a note, but his mother's plea for advice, neatly printed in blue ink on thin pink paper, was the second from the top of his pile of thirty-two letters. Laurie usually arranged them in her perceived order of importance and appropriateness for the *Gazette*'s aging, increasingly unhip readership.

Dear Kelly,

I've had a time of it lately and I'm in desperate need of your advice. I suppose every letter you receive begins this way, but it really is true.

  I'll get right to it (I know your time is valuable). My problem is that I'm afraid I'll stop loving my daughter if she continues to live with me. This is one of the most awful things a mother can say, I know, but I have to be honest with myself (and with you). Her second husband left her recently and she has a newborn daughter and one other child who is three. This older child is my daughter's first husband's son. This rotten ex-son-in-law never pays a penny of child support because we can't find him.

  The house is always a mess, my daughter has no job or any job prospects that I know of, and she spends all day watching TV and eating junk food as if she were still a teenager. My son is at least making something of himself, but there was a time (a long time, to be honest) when I worried he'd end up in prison (full disclosure: he did spend a few nights in jail a number of years ago because he used to be a heavy-drinking miscreant). That's beside the point, I suppose. I did the best I could, raising him and his sister on my own. I'm sure I made some mistakes, but who knows what genes they got from their cheating father—there was probably nothing I could have done aside from locking them in a dungeon from ages twelve to twenty-five.

*I want my daughter to find her own apartment
immediately but she can't afford to and I know that it would
be very uncharitable of me to put her and her children out on
the street. Even so, I'm going crazy and on some mornings I
can barely get out of bed and go to work.*

Yours sincerely,

K. Bennett

*P.S. If my son could turn his life around, I really do think that
my daughter should be able to too. He used to have a terrible
scratch-off lottery ticket addiction and along with being a
drunk, he slept around (like his father, unfortunately). Now,
he's no longer at the mercy of those habits, as far as I know.*

Colin sat with the letter in his unsteady hands, acutely aware of
the sounds all around him—the insect tick of the flickering light
above his cubicle, the soft chatter of people on their phones, the
steely mastication of a paper shredder, the nearby thwack of a coffee mug being set down with too much force. His stomach had
curled itself into a tight, abject ball and his eyes were so dry they
throbbed. None of what his mother had written was a surprise, but
as he'd read her words, it had felt as if she were standing behind
him, repeatedly jabbing hard at his kidneys, and this phantom
pain would not go away. He knew that up until a few years ago,
he'd deserved her dismal opinion of him; he also knew that he'd
surprised and pleased her by returning to college and managing
to graduate—and cum laude, by some miracle. But to be faced so
baldly with her previous grievances and fears, and as he perceived
it, her unvoiced worry that he might at any moment relapse into
his former drunken, lazy, pussy-hounding ways, stung badly.

Kelly Bloom, however, whom he'd begun in his private heart to
consider his better self, needed to see the situation differently—
this letter wasn't about him, Colin Bennett, not at all, and if he

chose to see it that way, he deserved these helpings of humble pie currently being force-fed to him.

While he was still sitting with the letter in his hands, Preston Dryden III called to him from his office. "Can you come in here for a minute, Colin?"

His boss was a short, wiry man in his mid-fifties with a full head of cloud-gray curls. He ran several triathlons a year, and his medals and bibs were framed and mounted on the wall behind his desk. His black leather desk chair was so large it looked as if he were poised at the mouth of a cave.

"Close the door," said Preston.

Colin obeyed, a nervous flutter in his chest.

His boss motioned for him to sit down. Colin sat and waited for him to speak. Preston waited for several disconcerting seconds before he said, "You're doing a fine job, Colin. You have a real future here at the *Gazette*."

Despite the unexpected praise, Colin could feel himself sweating. "Thank you, sir."

Preston shook his head. "No 'sir,' Colin. Just Preston." He paused, smiling without baring his teeth, which were yellow from fifteen years of chain-smoking before he'd become a boastful triathlete. "Kelly Bloom is one of our most popular features now. She gets almost as many clicks on our website as the police blotter."

"That's good to hear. Thank you, sir." Colin hesitated. "Preston, I mean."

"Keep up the good work, all right?"

Colin nodded. "I will. Thank you again."

Preston held his gaze for a long moment. "How do you like working with Laurie on the column?" he asked. "You two seem like a good team."

"I like it," he said. "It was nice of her to give me a chance."

"It was my idea to have you try out for the job," said Preston, his expression unreadable. "Not hers."

"Thank you, sir," said Colin. "Preston, I mean."

His boss waved an impatient hand. "It's in my nature to do people favors and to promote talent where I see it."

"Thank you," Colin repeated. He felt foolish and exposed. Preston turned his eyes to his computer screen, and without another word, Colin got up and left.

At his desk, his mother's letter mutely, threateningly, waited for him. Her anguished outpouring with its allusions to his past mistakes and his sister's more recent ones made him feel light-headed, as if he were looking at an overdue bill, one he knew he couldn't pay.

Within a few minutes an email from Laurie arrived, no subject or salutation: *What did Preston want?*

A loan, Colin replied.

Ha! What did he really want? asked Laurie.

He told me I was doing a good job. Colin would probably never tell her that Preston had claimed credit for giving him Kelly Bloom.

Nice that he noticed, Laurie replied. *He usually doesn't. Send me your picks for Kelly for next week before you leave today.*

He was tempted to tell her that one of the letters was from his mother, but she would ask which one or else would guess and then he would never hear the end of it: "Scratch-off tickets? Aren't there better ways to waste your money? What about cocaine?" Laurie would cackle. "And just how much of a lush and a playboy were you? Maybe I've misjudged you and you're more Mickey Rourke than Mr. Rogers."

The fact his mother had called him a miscreant, a word he couldn't remember ever hearing her say aloud, kept cycling through his thoughts. He supposed it was better than being called a loser. But not much.

He would answer the kind-hearted and long-suffering Kathryn Bennett's letter; he was all but certain Laurie would insist it be part of the week's picks. He emailed her his selections before he went home for the day and googled several of the women he had once dated or had sex with. He hadn't gone on a date in five months; he'd been living a monk's existence since taking the job at the *Gazette* and found that it wasn't such a hardship, his head cleared of the emotional calculus that accompanied any sexual relationship, no matter how short-lived. The rush of increased self-confidence, the temporary release of stepping out of his clothes and landing in a strange, willing woman's bed, the drinks consumed, the joints or cigarettes smoked before or after—he could go back to this mating dance if he wanted to, but for now, he didn't.

Around three in the morning, he was still awake, words from his mother's letter on an unstoppable loop in his head: *miscreant, drunk, addiction*. He could run a fucking triathlon too, if he put his mind to it, or a fucking third-rate newspaper office. He could show his mother and whoever else cared to notice that he wasn't a loser or a miscreant anymore.

At six thirty, not having slept all night and unsure what he was doing, he called his mother. It was Charlotte who answered, her voice cracking from hours of disuse. "What's the matter?" she asked, irritated. "Why are you calling so early?"

"I'm sorry if I woke you," he said.

"No, I was up."

"Is Mom there?"

She exhaled loudly. "Where else would she be?"

"Can I talk to her?"

His sister sighed again and dropped the phone. His mother was the only person he knew who still had a landline.

Somewhere in the background, he could hear a child whimpering above the hum of a humidifier or a fan.

"Colin, are you okay?" his mother asked as soon as the phone was in her hand.

"Yes, I'm okay, Mom."

"Well, then what's—"

"I just remembered something and figured I'd better call you before I forgot," he said. "You can have a free subscription to the

Gazette. Employees can request one for their families." It wasn't true, but he would get a discounted rate.

"That's why you're calling me at six thirty in the morning? Are you kidding?" she said, her laughter strained.

"I know how hard you work, Mom."

"Colin," she said, more worried now. "What's wrong? Are you at the police station?"

"What?" he said, taken aback. "No, of course not. I'm at home. Don't you have caller ID?"

"I didn't look at it. Your sister said it was you." She paused. "What's the matter, honey?"

"Nothing's the matter," he said. "Everything's fine. Better than it's been in a while, but I'm sorry you're having a hard time with Charlotte and her kids. I do want to help, but I know it probably hasn't seemed like I do. Maybe I can get someone to babysit while she goes out and looks for a job. Or if she wants to go back to college and finish her associate's degree, she could do that."

His mother said nothing for a moment. He could hear his nephew whining again, more plaintive now. "I don't know, Colin," she said. "I can't afford a babysitter. They charge so much. It's not like when you and Charlotte were kids and I could pay the girl down the street six dollars an hour and let her eat all the cookies in the house."

"We could split the cost," he said. "I'll figure it out."

She hesitated. "If you want to look into it, I won't stop you."

There was a thump in the background and Channing was now screaming. His mother squawked in distress and said, "Channing just fell off the bed. I have to go, sweetie." She hung up without saying goodbye, and Colin sat with the phone at his ear for a few more seconds, futilely asking if his nephew was okay. He felt groggy now and wasn't sure if he'd last the day at work, but he forced himself to go into the bathroom and turn on the shower. It was a relief to have somewhere to go each day where he was needed; for a long time he hadn't known if there ever would be such a place.

After his reply to his mother's letter ran, Colin received almost as much Kelly Bloom fan mail as he'd gotten for the reply to a woman asking what to do about her mother-in-law who, more than once, had arrived for a visit with a maid service in tow—and had the gall to stick her daughter-in-law with the bill.

The lines his fans cited as their favorites were almost all the same:

Until your daughter is able to afford a place of her own, perhaps you can establish some rules about household chores, bedtimes, and television viewing.

You might remind your daughter that as long as she's under your roof, you're in charge, just as you were when she was a child.

You might also consider complimenting both of your children when they do something you appreciate and/or hope to encourage them to do more of. This could go a long way in boosting their self-esteem.

No junk food, unless it's the kind coming out of your own oven.

Within the month, Laurie told Colin that if he kept up the good work, Kelly Bloom might one day be a syndicated columnist.

"Does that mean I'd get a raise?" he asked.

"Yes," she said with a sly smile. "Do you want it in scratch-off lottery tickets?"

His breath caught in his throat. "Why—why would you think that?"

"Oh, come on, there are no secrets here. Your mother's name and address were on the return address label on her envelope. I looked her up."

He opened his mouth but no words came out.

"It only adds to your mystique," she said. "A good thing for a young man to have."

"I was kind of a fuck-up for a while," he said.

She nodded. "That's okay. It teaches humility. Another good thing for a young man to have."

"I guess it is."

She was already several steps away, no sign she'd heard his reply. A little while later, Preston summoned Colin to his office and closed the door, but instead of congratulating him on his continuing success as Kelly Bloom, he asked Colin to hang another framed triathlon medal on the wall behind his desk. Colin spent nearly an hour making minute adjustments to the nail and wire on the back of the medal's frame until his boss was satisfied.

At his desk, a voice mail from his mother awaited him. In it, she reported that Charlotte had somehow already acquired a new boyfriend. She sounded distressed, adding that she and Charlotte were getting along better since she'd started following Kelly Bloom's advice, but if Charlotte invited the new boyfriend to stay the night, someone in the house would not survive to greet the new day.

Colin started to call his mother back but reconsidered. He didn't know what he could say to console her. His sister would go on creating new problems and drawing people into them. His mother would probably write to Kelly Bloom again. Laurie would love this, but he tried not to think about it. Kelly Bloom had advised someone only a few days ago not to make a habit of soliciting trouble from the future. It was better to let bad news take you by surprise, because it usually didn't arrive too often anyway. He wasn't sure if he agreed with Kelly on this last point, but he wanted to.

Wedding Party

1

It was the bride's second marriage, the groom's third. They were both in their thirties, but Kim wasn't sure if the groom was fibbing about his age—half of his face was hidden behind a dark beard, and he kept his hair, thick and shiny, tied in a youthful ponytail. She hadn't searched for him online, having managed to break this habit after looking up a different client several months earlier and discovering he was semi-famous for a series of YouTube videos he'd posted of himself performing homegrown stunts in the *Jackass* vein which included swallowing half a bottle of motor oil mixed with Bailey's Irish Cream and dangling heavy objects from his penis while, off-camera, others howled with drunken laughter. After watching four of these clips for reasons Kim still didn't understand, she'd had trouble looking him and the bride in the eye.

These new clients, Ryan and Emily Ann, had money and divorced parents, several half- and step-siblings, and, for the moment, good attitudes. Kim had a feeling the groom was stoned every time she met with him and the bride, but he wasn't inarticulate or dopey, only vague and smiling. She wondered why they were in such a hurry to marry—they'd met only seven months earlier, when the ink on Ryan's second set of divorce papers wasn't yet dry and Emily Ann had just joined Gamblers Anonymous and was trying to adopt a child from Guatemala, a quest Ryan had convinced her to set aside in favor of adopting two puggles. He liked other people's children just fine, he'd told Kim during their second meeting, his fiancée's expression blank as he talked, but he didn't want any of his own—lucky for him because his sperm count wasn't the greatest, possibly because he was born during a period of intense solar flares, and his mother had eaten a lot of seaweed while pregnant with him.

Kim had learned to take in the superstitions and idiosyncratic details couples shared with her without letting her surprise or boredom show. She knew they couldn't help themselves—most of them were young and in the habit of posting every thought and whim online. One couple she'd worked with the previous year had wanted to marry on a rocket blasting into space—did Kim know if anyone had ever done this? (She did not, nor had she ever heard of it—though with billionaires now taking rides on the space shuttle, she supposed space weddings were coming.) Another couple wanted a silent wedding with their vows and the priest's words projected onto a big screen suspended above the altar. Another wanted to marry on the ocean with everyone floating on air mattresses while dolphins leapt in the distance against the setting sun.

Ryan and Emily Ann were less dramatic and ambitious, but they'd decided to host their ceremony on the lakefront and had a guest list of a hundred and fifty people, most of whom were bringing a plus one. In late September, an outdoor wedding was risky, but the bride and groom had agreed to use a tent for the reception and a half dozen portable heaters in case of a cold night. As a rule, outdoor weddings made Kim nervous, especially when the guest list was large—even in the summer, Chicago weather was unpredictable. Her feeling was that if people wanted to get married outdoors, they should move to San Diego, or at least hold their wedding there.

2

Clay did not understand his nephew. Two divorces already, and now a third wedding, and the boy wasn't even close to the age when AARP started sending out those membership forms that looked like a check might be inside but of course there never was a check. Why couldn't Ryan simply live with a woman and keep lawyers out of it when one of them got sick of the other? No one batted an eye these days over unmarried cohabitation unless they were pious hypocrites, but who cared what those reprobates thought anyway. In his experience, those folks routinely cheated on their taxes and sent their gay sons off to be deprogrammed by scripture-spouting maniacs.

Clay had only been married once, and that was back in his idiotic mid-twenties when he rode a motorcycle and kept an iguana named Clint Eastwood as a pet. The marriage hadn't been his idea, but he'd thought it might be fun and for a couple of years it was, but then his wife's sister moved in with them, after she'd left the commune in rural Oregon where she'd learned to cook without meat and had stopped shaving her legs and armpits. He'd gotten into some trouble with her, and for a year and a half he and the sister had lived in a tent in whichever friend's yard they could pitch it. It had been tough to hold down a job when he couldn't shower very often and didn't have a washer, and on top of this, his dental hygiene was on the questionable side, but all that nonsense was more than thirty years ago now, and in the end, he'd managed to hold on to most of his teeth and had been waking up alone for nearly ten years. Much of the time, it wasn't as bad as you'd think it would be.

3

Ryan had asked his uncle Clay to be his best man—his two closest friends had already filled that position in one of his previous weddings, and he thought it might jinx the whole thing if he were to ask one of them to stand up again. If he were called before God or some sort of almighty bogeyman to reveal who his favorite family member was, he'd have to say Clay because his parents were batshit, his grandparents were dead, and even though he got along all right with his brother and sister, Sebastian was a little off and possibly a peeping Tom, and Jill's house was crammed full of so much crap from flea markets and yard sales you could barely move from one room to the next without knocking something over, and she was only forty-two. She had too many pets, and the place smelled terrible. Although Ryan appreciated her soft spot for birds and various four-legged creatures, he kept his house pet acquisitions firmly in the dog realm.

But he wasn't prone to throwing stones—he had his own set of problems, and one of them was he didn't like being alone and certainly couldn't live alone for more than a week or two without sort of losing his mind and joining chat rooms about owl migration routes and French cooking and other topics he knew nothing about. His therapist had told him this was something of a Trojan-horse problem, with other problems living like stowaways inside a bigger problem. His therapist had advised him not to remarry so quickly—couldn't he and Emily Ann take it slower than Ryan had with his two ex-wives?

Well, a year and a half into his first marriage, his wife realized she was still in love with her college girlfriend, and three years into his next marriage, his second wife, Gabrielle, slept with one of her coworkers, and despite saying it wouldn't happen again, it did happen again, and even though Ryan knew he was still in love with her, he also knew he would never trust her again. She hadn't wanted the divorce, but he wasn't able to sleep the night through without waking up in a blind rage after he found out she was still having sex with her coworker. He didn't like worrying that his fury at being cuckolded might jump the wall at some point and make a lunge for her. And because he was still in love with her, he realized he would probably be a confused wreck for a while.

When he was with Emily Ann, however, he felt saner and relatively happy. So far, she'd been extremely loyal, and even better than her loyalty was the fact that men did not ogle her like they did Gabrielle. Emily Ann was pretty but not a knockout. No other guy ever stared at her as if Ryan, with his arm around her as they entered a restaurant or a party, were invisible.

His secret thought was that one day he and Gabrielle might get back together—when they were both in their sixties or seventies, and she was done screwing around. After her looks had faded and she'd had a cancer scare and come through it a more humble person who understood how deeply her lust for the bonehead at work who played drums in a Doors cover band had hurt and tormented her adoring, occasionally stoned former husband.

4

Emily Ann was her father's third daughter and the fifth child of six. She was her mother's only daughter and first of her three children. She was glad Ryan had only two siblings and was the calmest guy she'd ever dated seriously, but it worried her a little that he didn't seem to want kids. She wasn't entirely sure she wanted them either, although she did think she might at some point. Her first husband had wanted kids, but he'd also wanted to live in Alaska, and when he insisted they move from Chicago to Anchorage, she'd become very depressed. She couldn't stand exceedingly cold weather, and this had turned out to be only one of several major problems. The biggest wasn't his fault, but hers—she'd lost all their money playing online poker at the beginning of the pandemic, a period of collective quasi-insanity that wasn't over yet. The virus was also the reason why she and Ryan had decided to hold their wedding outside. She sensed the wedding planner would have preferred a banquet hall or a hotel ballroom, but at least she wasn't being pushy about it.

When they had their first meeting with the wedding planner, Ryan mentioned the idea of hiring a psychic for the reception, and he wouldn't let it go like Emily Ann had initially hoped. She knew without doubt it was a bad idea because no matter what the psychic said, at least a few people would end up angry or traumatized, and Emily Ann really didn't want any of the guests to remember their wedding as the night they were told their house would burn down or their teenage daughter would run off with the father of three who lived two doors away. She'd been at a New Year's Eve party a few years ago where this very thing had occurred. It had taken a couple of months for the psychic's predictions to come true, but this had only heightened the suspense, and one person was still talking about suing the host for psychological damages.

She wasn't sure why Ryan had proposed so quickly, even though she'd been hoping since their fourth date he would. On that date, he'd taken her to a pottery shop and they'd both crafted little animals—a lion, a seal, a fox, and a frog—and she supposed she'd fallen in love with him on the spot. His second ex-wife was still calling him, and although Ryan said it was only because they shared custody of a dog, a high-strung German shepherd mix named Horst, he seemed happy whenever she called or texted, which was at least once nearly every time he and Emily Ann were together.

5

Poor Emily Ann—even though she was the firstborn, she was the most lost of Julia's three children. It didn't help that Bill, Emily Ann's father, was a blowhard and a fool who had spoiled her rotten until she was thirteen—the year he'd left Julia for another woman—after which he'd neglected Emily Ann and her brother Zachary obscenely. No wonder their daughter was so confused and unhappy and had had that awful gambling problem in the early months of the pandemic. Fortunately, Zachary had stronger self-esteem—maybe a little too strong, but at least he knew he didn't have to turn himself inside out to please everyone who crossed his path, nor did he go chasing after validation in virtual casinos. It did bother her that he was a musician, but he hadn't impregnated anyone yet, as far as Julia knew.

She hoped this second marriage of Emily Ann's would last—her own second marriage was a solid, waterproof vessel, and much of this, she felt certain, was due to her loving husband's strong moral compass and distrust of the internet (thank goodness—Bill had met the woman he'd dumped her for online!). Stewart did not leer at other women, nor did he make up stories about the year he served in the Vietnam War. He didn't have the supplest sense of humor, but she would take his steady seriousness any day over Bill's dumb jokiness and wandering eye. It was a wonder he hadn't been MeToo'd with all the other would-be Casanovas, though for all she knew, he had but had quietly settled with whatever women he'd made a grab for. She hadn't seen him in four years—not since Emily Ann's first wedding—and Julia wasn't exactly looking forward to seeing him again, but it couldn't be helped. At least she'd held on to her figure, despite having three babies—the third, Stewart's and her good-natured Benjamin, arriving when she was forty-one—and on the whole, she liked weddings but would have preferred her only daughter to have had just one.

As for her son-in-law-to-be, he was a cheerful bore who seemed not to let things get under his skin, but Stewart worried Ryan would never amount to anything and wished he had some sort of career. Ryan had family money and technically didn't need to work, so, well, he didn't, though he pretended to—apparently he did something nebulous in the field of graphic design. Trust funds corrupted the mind, in Stewart's view. Julia didn't share this opinion, and all things being equal, she would rather Emily Ann have a rich husband than a poor one (but she hoped Ryan wasn't planning to give her unfettered access to his bank account because he would surely regret it).

It didn't seem likely he intended to, in any case—there was a prenup, which, although coldhearted, was never a bad idea, in

Julia's view. The world was coldhearted. People didn't like to hear this, but it was nonetheless true.

6

To Kim's great relief, the day of the wedding was clear, the temperature in the mid-seventies—San Diego weather having been bestowed by the weather gods upon Chicago's North Shore—a perfect early autumn Saturday. The tent had been pitched with no snafus, the tables and chairs unpacked and set up on time, the flowers, the caterers—everything had come together like a well-rehearsed symphony of moneyed goodwill and bracing competence. She really could not believe it.

Ryan and Emily Ann had rented a house with beachfront property for the ceremony and reception—a good tactical choice, as the house also served as the launch pad for the wedding party. Kim had been assigned a small, sunny room off the kitchen as her base of operations. There was one bizarre, slightly sinister occurrence, however, something Kim had never before encountered while on the job: she witnessed the groom's sister stuffing a small, triangular throw pillow from the living room sofa into a black duffel bag and scurrying out of the room with surprising nimbleness, despite the air cast on her ankle. Perhaps the cast was subterfuge, meant to keep Jill from being enlisted last-minute as an usher or a gofer, or perhaps she had a phobia about dancing in public?

Regardless of the reason, Kim was annoyed that she now had to decide if she should report Jill's crime to the groom or confront the thief directly. Neither scenario promised anything but awkwardness at best, and at worst, she risked being shown the door if she embroiled herself in what was likely some ongoing family drama over Jill's ostensible kleptomania. Better to say nothing at all.

Yet, she did wonder what else was in the duffel and hoped Jill's light fingers would not find their way into her or anyone else's wallet. The duffel's lumpish appearance certainly implied it held more cargo than a small throw pillow. If Kim herself were prone to stealing, she would already have filched the five-pound bag of white Jordan almonds that sat unattended ten feet away from her office doorway on the kitchen counter. If she craned her neck from where she sat at her temporary antique walnut desk, the candy was right in her sightline. Her mouth tingled at the thought of the hard candy shell softening on her tongue.

She got up and tiptoed over to the bag, nodding at the caterer who stood rolling silverware into white cloth napkins. The bag of almonds wasn't yet opened. "May I have a few? I didn't eat lunch," said Kim, pointing at the still-pristine bag.

The caterer, a woman in her fifties with the sinewy look of a distance runner, nodded. "Help yourself. You actually like those things?"

"I do," said Kim, with a diffident laugh.

"They taste like wood to me," said the caterer.

The bag's seal wouldn't yield to Kim's slippery hands. Flustered, she pulled a knife from the wooden block of Chicago Cutlery next to the enormous stainless steel sink and sawed into the bag. The caterer watched with benign interest. "You're the wedding planner, right?" she said.

Kim nodded as the knife finally breached the bag and the sugary, plasticine smell of the candied almonds streamed out. She inhaled greedily as she poured several almonds into her palm. They were flawless—the Platonic ideal of candied nuts. Kim held her breath to keep herself from sighing.

"How'd you get into this line of work?" the caterer asked, as she placed a fresh silverware roll at the apex of a lopsided pyramid.

An almond's coating was melting on Kim's tongue now, her saliva glands tingling. It was almost too blissful to be borne. She looked at the caterer through misty eyes. "I've loved weddings since I was a little girl. I remember watching Prince Charles and Lady Diana's wedding on television when I was visiting my grandmother, and she woke me up very early. We sat in our pajamas, eating raspberry coffee cake as we watched, and Grandma cried and said she had never witnessed a more perfect wedding."

The caterer gave her a pitying look. "A shame how that one turned out."

7

Clay didn't mind public speaking, but he hadn't done any since high school speech class, when he'd written a report on how to make a peanut butter and jelly sandwich with one hand tied behind your back and another on how to give a cat a bath. (The answer was you didn't—that was the whole speech, but the teacher didn't think Clay was funny.) Now that his nephew and this shy girl with nice legs were officially married—the bride, to everyone's amusement but her own, had had hiccups the whole time they were saying their vows—Clay hoped to make a best-man speech people might fondly reminisce about for years. He'd spent many hours writing it and had practiced several times in front of the mirror and had also read it to the Comcast repairman as he fixed Clay's Wi-Fi, which had gone on the blink when he was trying to order Ryan's wedding gift (a year's supply of eco-friendly laundry soap—it wasn't on their registry but he was sure they'd need it, unlike the fancy placemats from Provence which cost twice as much as his monthly cable and Wi-Fi bill!). When he was done reading his speech, the Comcast guy had said, "That was a whole lot better than the one I got at my wedding."

Now, under the big white circus tent, Clay looked out at the expanse of shining faces, some alert and receptive, others bleary from all the free liquor—he'd overheard someone losing his lunch on the other side of the canvas wall a few minutes earlier (if you didn't charge at least a few dollars for the hard liquor, the whole evening would of course turn into a goddamn fraternity party).

Clay noticed his sister giving him an apprehensive look as he stood up from the table and pulled his speech from the inside pocket of his tuxedo jacket. He knew she'd opposed Ryan's decision to ask him to be in the wedding party, but Stephanie had always been a wet blanket, and Clay was going to claim his moment in the proverbial sun whether she liked it or not.

He cleared his throat and glanced at Ryan, who lifted his champagne glass merrily. Clay raised the microphone to his mouth and peered down at his speech, which he saw was not his speech at all. He'd brought the goddamn power bill.

"Fuck me," he said. Some of the guests tittered nervously. He hadn't meant to say the words aloud. "Sorry, everyone," he muttered. "I brought a utility bill instead of my speech. At least I can stop by the library later and renew my card."

Clay smiled uncertainly at Ryan, who seemed to be enjoying himself. Emily Ann looked wary. He didn't risk another glance at Stephanie—even several yards away, he could feel the scorn and fear rolling off of his sister. "Don't worry, young lady," he said to the bride. "You and your groom are in good hands." He turned back to the tent full of guests, sensing their sharpened attention. He would not fuck this up. Objectively speaking, he'd probably fucked up a lot in his life, but tonight he would do his best not to humiliate himself or anyone else.

"My nephew, Ryan Alexander Fisher, is someone I've known from the day he was born. When his mother was in labor at the hospital, I was there, waiting with his father, for Ryan's big debut. After several hours in the waiting room, flipping through *Reader's Digest*s and *Prevention* magazines, I got up to stretch my legs and ended up having a minor run-in with a bad-tempered nurse who reprimanded me for loitering—her words, not mine—by the vending machines, but my view was, you never knew when someone would forget to grab their change or a second bag of barbecue chips might drop down into the well—and bingo! Your lucky day."

People were laughing, including both members of the bridal couple. Clay looked down at the power bill and noticed it was his next-door neighbor's—the mailman had misdelivered it once before—and payment was two weeks overdue.

"I knew you'd all know what I meant," he said, smiling at a dark-haired woman a few tables away whose breasts were loose in her top. His ex-wife's sister hadn't worn a bra either, saying they'd been invented by a man (which Clay later learned wasn't true) to serve the male gaze.

He glanced over at Stephanie, whose eyes were wide and staring. She looked a little like one of those life-sized first-aid dolls. He gave her a reassuring smile, but her expression didn't change.

"As you all know," he said. "Ryan's birth was a success, because here he is, and here we all are tonight, some of us actually enjoying ourselves and not wondering how early is too early to leave. Any time before ten o'clock. That's the answer." He paused, unable to remember what he was supposed to say next. "I guess I should wrap this up—"

A female voice in the back screamed, "Yes!" followed by two male voices shouting, "No! Keep going!"

"—so those of you who don't intend to stay until ten o'clock can make your excuses and head out into the night. Wedding cake and Lyle Lovett cover band be damned. Let me close by saying I wish my nephew Ryan and his lovely new bride Emily Ann lasting happiness, no flat tires, lifelong fidelity, a steadfast sense of humor, no lawsuits, and no mass shootings."

Emily Ann appeared to be exhaling slowly, and Ryan was grinning and nodding like a man who knew the best answers. Many of the guests looked perplexed, but some were gamely chuckling, and one guy, maybe one of the "Keep going!" shouters, was guffawing. Clay took a bow and sunk into his seat, his face flushed with victory. He didn't look over at Stephanie or try to locate Griffin, Ryan's father, who had divorced Stephanie fifteen years earlier and subsequently begun camping in a Utah cave, living in it on and off for several years before he'd fully reentered society six years ago.

Clay knew his sister wouldn't smile back, and Griffin was probably in the bathroom or on the beach, staring out at the dark lake—he hated chairs and had stayed on his feet behind the rows of seated guests during the exchange of vows. He'd likely missed the whole speech. Clay owed him money and although Griffin no longer brought up the unpaid debt on the rare occasion their paths crossed, Clay doubted he'd forgotten about it. He'd brought some of the money he owed Griffin with him tonight. Before the wedding, he'd sold two old LPs, one a pristine early Dylan and the other a Janis Joplin. He'd gotten a fair price too.

He was aware that a man who didn't pay his debts (or at least try to) wasn't worth knowing, and Griffin, Clay was sure, had already written him off.

8

Sebastian knew his sister was at it again—he'd seen her putting a box of votive candles into the black duffel she was carrying around, pretending it was her purse. The air cast was also doubtless pure theater: he did not believe she had a sprain. He stood behind her as she clomped to their assigned table after the vows and discreetly groped the duffel's nether regions, his hand finding the hard edges of what felt like a picture frame and another object with the contours of an apple or a pomegranate, along with a third object, soft and dense, some kind of small cushion.

When she sensed his hand on the duffel, she yanked it closer and hissed, "Degenerate."

He wasn't sure why he still talked to her. A few years ago, when she was angry with him for telling their parents about her klepto tendencies, she'd retaliated by making up a malicious lie, one he probably could have sued her over if he were a litigious person unafraid of bad publicity. She'd told them she'd caught him spying on her neighbor's teenage daughter while the girl undressed for bed. Their father hadn't believed her, but their mother was less sure, probably because she'd once caught him in a vulnerable moment in front of his iMac, the actress in the porn clip he'd cued up dressed like a Catholic schoolgirl. It was all so absurd and unfair—he was only sixteen at the time, not some creepy pedophile in his fifties!

At the reception, Sebastian was seated one table over from Jill. When she got up and limped across the tent for a second piece of cake, she left the duffel under her chair, and it was then that he pounced. The three other people at her table, their cousins, looked on with curiosity as he unzipped the duffel. Out tumbled a small triangular pillow, a framed picture of a beach at sunset, and an apple-shaped candle, along with the box of votives, a package of floral paper hand towels, a small blue frog figurine, a pizza cutter, two tampons, and a pair of purple flip-flops.

Behind him he heard a screech and recognized the pitch as Jill's. She was two tables away and tried to run toward him but tripped over the leg of their great-aunt Lucy's date's chair and fell in a heap onto this frail-looking man's lap, her cake plate exploding into shards and greasy clumps at the edge of the dance floor. Sebastian raised the triangular pillow and waved it at her.

"That's mine," she cried as she freed herself from Lucy's date's lap and ran toward Sebastian, her air cast flapping loosely around her ankle. "Give it back!"

People were watching them, but not as many as might have been—half the wedding guests were on the dance floor, shuffling along to "If I Had a Boat." The band was good, but he wondered when Ryan had become a Lyle Lovett fan. Or maybe Emily Ann was the one.

"I very much doubt it's yours," said Sebastian, suddenly furious, tightening his grip on the duffel and the pillow. "You're a liar and a thief and you need help."

Jill pulled back, doubt in her eyes. Before she could come up with a retort, the wedding planner was at their sides, gently extricating the pillow from Sebastian's grasp. "This needs to go back in the house," she said gently, as if calming frightened children. "Where it came from."

Jill and Sebastian both looked at her dumbly.

"The rental house," said the wedding planner, pointing behind them. "I'll put it back where it belongs."

"Thank you," said Sebastian.

The wedding planner nodded. She was pretty and wasn't wearing a wedding ring. He liked the way she stood before them with authority but no meanness. He wondered if she had a boyfriend.

The band segued into another song, something about skinny legs—that was its title too, Sebastian was fairly sure. The bassist, he remembered now, was Emily Ann's brother.

Jill looked as if she was about to cry after the wedding planner left the tent, the small pillow wedged under her arm. She turned away and began stuffing the other purloined objects back into her duffel. Sebastian met the gazes of their cousins, each having watched the scene in silence.

Mickey, the youngest, finally spoke up. "Man, you guys never change." His laugh was rueful.

9

The psychic had been told to set up in a small room off the foyer, but no one came to see her, and after forty-five minutes of sitting alone with her phone on silent and no signs of life in the hall, she realized they'd changed their minds about needing her services but hadn't bothered to tell her. The one fortunate thing was they'd paid two-thirds of her fee in advance and the other third she'd insist on collecting before she went home.

Out the window she could see a large tent lit from within, people silhouetted as they moved around inside. A song she recognized but didn't know the name of filtered in through the open window, and she closed her eyes for a moment before she stood up and went into the hall. She passed two servers, both in spotless white button-downs and knee-length black skirts, carrying metal trays loaded with soiled cake plates.

The psychic wondered if there was any cake left, and a minute later, when she slipped into the tent, she saw the bride and groom embarking on their first dance as a married couple. She studied the bride's hopeful face and the groom's less hopeful face and recognized that he was more afraid of the future than his bride was, but the psychic thought they might outlast his ambivalence and depression (as yet undiagnosed) and the bride's bad habits with money. Except the past was pulling at him particularly hard, which was often the case with grooms. In her experience, the secrets men guarded most closely were rooted in nostalgia and sentimentality. Much would depend on whom they decided to let into the marriage and whom they kept out. Their families were dark vortices swirling around them—trouble, pain, resentment, confusion.

This was nothing new. Even though her own family was small and most of its members were now in the ground, she could still feel her mother's gaze upon her from beyond the grave, the impassive crow on the high branch staring down at her in silent judgment.

The cake was delicious—chocolate with vanilla icing and fresh raspberries in between layers. The psychic ate greedily, having skipped dinner because she'd hoped to be showered with leftovers from the wedding banquet. She'd predicted this poorly, however, and although she'd been certain before she set out for this job in her little red Fiat (a car she loved as much as any person she'd ever known) that the night would feature some surprises, she hadn't been able to foresee what kind. Her own future was generally a fog to her, whereas other people's future successes and disappointments were often discernible, like shapes in the clouds, as she'd discovered in college when, one drunken night around Halloween, her roommate dragged her to see a tarot card reader, who, after laying out the cards, looked at the psychic and told her she had the gift too. At the time, the psychic had laughed it off, but the tarot reader was undeterred. "Don't mock your gift," he said. "It's as much a part of you as your spine."

As she savored the last bite of cake, she watched the wedding planner approach her from the other side of the tent. The wedding planner did not, as the psychic expected, shoo her back into the house. "Would you tell my fortune?" she asked shyly.

"Follow me," said the psychic with a nod, before leading the wedding planner out of the tent, down the flagstone path to the back door, and into her temporary room. She motioned for the wedding planner to sit on one of the two velvet cushions she'd arranged on the floor nearly an hour ago.

The wedding planner settled onto a cushion, tucking her slim legs beneath her, her expression timidly expectant. The psychic sat down across from her and reached for her hand, turning it palm up. She peered in silence at the wedding planner's soft pink skin with its forking lines, several seconds passing before she said, "Let me see your other hand."

The wedding planner offered it with a nervous laugh. "I don't know how much I believe in any of this."

"We all want answers to questions we doubt anyone has the answers to, but we ask them anyway." She traced the younger woman's left-hand lifeline and looked into her face. She sensed the wedding planner's kindness, and the fact she had less self-interest than the psychic expected of someone in her line of work. "Your mother died not long ago," she said.

The wedding planner blinked. "Did someone tell you?"

The psychic shook her head. "No one told me. There's someone here you should get to know better. You've already met him," she said. "Your father's ill but he'll get better. You should say no more often than you do."

"My father's ill?" said the wedding planner, alarmed.

"Make him go to the doctor. There's still enough time."

The wedding planner gave her a stricken look. "I can't lose him so soon after my mother. If no one has the answers to our questions, why are you pretending you do?"

"I'm not pretending. What I said was we doubt anyone has the answers. That doesn't mean no one does."

The wedding planner hesitated before she said, "Is the man I'm supposed to meet the brother of the groom?"

The psychic nodded. "That's my impression."

"I'm not sure I want to get mixed up in this."

"You'll figure out what to do."

The wedding planner did not look convinced. "Let me get the remainder of your payment," she said. "And after that, you're free to go unless you want to stay and listen to the band."

The psychic didn't ask why the bride and groom had changed their minds about hiring her. It wasn't the first time a client had gotten cold feet, but usually they did not make her wait so long before telling her she could leave.

The moon was visible above the treetops as she made her way back to her car. Someone had left a flyer for a doughnut shop under a windshield wiper. The psychic folded it up and put it in her shoulder bag. Other drivers had thrown theirs onto the pavement.

Down the street, a woman stared at her phone as her dog sniffed at the base of a tree, her face ghostly in the phone's thin light. The psychic had made six hundred dollars for two hours of her time. Her mother had called her a grifter, never once taking it back. Some people would not love you, or not love you enough, no matter what you did. The sooner you understood that, the psychic knew, the better off you'd be.

The Common Cold

We were sixteen, twenty-six, and then, somehow, forty-six. I wasn't sure where thirty-six had gone, and on bad days, I thought about it more than I knew to be healthy. Thirty-six seemed to me the ideal age: the drunken confusion and missteps of your twenties far enough behind you as to almost seem to have happened to someone else, but the soundness of your thirty-something body still permitted you to spring out of bed in the morning, if you had that sort of temperament. At 8 A.M., unlike at 8 P.M., you still believed you would clean the entire house and do every scrap of laundry and answer a hundred emails and not eat the rest of the sheet cake left over from the family reunion.

By the time we turned thirty-six, Greeley, my closest friend, had been married twice and given birth to two children. At forty-six, she was still married to her second husband, albeit barely. I'd never married, nor did I have any children. (As a woman, you knew these things absolutely, whereas a man could get by claiming ignorance, a child or two of his possibly floating around in the world, waiting to ambush him with accusations or requests for love and attention, possibly all of the above. I suppose this condition colored the lives of some men with a kind of suspense, and hope too, perhaps.)

It helped to be rich if you intended to marry, let alone divorce. Any indignities you might suffer would be attenuated by new cars and good views and well-equipped kitchens. Greeley wasn't rich but she was brave, and I suppose in most circumstances bravery was as useful as money, if not more so.

Her husband, Hart, was often sickly. He was also depressed and obsessive about timepieces. I thought the two conditions were related, but for years Greeley scoffed at this, until she started agreeing with me, after he stopped being able to get out of bed before noon and began to lose one job after another.

Hart was a tall, bowlegged man with evasive, watery blue eyes and pale hair that grew in tufts on his head and the backs of his hands. He walked around the house in two pairs of socks, regardless of the season, and wore watches on both wrists. I knew from Greeley that he slept with his watches on, only taking them off when he bathed. His mother had raised him on her own and never told him who his father was. Greeley assumed the watches were an attempt at control after a childhood full of uncertainty. She was patient and kind, one reason why she put up with Hart, and with me.

Every room in their house, including the three bathrooms and the closet in the master bedroom, had at least one wall clock, often more. Many of these clocks didn't work, Hart having let the batteries run down, and no one—not Hart nor Greeley nor their son or daughter—ever bothering to replace them. I didn't go over to their house very often, but the year Greeley and I both turned forty-six, I was lovesick and desperately unhappy and began to go wherever someone familiar would let me in and permit me to talk about the man who was at the root of my misery. More often than not, it was Greeley and Hart's house I went to, fleeing my apartment with its dying houseplants and rattling, leaky windows.

I should have moved out years ago but hadn't yet been able to bring myself to do it. The ceiling appeared to have developed new cracks in the last few months, and I had new neighbors below me whose arguments I could hear through the floorboards most nights. On the four-lane road our building faced, ambulances shrieked by at all hours. Dogs barked disconsolately from behind the locked gate of the building across the alley, and irate loud-mouths often shouted at each other by the dumpsters that were emptied by lumbering trucks before first light on Tuesdays and Fridays. Whenever I was home, and not preoccupied with clean-ing or cooking or sleeping, I'd be seized by the ruinous urge to call the home of the man I was in love with and tell his other girl-friend, the one he took around in public, that he was a liar and a fraud, and she should know their relationship was doomed.

Hart and Greeley's children, Liza and Matt, affably tolerated me when I showed up at their house, which was fourteen miles through city traffic from where I lived. Hart usually hid in the basement during my visits, watching old movies and playing online Scrabble. Greeley was planning to divorce him but hadn't yet told anyone other than her widowed mother and me. She was waiting for both their kids to finish high school, she said, which was still a few years away.

One Saturday in mid-November, when the sky was hurl-ing down dingy clumps of snow and Greeley was late returning home from taking her mother, who lived a few miles away, to the library, I found myself alone at her house with Hart. He answered my knock and after a moment's indecision let me inside, and to my annoyance, he announced his intention to keep me company until Greeley's return. I'd been the maid of honor at their wedding nineteen years earlier. Hart and I had liked each other for a long time, but somewhere in our early forties, our mutual goodwill had turned to apathy on his end, chafing forbearance on mine. Respect, sympathy, curiosity—whatever it was that governed our relationship—had apparently been exhausted. It was similar to how for years I'd found the Peter Sellers movie *Being There* hilari-ous, but then unaccountably, it began to seem tragic.

I sat down on their pumpkin-colored velvet sofa, with one of their two cats, the white one named Natasha, curled up on the cushion next to mine. Her green eyes opened halfway as she felt my weight settling near her. Hart sat in a matching armchair across from me, and I smiled at him tentatively, wondering what had gotten into him. It was possible Greeley had ordered him to keep me company while she finished the errand with her mother.

"So," he said.

I peered at him, anxious and tired. I had no idea what he would come up with next. "Yes?" I said.

"So." He laughed self-consciously.

We looked at each other some more. Natasha yawned, her throat emitting a tiny squeak.

"Did you know there are literally thousands of strains of the cold virus circulating among us every year?" he said.

"I don't know if I did."

"That's why there's no shot for the common cold. There are fewer flu viruses, and it's easier for immunologists to guess which ones will cause the most trouble."

"Interesting," I said. This trivia did interest me. For one, I didn't like colds, but I couldn't think of anyone who did. "Do you get a flu shot every year?"

"No."

"I do," I said. "But not yet this year."

He looked at one of his watches. He had two on his right wrist today, one on his left. His and Greeley's son looked like him—blond, tall, and blue-eyed, but Matt didn't share his father's obsession with clocks. Nor did he appear to be depressed. He was sixteen and good-looking and girls called him at all hours; Greeley had started to take away his phone after 10 P.M. His sister Liza, fifteen and less popular, took after Greeley; she was petite and dark-haired. She wasn't interested in timepieces either, which Greeley was relieved about.

"I wonder what's keeping them," said Hart. "My mother-in-law must have wanted to go to the grocery store."

"It's okay," I said too brightly. "You don't have to keep me company. I brought something to read." Matt and Liza were out with friends. The house was quiet.

Hart had a crumb at the corner of his mouth. I wanted to tell him but worried it would embarrass him. I hoped it would fall off on its own without either of us having to do anything about it.

"I don't mind," he said. He looked at one of his other watches, pretending to adjust it, or maybe he actually was adjusting it. If it was the kind you had to wind, he'd probably let it run down.

He hadn't worked in over a year. Greeley was paying all the bills and resented this enormously. I'd told her the other day that I wished I could take us to the South of France for a month, where we might meet beautiful young Frenchmen who would sponge off us unapologetically while we used them for sex. "I can't leave my mother for a whole month," she'd said, thinking I was serious. "Hart could probably take care of the kids, but Mom needs me."

Hart and I sat in silence, me petting the cat, who was now purring loudly, Hart glancing from his watches to the windows that overlooked the street. Greeley's real name was Bethany, but she had always disliked it and as a joke had renamed herself after the novelist and Catholic priest Andrew M. Greeley, whose books had almost no sex in them despite their provocative covers, as we'd discovered, to our serious disappointment, when we'd read them in high school. The nickname stuck, but her mother continued to call her Bethany and her father did too, until he died two years ago from a heart attack at the dentist's office. He was in the waiting room looking at an old issue of *People* when he died, not in the chair with the drill whirring in his ear. He had gone quickly, the receptionist later assured Greeley and her mother. He'd stood up suddenly before falling down and dying, a look of terrible surprise on his face, as I imagined it.

"Greeley told me about the guy," said Hart, his gaze lit by mischief. "The one you've been writing poems for."

A truck rumbled by in the street, but it took me a moment to sort out where the sound was coming from. I should have known Greeley would tell him. Why wouldn't she? They weren't divorced yet and continued to sleep in the same bed, probably having sex in it too, once in a while.

I couldn't think of anything to say.

"It's good you let him know how you feel," said Hart. "As they say, nothing ventured, nothing gained."

Who says this? I thought, suppressing the impulse to roll my eyes. A second later, I felt like breaking into tears, but I suppressed that too.

"You could always ask him to marry you," he said. "I bet that would throw him for a loop. And who knows, maybe he'd say yes."

"That would not be a good idea," I said, incredulous. "I don't want to marry him."

He tilted his chin at me. "That's what you say."

"And that's what I mean."

We were each taking the measure of the other, he having decided when he let me in, I suppose, that he had something to prove to me, that he was on an upswing or at least was frozen mid-decline. The crumb was still by his mouth.

I felt my own mouth twitch, sending an inadvertent signal that Hart failed to read. The man I was in love with was named Dawoud. He was extremely good-looking, morally protean, generous in bed, and promiscuous with promises. He was ten years older than I was, but still behaved like a college boy, with his cargo pants and blithe cheating and impromptu camping trips. This had been going on for over a year. I had never suffered so much in my life.

I had to make it stop. It was also feasible his girlfriend would murder one of us when she found out what we were doing, mostly on Thursday evenings and Sunday mornings when Dawoud would sneak over to my apartment while this public girlfriend was in a water yoga class at the gym we all belonged to.

She had a silky blond ponytail and was purportedly only a few years younger than Dawoud, although she looked my age. She had much larger breasts than I did—I'd seen them in the locker room and tried not to gawk. I was excruciatingly jealous, but also thinner than she was. And I had thunderous orgasms, which Dawoud was very proud of, sometimes speechless over, as was I. We spent most of our time at my place naked and panting and laughing together. I hated when he left, never really sure if he would come back. He might get hit by a train or choke on a piece of apple or his girlfriend really would murder him before she came for me. He might change his mind about me and find someone else.

"But what if he proposed to you?" asked Hart. "Would you say no?"

I sensed something in Hart then that I probably hadn't ever sensed before in anyone. What it was was this: he had once been a tree—most of the molecules in his body, I strongly felt, had belonged to a conifer in another, very distant age. I felt a wave of compassion for him and smiled tentatively, seeing him differently, more appreciatively. Did he have any idea what he'd once been? I doubted it. "I would say no," I said.

Greeley came in the door a few seconds later, pausing when she saw us together in the front room. I went over to her and hugged her. She smelled like lavender soap and her cheeks were cold. Hart stayed in the chair. Natasha leapt down from the sofa and ran into the kitchen where her food and water bowls were waiting to be kicked over by the next clumsy human, often me.

"I want Trish to read us one of her love poems," said Hart. "For that guy. You know, Dawoud." He pronounced his name da-wad.

Greeley stared at him, appalled.

"Dawoud," I said.

"Ignore him," said Greeley. "I'm sorry, Trish."

"It's okay. I don't have any of those poems with me anyway," I said, trying to keep the peace.

Greeley was shaking her head. She took off her coat and hung it in the closet by the front door. "Have you had lunch yet?' she asked.

"I haven't," said Hart.

"I wasn't asking you," she said.

"I haven't either," I admitted.

"You need to eat," she said sternly. "I'm ordering a pizza."

"No, no, don't do that," I said.

"I'd eat some," said Hart.

She ordered a pizza—spinach and mushroom—along with a dozen garlic breadsticks. She knew this was my favorite order, especially the breadsticks. I wanted to move in with her. It was like this every time I came over. I had known her since we were nine years old, when she had enormous eyeglasses and so did I. The first summer I knew her, we'd put water balloons in the fronts of our bathing suits and stood in the backyard, her mother taking our picture, all of us laughing. Neither Greeley nor I had big boobs, though she did for a time when she was pregnant and she lorded it over me then, but not very seriously.

The pizza was delivered a half hour later. The delivery boy was a man in his seventies. I wanted to ask if he was doing this because he was bored with retirement. I hoped it wasn't because he needed the money, but I had a feeling it was. I tipped him eight dollars and paid for the order, ignoring Greeley's protests. I had more money than she did and much lower overhead. It was all a fluke, really. My father had left me some money when he died, the year before her father died. He and my mother had been divorced for years and I was his sole heir. He'd left money to PETA too, although he wasn't even a vegetarian, and to the public library in the central Wisconsin farming town where he'd spent the last fourteen years of his life. He'd never remarried, but had gone on elderly singles' cruises a few times a year; he'd said he didn't want the "hassle" of commitment after he and my mother divorced.

Going through his papers after he died, I'd discovered he'd had relations with women who were probably sex workers. I wasn't scandalized, but I did think about it fairly often. It was like knowing too much about your neighbors' sexual habits, except, like it or not, I would never again have to look upon my father burdened with this knowledge.

While we were eating the pizza, my phone started ringing. When I took it out of my bag to investigate, I saw with a stab of alarm and desire that it was Dawoud. If he was calling to say he wanted to come over, I would feel both bereft and angry. Sometimes he did this—call out of nowhere and ask if I was free, always expecting that I would be, but sometimes I wasn't, and he would hang up abruptly after saying, "It's fine, Trish. It's fine! Talk to you later." It would take me a day to recover from this exchange, mostly due to my fear that he would never call again.

Greeley recognized this as the response of a woman with no self-esteem. And what exactly did I think having an affair meant? She'd say, "Why do you let him have so much power over you?" I'd tell her I didn't let him, per se—it was just what happened when you were in love with someone who was trying to hide you from everyone else in his life.

I let his call go to voice mail. Greeley patted my hand when I put the phone back in my bag. "Good girl," she said.

Hart perked up. "Was that him? The guy you write poems for?"

Greeley frowned at him.

"Yes," I said wretchedly.

"You should have let me talk to him," he said.

Greeley shook her head. "No," she said. "Not funny."

He looked at us, hurt. "What? It could have been a man-to-man conversation. I could ask him the kinds of questions Trish probably never has the courage to."

I noticed the crumb was finally gone from the corner of his mouth, but he had a small smear of pizza sauce on his chin now.

He looked like a giant baby—his face pink-skinned, his thinning, tufted blond hair nearly as delicate as an infant's fluff.

I smiled at him and shook my head. "Dawoud isn't big on revealing his hand. But it's nice of you to suggest this."

"Do you want to call him back?" asked Hart.

"No."

"It might have been important," he said.

"It wasn't important," snapped Greeley. "He's a selfish asshole. He's only using Trish for sex."

Her vehemence startled me a little. Even if what she'd said was probably accurate, I didn't want to hear her say it aloud, especially in front of her unraveling husband who, the other day, had washed his blue jeans with Greeley's new white bras and turned them all a grubby blue-gray. He had also run over a pile of rocks while mowing the lawn last month and ruined the blades. Their oven had so much food crusted on the bottom that every time Greeley turned it on, the smoke alarm went off, but she refused to clean it herself because Hart had promised to do it, and she was waiting for him to keep his word and swore she would keep waiting until he did.

I was afraid that, like Dawoud's public girlfriend, Greeley had murder in her heart and would snap in some violent, irrevocable way if Hart kept bumbling along and ruining their expensive household appliances.

"How do you know that for sure? Have you met him?" Hart asked Greeley.

"Hart, honestly. Go away and let Trish and me talk by ourselves," she said.

I really wanted him to leave us alone too, but I felt bad when he took his plate and went down to the basement without another word.

She squeezed my arm. "If you want to call him back, go ahead," she said.

I shook my head. "No, it's okay. Hart said I should ask Dawoud to marry me."

She looked at me, her face grim. "He's getting worse, Trish. I don't know what to do. Yesterday I caught him in a chat room for labradoodle owners. We don't own a labradoodle, as you know. But he was acting like we did."

"I'm sorry," I said. I assumed he was either bored or delusional. I hoped it was the former. Greeley was crying now, her face suddenly wet with tears. I reached over and hugged her and soon we were both crying.

When we stopped, I shared with her what Hart had told me about the common cold. "He does know a lot of trivia," she said glumly, wiping her eyes. "I'll give him that."

A second or two later, she whispered, "I have to divorce him. I'm not sure what will happen to him after I do, and it's going to upset the kids very much, but I have to do it. I can't wait much longer."

I took her hand and we sat in silence, listening to the drone of the TV in the basement. "He seemed less depressed than the last time I saw him, at least," I finally said.

She nodded. "Yes. But it's unpredictable. He'll be okay for a week but then without warning he'll stop showering and picking up after himself and talking to me or the kids. He won't exercise, even though on the rare occasions he does, he always feels better."

"What about antidepressants?"

"He won't take them," she said. "Not regularly. Whatever you do, don't ask Dawoud to marry you."

"No, of course not. It's never even crossed my mind."

"Because if you did marry him, he'd cheat on you too."

"I know."

She put her face in her hands. "But I envy you," she said, her voice muffled. "You have not chosen to marry the wrong man."

"For a while he was the right man, wasn't he?" I said softly.

She put her hands in her lap and looked down. I had a picture in my mind right then of her and Hart at Halloween six or seven years ago. He was dressed as a zucchini, she as a chef's knife. I'd come over to help them hand out chocolate bars to all the kids in the neighborhood, dozens and dozens of them, red-faced and grinning and manic on sugar. One little girl who reminded me of me pointed at Hart and asked Greeley, "Will he get to be the knife next year?" And Greeley replied, "You're a sharp one, aren't you." The girl blinked, not getting the pun, but Hart and I laughed. "I hope this woman will always be my knife," he said to the little girl, his arm around Greeley's shoulders. "And that I can always be her vegetable." Greeley made a comical face. I could see she was very happy.

"Yes, he was the right man for a while," she said. "But now he isn't."

Driving home later, I thought about Hart in the basement and Greeley on the first floor with the crusted-over oven and her ruined bras upstairs in the bedroom and the damaged lawn mower in the garage and all the other frustrations of her long marriage to Hart. I knew he deserved some compassion too—he wasn't evil, just beaten down and sick and weaker than she was. They'd had some good years, and their kids weren't jerks. Greeley liked her house too, but right now I knew it wasn't much comfort when she thought of the failings of the husband she shared it with, a man who was not looking for a new job and had slipped into midlife depression and might not be able to pull himself back together anytime soon, if ever.

And at forty-six, what did I have? I'd tried to keep it simple, as Greeley purported to envy. I'd held myself back from binding attachments when they were offered—I'd turned down two marriage proposals, the first in my twenties, the second in my thirties. Both men had gone on to marry other women and have children. I didn't regret this, though. You took your chances no matter what you did.

I believed I had been a tree once too. I had lived outside in all seasons, witnessing the comings and goings of birds and rabbits and wolves and people who were always arguing or feeling put-upon or who knew what—maybe not much of anything. I was responsible for the care and upkeep of my own bras and had no lawn to mow. To be honest, this was a relief.

Just before I'd left Greeley and Hart's place, Hart had emerged from the basement to say goodbye. He must have heard us talking or else simply guessed I was ready to go home. Greeley didn't care anymore if he heard her saying unflattering things about him. He was like a cement wall now, she said, nothing penetrated him.

He came up from downstairs and stood in the doorway, studying us for a second before he said, "Keep writing poems, Trish, and be sure to wash your hands with soap and hot water. You need to guard against the common cold. It's almost winter now."

"I will," I said, smiling at him as kindly as I could.

I didn't return Dawoud's call that night after I got home. When he called again the next morning to confirm our usual X-rated Sunday gymnastics, I didn't answer. I went out instead and stayed away all day. He called again. Again, I didn't answer. *It's over*, I typed into our ongoing text thread, though I couldn't bring myself to hit send. I was going to sell my depressing apartment, I realized. I was going to take a leave of absence from work and travel for a while. It was something I'd been intending to do for many years.

The next morning, Greeley texted me a picture of her espresso machine with the caption *The latest casualty of my marriage*. I sent back a frowning face, adding *I'm sorry, G.*

It's over, I typed again, and this time I hit send. It wouldn't be enough, but it was a start. I looked out the window, down into the alley, where a man in gray sweats was foraging in the recycling bins for aluminum cans, his bike basket already teeming with his finds. I watched him, drinking my morning cup of strong black coffee, ignoring the urge to check my phone. After the coffee was gone, I got ready for work and the drive to the high school where I was the assistant principal. It was Monday, after all. I was good at this job, despite the chaos of my private life, and liked most of the students and teachers, and my boss, Principal Brynne, who had the same birthday and hairstyle as my mother. At school I was organized and punctual and people came to me when they needed things, which I wanted them to do.

During lunch, I ordered a new espresso machine for Greeley. I didn't include a gift message. She would quickly figure out who'd sent it, but I wanted it, at least for a little while, to be a surprise.

ACKNOWLEDGMENTS

"The Swami Buchu Trungpa" appeared in *New England Review* 41, no. 1 (2020), and was cited as a distinguished story of 2020 in *The Best American Short Stories 2021*.

"Where Do You Last Remember Holding It?" appeared in *New England Review* 43, no. 2 (2022).

"The Monkey's Uncle Louis" appeared in *New England Review* 39, no. 3 (2018), was reprinted in *Litbop: Art and Literature in the Groove* 1, no. 1 (2021), and received a special mention in the Pushcart Prize XLIV anthology (2020).

"Direct Sunlight" appeared in *Boulevard* 36, no. 1 (Fall 2020).

"In the Park" appeared in *LitMag* 1 (2017) and received a special mention in the *Pushcart Prize XLIII* anthology (2019).

"House of Paine" appeared in *Story*, no. 7 (Spring 2020).

"The Petting Zoo" appeared in *ZYZZYVA*, no. 109 (Spring and Summer 2017).

"Mega Millions" appeared in *Hunger Mountain*, no. 26 (Summer 2022).

"Dear Kelly Bloom" appeared in *Massachusetts Review* 57, no. 3 (Fall 2016).

"The Common Cold" appeared in *The Literary Review* 62, no. 2 (Fall 2019).

The story "Direct Sunlight" was inspired by an April 2019 *Without Fail* podcast interview with Kenneth Feinberg.

I am grateful to the editors who first published these stories: Carolyn Kuebler at *New England Review*, Michael Nye at *Story*, Minna Proctor at *The Literary Review*, Adam McOmber at *Hunger Mountain*, Jim Hicks at *Massachusetts Review*, Marc Berley at *LitMag*, Oscar Villalon and Laura Cogan at *ZYZZYVA*, Jessica Rogen and Dusty Freund at *Boulevard*.

And to Marisa Siegel, the editor at Northwestern University Press who has shepherded this book so generously and expertly to publication. Thank you to Anne Gendler for her discerning eye and early encouragement, and to press director Parneshia Jones and her staff for their ongoing guidance and generosity.

I also owe a perennial thank-you to the booksellers in Chicago and beyond who have championed my work over the years, and to my parents, Susan Sneed and Terry Webb. A special thank-you is also owed to Sheryl Johnston, publicist and good friend, and to my partner Adam Tinkham. His keen eye and ear never fail to catch what's working and what's not yet there. (He also makes me a much-needed espresso every single morning.)

Lastly, much gratitude and affection to my supportive friends and family in Chicago, Los Angeles, and beyond, to my students past and present, and to my colleagues and fellow writers at Northwestern University and Regis University.